The Disquieting Dandy

Lady Meriel had heard about such London dandies as Sir Antony Davies indisputably was.

Here was a fop who clearly cared about the cut of his coat and the knot of his cravat more than about anything else on earth. Here was a libertine who thought no more about stealing a woman's honor than about flicking off the head of a daisy with his riding whip. Here was a gentleman who quite possibly might be spying against his own country for the funds necessary to maintain himself in his insufferably sumptuous style of self-indulgence.

And it was a testament to Meriel's firmness of character that she resolved to ignore Sir Antony's startling good looks and maddeningly smooth charm . . . for otherwise it would be too dreadfully easy to fall in love with him. . . .

For a list of other Signet Regency Romances by Amanda Scott, please turn page. . . .

LADY MERIEL'S DUTY

by
Amanda Scott

A SIGNET BOOK

NEW AMERICAN LIBRARY

PUBLISHED BY
THE NEW AMERICAN LIBRARY
OF CANADA LIMITED

NAL BOOKS ARE AVAILABLE AT QUANTITY DISCOUNTS WHEN USED TO PROMOTE PRODUCTS OR SERVICES. FOR INFORMATION PLEASE WRITE TO PREMIUM MARKETING DIVISION, NEW AMERICAN LIBRARY, 1633 BROADWAY, NEW YORK, NEW YORK 10019.

First Printing, September, 1987

2 3 4 5 6 7 8 9

SIGNET, SIGNET CLASSIC, MENTOR, ONYX, PLUME, MERIDIAN AND NAL BOOKS are published in Canada by The New American Library of Canada, Limited, 81 Mack Avenue, Scarborough, Ontario, Canada M1L 1M8

PRINTED IN CANADA
COVER PRINTED IN U.S.A.

For Carolyn,
whose generosity has provided months of
clean air and freedom to confer with the Muse

1

"Will we go all the way to the top, Meri?"

The boy's high-pitched voice drifted back to Lady Meriel Traherne as she paused for a moment on the precipitous rock-strewn path halfway up the northern slope of that mighty Welsh mountain known as Cader Idris, or Arthur's Chair. Looking up at him with a grin, Meriel pushed wisps of light brown hair away from her face and called back laughingly, "Ask me that question when we reach Llyn-y-cau, Davy. Once you see how steep the Fox's Path is at that point, you may decide you have no wish to climb higher."

Davy's chuckle floated back on the light westerly breeze wafting across the slope from Cardigan Bay. From where Meriel stood, the village of Dolgellau below looked like a collection of dolls' houses along a blue-and-white ribbon that was the Wnion River, and she could see the boats in Barmouth harbor ten miles to the west. Ravens soared overhead in the clear blue sky, and the sound of water tumbling over rocks came from a rill a short distance away.

Three-quarters of an hour later, when they reached the shore of the dark lake known as Llyn-y-cau, the view was even more impressive, for they could now see over the ridges in the middle distance to the north as far as the majestic snow-covered peak of Mount Snowdon, thirty-five miles away. The boy dropped to his stomach beside the small tarn, leaning down to splash water on his thin freckled face. "Climbing is hard work," he said over his shoulder.

"Aye," she responded, sitting down beside him and wishing, not for the first time, that a lady could wear nankeen breeches and a simple open-necked cotton shirt when she took her exercise in such a strenuous form as this. Her moss-green frock was lightweight, but its full gathered skirts encumbered her legs, and her shawl tended to slip off her shoulders at inconvenient moments. Still, her footwear was good enough, a pair of stout boots long since outgrown by her elder brother, Jocelyn, yet still too large for Davy.

The boy made a cup with his hands, slurping noisily from the lake. When he straightened at last, water streamed down his pointed chin, making water spots on his shirt front. He turned to gaze at the twin-peaked summit rising nine hundred feet above them, its perpendicular golden rock face making a shadowy, pointed backdrop for the dark lake. Meriel had often thought it looked much like a piece of broken crockery with sharp, jagged edges rounding inward to contain the lake.

"Do you know what the other side looks like, Davy?"

"Well, I've not come up here with you before, have I?"

"I ought to have brought you long ago," she said, bending to splash water over her hot cheeks, and thinking how different he was from what she had been at his age. She had not waited for someone else to bring her onto the mountain, but had been drawn to it irresistibly from her earliest years, despite all attempts on the part of those in authority over her to discourage such expeditions. Smiling apologetically, she explained, " 'Tis merely that when I come here myself, I am searching for peace and solitude—two things one does not find in the company of one's sisters and small brother."

"Is that what you sought today?" the boy asked, his tone one of simple curiosity.

She grinned at him. "Much you would care. I could scarcely send you home again when you ran after and pleaded so eloquently to accompany me. However, I did wish to come for a last bit of real peace before we all leave Plas Tallyn."

"Will I like London, Meri?"

"I daresay you will," she replied. "There are any number of things to do and places to see, you know. And then, too, you will be going to school soon. You will like that."

"Will we be taking Mr. Glendower?"

"Only as Auntie Wynne's chaplain and as a sort of courier to arrange things for you along the way. In London you will need a tutor who is younger and more willing to enter into those activities that you enjoy, Davy." She paused, crinkling her eyes as she gazed at him more searchingly. "I thought we had been over this point before."

The boy looked up at her from under eyebrows so blond as to appear white, making his thick dark lashes startling by contrast. His light blue eyes twinkled. "I wanted to be certain," he said. "I've had my fill of Mr. Glower Glendower."

Meriel didn't reply. There was nothing she could say that would be appropriate. Davy was, after all, only twelve. One simply could not agree with his sentiments outright, however much one might wish to do so.

The silence lengthened. Anyone seeing the two of them at that moment would have had no trouble recognizing their relationship. Although Meriel was more than twice Davy's age and a head taller, they each had the same determined chin and the same finely chiseled features. Both had fair hair, though hers was several shades darker than his, with deep golden highlights, and like his, her eyebrows were lighter than her hair, and her lashes darker. Instead of light blue eyes, however, hers were the gray-green of soft, velvety heather leaves.

One other trait that Meriel would as soon not have shared with her brother was a pair of shoulders broader than her hips. With wide skirts, no one noticed her slim, boyish figure, but according to her aunt, newer fashions boasted more revealing, pencil-slim skirts instead. Fatal, she thought. Not that such things mattered to her any longer. At twenty-six she was long past the age of being on the lookout for a husband. Her primary interest now was her family. Still, she thought, it might be amusing to cut a dash when she reached Paris. Her sister Nest, by all accounts, had not found slim hips a disadvantage in that great city.

"What *is* on the other side?" Davy asked suddenly, breaking into her thoughts.

Meriel stared at him blankly for several seconds, then chuckled. "Grassy slopes and no cliffs," she said. "The land descends abruptly, to be sure, but it looks as if one could slide all the way into the Dysynni Valley on one's backside without hitting a single rock."

Davy's eyes widened as he looked back the way they had come, and she knew what he was thinking as though he had expressed himself aloud. In many places the walls of rock along the northern face of Cader Indris were perpendicular.

"I want to see," the boy said, getting to his feet.

"Oh, Davy, it will take us nearly two hours to get back as it is," she protested.

"How long to get to the top?"

"Forty minutes, maybe."

"And down to the lake again?"

"Less than half that time."

"An hour, then. Please, Meri?"

She shook her head, but it was a token gesture, and he knew it. Lady Meriel had been mother and father to her younger sisters and brother for nearly two years now, and while she could be strict with them when necessary, she always found it difficult to deny them pleasure. Particularly Davy. He had been her special child practically from the cradle, for her mother had been ill after his birth and had never truly recovered her strength. Then, when the typhus had struck northern Wales two years previously, her mother had succumbed within a week, and her father, stout though he had been, had followed her to the grave within the month, leaving the four of his six children who remained at Plas Tallyn to fend for themselves.

War in France had made it impossible for them to seek refuge with their sister Nest, who had accompanied her husband, the Comte de Prévenu, to Paris several months before her mama's death, when the *comte* and his family had been granted amnesty by Napoleon Bonaparte. And Jocelyn, their elder brother, now the twelfth Earl of Tallyn, was somewhere in the wilds of America, unreachable seemingly, for Meriel had written to tell him of their predicament—and incidentally, to inform him of his own inheritance—immediately after her father's demise.

She got to her feet now, smiling at her small brother. "Be careful now, Davy, for the upper path is difficult. Auntie Wynne is distracted enough, what with all the travel arrangements and worrying about what mischief you and Gwen will get into, as well as Eliza's come-out. I don't want to have to tell her you fell off a mountain."

"Pooh," said the boy scornfully. "As if I should do anything so daft as to fall. And come-outs are paltry things, by what I hear. Eliza don't want to leave Bugg Dewsall, so I don't see why she should have to go to London to catch a husband anyhow. You didn't find one there."

"Mr. Dewsall's name is Gwilym," Meriel corrected automatically, "and we have all been over and over why Eliza mustn't marry him. She is too young."

"Too young for Bugg but not for some London beau," Davy said in the same scornful tone. "I know."

"You know a deal too much, young man," Meriel said sternly. "If you mean to reach the summit, you'd best get moving before I change my mind."

He threw her a saucy grin and scrambled away, moving upward over the narrow, rocky, scarcely discernible path as though he were part goat. Meriel followed at a more leisurely pace, cursing her skirts again each time they caught on a bit of scrub or got in the way of her feet as she clambered over the rocks, but savoring the sweet, clear air and the familiar sense of freedom the mountain always gave her.

At the summit they paused to scan the magnificent view. To the south lay the green-and-golden Dysynni Valley, and to the west, the olive-green Mawddach estuary, stretching to Barmouth and the broad inward sweep of Cardigan Bay. Beyond the rippling ridges to the north they could see the glorious snow-covered summit of Mount Snowdon. And to the east the sharp depths of the Dovey river valley wound north and south with ridges on either side thick with hazel, beech, and elm trees. Nearer, practically at the northeast foot of the mountain, lay the great sprawling stone house at Plas Tallyn, home of the Traherne family for centuries, looking now like a child's toy. Meriel drank in the view and knew from the deep sigh of appreciation that her small brother was as awestruck as she was.

The sensation was a familiar one, but in a way it seemed brand new each time. She had been climbing this mountain ever since she was a tiny lass, sometimes tagging after her brother Jocelyn and his friends, but more often alone. Over the years the mountain had continued to call to her, to offer strength when she needed strength, comfort when there was none to be had elsewhere. In many ways, the mountain was home in a way that even Plas Tallyn was not.

"We've got to go, Davy," she said abruptly. "The others will wonder where we are, you know, and it does not do to worry Auntie Wynne."

"I don't believe she really worries all that much," said the boy, regarding her placidly. "Not, in any event, when she has her books to read and her yarns for stitching. Still, 'tis a pity you do not mean to travel with us to London. We will miss you, Meri."

"I know, love," she said, giving him a quick hug," but I'll be back before you know it. I must go to France to look into that school Auntie Wynne is so set on for Gwenyth now that we've got peace, but I'll be back in the twinkling of a bedpost."

"After you go to Paris to see Nest," he pointed out with a grimace.

"Yes, well, we must be certain that all is well with her, you know."

"She says all is well, and she ought to know. She is there and you are not."

"Don't be impertinent, Davy."

The boy fell silent, and they soon turned their footsteps toward home.

Upon their return to the great graystone house, they discovered the rest of the family in the vast draft-ridden ground-floor with drawing room, the ladies occupied in various ways while willowy Mr. Glendower read aloud to them in his carrying voice from a book of sermons. Auburn-haired Wynnefreda, Lady Cadogan, sat with her tambour frame near the roaring fire, setting neat stitches, her needle and frame held firmly in long, slender fingers.

"Merciful heavens, Meriel," she said, her strident but carefully cultivated tones cutting without ceremony through the chaplain's well-modulated ones when she saw her niece and nephew on the threshold, "what an example to set for your sisters, coming into this room looking like a shag rag. And you, Dafydd, in all your dirt. Wherever have the pair of you been all the afternoon?"

"I wonder, ma'am," said Meriel, smiling fondly at that upright dame, "if you know what a shag rag is."

"Why, I haven't the least notion," said her ladyship, diverted and somewhat surprised, since she knew herself to be well-educated for a female, and was particularly proud of her extensive vocabulary. "I do know, however, that it is something one does not wish to discover in one's drawing room."

"No, indeed," Meriel agreed, her smile widening. " 'Tis a rag kept in a fighting cock's bag and used to polish his spurs and beak before he is brought up to scratch."

"My lady!"

"Meriel!"

Both the chaplain and Lady Cadogan looked properly scandalized, but Meriel, her gray-green eyes atwinkle, merely turned away from them toward the two other female inhabitants of the room.

"Are you both prepared to depart in the morning?" she inquired.

Flaxen-haired Lady Gwenyth, who at the age of fourteen was looking forward to her first trip to London with much the same air of excitement as her younger brother, fairly bounced up and down upon her brocade pouffe, the mending she had been pretending to attend to sliding unnoticed to her feet. "Shall we truly ride on a great boat?" she demanded.

"Indeed, love, all the way from Barmouth to Bristol, where Mr. Glendower will hire a post chaise for the rest of your journey to London. It will be very exciting, will it not, Eliza?" She turned to the elder of the two girls, a young lady of seventeen summers, who had closed the book in her lap that she had been reading in defiance of Mr. Glendower's choice, and who was attempting to behave as if trips to London were quite commonplace occurrences in her experience.

Lady Eliza pushed a strand of honey-colored hair away from her gray eyes and regarded her eldest sister with a long-suffering air. "I suppose it will be pleasant," she said, "though I shall quite naturally miss Gwilym dreadfully."

"Dear me, why ever should you?" inquired Lady Cadogan, wide-eyed. "I am certain I never missed Cadogan, and I was married to him, after all, which will never be the case with you and young Dewlap."

"Dewsall, Auntie Wynne," corrected Gwenyth, chuckling. "His name is Dewsall, and I am persuaded he's ever so much more handsome than Viscount Cadogan, for though I never saw him, you have always said he squinted like a bag of nails and had teeth which stuck out, which Bugg does not."

"Gwenyth," said Eliza awfully, "if you cannot keep a still tongue in your head, you will be sent to your bedchamber without your supper."

"By whom, Miss Prim and Proper?" demanded Gwenyth. "You are not my guardian, and Meri has said nothing at all."

"Well, I'm sure I am as much your guardian as she is," said Eliza, "for she is nothing of the sort. Jocelyn is our guardian."

"Fiddle. A fine one he is, I must say, off in America these seven years past, maybe even dead for all we know, and leaving Meri to manage his estates and us as well."

"That will do, Gwen," said Meriel evenly. "Please pick up your mending off the floor and do not speak so of our brother. 'Tis most unbecoming."

"Well, I honor his principles, of course, though I do think he might have done better to have fought for the equality of men right here in Wales instead of running off to America to spite Papa," Gwenyth said unrepentantly. "In any event, I do think he might have written at least once in all these years, if not before Papa died, then certainly afterward. One would think he might care something about being an earl, for pity's sake."

"Yes, one might," agreed Lady Cadogan. "After all, many men go to their reward without ever having enjoyed that privilege."

"Well, I should think they do," said Eliza, losing her die-away air completely as she sat up straight and looked with amazement at her aunt.

"You know perfectly well that she is referring to Lord Cadogan and not to men in general," Meriel said, hiding her amusement with difficulty. It was a sore point with Lady Cadogan that her husband had had the misfortune to predecease his father and thus had failed to come into the earldom that would have made her a countess instead of a mere viscountess. She had behaved bravely however, not mentioning her misfortune above once or twice a week since her removal from London to Plas Tallyn the previous year. Her duty at that time had been clear to herself if to no one else. With Cadogan dead and yet another year of mourning stretching before her, she had been unable to think of a better way to spend it than in looking after her orphaned nieces and nephew. If she had been grateful to find that Meriel had things well in hand at Plas Tallyn, she had said nothing about it, preferring to make gentle suggestions as to how things might be improved, without lifting a finger herself to improve them. She had found an ally in Mr. Glendower, her late brother's chaplain, who had encouraged her to believe that her grief was great and that she ought to seek solace under his spiritual guidance. Until the weather had begun to clear, bringing thoughts of the forthcoming London Season to her mind, she had been content.

Now she recalled a continuing grievance and looked askance at her eldest niece. "I do not know how you can think of going off to France and leaving me to deal with all these children on my own, Meriel. Such an impertinent lot. I cannot think they will behave if you are not by."

"They will give you no difficulty, ma'am," said Meriel, glancing from one to the other of her siblings. "They know their duty."

"Yes, no doubt." Lady Cadogan looked at each one much as Meriel had done, but finding no comfort in what she saw, she sighed, looking first at Mr. Glendower, who was regarding her sympathetically, and then back at Meriel, who was not. "I daresay you do not wish to discuss it further at present, for you will wish to rid yourself of the dirt you collected on your precious mountain," she said, sighing more deeply yet. " 'Tis the unnatural freedom you enjoy here at Plas Tallyn, I suppose, that puts such hoydenish notions as this journey into France into your head. But I shall say no more. Marwyn will be announcing supper at any moment, and you will certainly not sit down looking like a . . . like a Gypsy," she finished triumphantly.

"No, ma'am." Meriel smiled down at the boy, who had been standing beside her, an interested but silent spectator of the scene. "Come, Davy. You will dine with us tonight."

He shot her a grateful glance, then turned with a tiny smirk to inform his other sisters that he too had climbed Cader Idris. "All the way to the top," he added smugly.

"Yes, well you look it," said Eliza, unimpressed. "Do go away and change, Davy, there's a good boy."

The look he gave her was anything but angelic. Meriel, intercepting it, felt an urge to warn him to do nothing foolish, but she held her tongue. It was her policy, whenever possible, not to interfere. Not that it was always possible, despite her good intentions. Which was why she was going to France. A glance at her aunt showed clearly that that topic was anything but finished.

Indeed, they had scarcely seated themselves at the supper table before Lady Cadogan said shortly, "I have received word from Lord Uxbridge that he will have your passport, French money, and some useful letters of introduction ready for you when we reach Barmouth, Meriel, but he agrees with me that you ought to have a footman by you as well as your maid, and he recommends going no farther than Rouen. He mentions the state of the political situation, but he does not go into detail, so I do not know what he can mean. Still, he is perfectly right. You've no business to be traveling alone."

"I shall not be alone, ma'am," Meriel said equably. "I shall have Gladys Peat with me, and my pistol as well."

"A female with a pistol," wailed Lady Cadogan. "Whoever heard of such a thing?"

"Well, it will be far more use to me than a footman, who would have to be a stranger, for none of our menservants would go. Nor would I wish to take any of them. Gladys and I shall do very well. As for the political situation, since we are now at peace with France, I cannot think there will be any danger there."

"Perhaps we are no longer at peace," suggested Lady Cadogan. "It has been weeks since anyone here saw a newspaper, after all, and any letters we have received have contained only gossipy news."

"Come now, ma'am," Meriel said, smiling, "you know we should certainly have heard if England and France were at war again. Uxbridge merely expresses a typical male belief that women need men to protect them. I have learned better these past years, I promise you. My sole concern has been for the children, but with them safe under your capable wing, I know I need only enjoy my journey. And so I shall, thank you."

"You needn't think to get round me with cajolery," Lady Cadogan said tartly.

"I don't cajole, ma'am."

Davy and Gwenyth laughed, and even Eliza allowed herself a smile.

"I don't see why any of us need go anywhere," that young lady said. "Dolgellau is town enough for me. And here we sit in a magnificent house at the foot of one of the world's most beautiful mountains, in the midst of our particular friends—"

"*O, Liza, dal dy dafod!*" said Gwenyth rudely as she helped herself from a plate of grilled trout. "Our particular friends, indeed. Only Bugg Dewsall, that's who. And he's no particular friend of mine, or of Meri's, or of anyone but you."

"Gwenyth," said Meriel calmly, "if you must request

that your sister hold her tongue, pray do so in a civil manner and in English. To be flinging Welsh expressions about at a London dinner table where they will not be understood will never do."

"Stuff," said Gwenyth, wrinkling her nose. "Welsh is a perfectly good language. Moreover, I shall not be allowed to dine in company in London."

"Very true, my dear," said Lady Cadogan, "but when you get to l'École de Bonté in Rouen, you will not want to blush for your manners, you know. The French are most particular. And as for your friend Mr. Dewlap," she added sternly, turning to glare at Eliza, "we must certainly hope that in London you will quickly come to see the error of your ways, my dear. Entirely unsuitable, I assure you."

Before Eliza could speak the words that had clearly leapt to her tongue, words that must have seen her banished from the table, Meriel said in her soft-spoken way, "He is quite unsuitable, Eliza. You know he is. His father is little more than a coal miner. Jocelyn will never permit the connection."

"Gwilym's father owns three slate mines," Eliza said defiantly. "Even Jocelyn owns but two."

"That is quite a different matter," Lady Cadogan said, peering at one of the dishes before her, then looking directly at Eliza. "Your brother is not dependent upon the income from his mines for his well-being. Mr. Dew-whatever is. What is more important, his son is not quality."

"I don't care," said Eliza stoutly. "You will soon be made to see that even separating us by thousands of miles will not quell our deep passions!"

With a ponderous laugh Mr. Glendower observed from the foot of the table that Lady Eliza had not seemed to grasp the geography lessons he had so carefully prepared for her perusal. "For I daresay that London is not quite so far as a thousand miles from Dolgellau, you know."

"Dear me," put in Lady Cadogan, "it is certainly no more than three hundred and fifty. If you know what the foolish child is nattering about, Mr. Glendower, I wish you will tell the rest of us. Meriel, do you follow her meaning?"

"Indeed, ma'am, she has been reading more of those foolish books of hers. Truly, Eliza, people do not fall head over ears in love upon first seeing one another. Moreover, love has little to do with marrying suitably, since one simply must live according to one's station in life."

"Joss didn't," Davy said. "He left everything behind."

Meriel looked at him for a moment, then said gently, "Our brother Jocelyn was carried away by local sympathy for the French republic, my dear. You will not remember, but many people left Merioneth for America then because times were hard and the common people blamed the landowners, much the way the French peasants did before their revolution. Joss took their side, engaging in one dreadful row with Papa after another, all of them over stupid matters of politics. In the end he went off in high dudgeon to join the others. He may have found what he was looking for, or he may not, but he will discover that he cannot elude his responsibilities here forever. One way or another, he must deal with them."

"Then why have we not had word from him?" demanded Gwenyth. "Two years, for pity's sake, since Papa's death. Is Joss dead too, do you think, Meri?"

Meriel did not answer the question immediately for the simple reason that she could not offer a flat denial. Her first letter had been followed by several others, one of which, at least, he must have received if he was still alive.

"I cannot answer you with certainty, Gwen," she said at last, softly. "Somehow I know he will be with us again one day, but I have no proof other than my own belief that he is not dead."

"You have had no news," said Lady Cadogan, signing to the footman to clear her place. "Had he died, I assure you that someone would have written to inform you of the fact."

She had used the same argument before, and as always Meriel took comfort from it. But knowing that her brother had emigrated to the colonies with a band of Welsh dissidents caught up in a cause she had never truly understood or sympathized with didn't encourage her to believe anyone would have taken time to send word home if Jocelyn had died. And although letters arrived in Merioneth from the New World occasionally, she knew that most of them were brief requests for money. Any gossip they contained was mostly family news, and no other Trahernes had sailed with Jocelyn. Nor would he have expected his father to send him money. Lord Tallyn had cut the connection upon Jocelyn's departure, and had there been a way to disinherit his son, Meriel had no doubt he would have found it.

Happily, there had been none. The Tallyn estate had been entailed right along with the title from the time Edward I had awarded Tallyn to Henry Traherne, Baron Beaufort of Shropshire, one of his favorites. Merioneth was then a center of Welsh resistance to King Edward's dreams of conquest, for it was just over the hill in nearby Denbighshire that Dafydd, brother of Llewelyn the Last, had had his headquarters. After Dafydd's defeat, the defense of the district was entrusted to Traherne, later first Earl of Tallyn, with his king commanding that the fortified manor house at Plas Tallyn be fully garrisoned to keep the surrounding countryside loyal to the crown. The task of taming the Welsh had proved from time to time to be nearly impossible, and it had been said more than once that they were scarcely more civilized in this new century than they had been in centuries past.

"We have strayed somewhat from the subject," said Lady Cadogan severely, bending a basilisk eye upon Meriel that effectively startled her from her musing. "Your brother's whereabouts need not concern us at the moment, but I can certainly assure you that he would never countenance your traveling into France. To go to Rouen is bad enough, when you might employ another to attend to the matter, but to go on to Paris—"

"Indeed, ma'am, I must."

"Poppycock. Your sister is perfectly safe. Indeed, her most recent letter indicates that she is misbehaving quite as much as ever she did. Parties and balls, with her poor husband locked away in the Bastille or wherever that dreadful Bonaparte is keeping him."

Meriel smiled. "I doubt the Bastille, ma'am, but you are correct in saying that Nest sounds undistressed. She is such a shatterbrain, you know, thinking of little beyond her own pleasure. Still, she loves her husband, so I fear she is merely putting a good face on the matter. I must see for myself."

"Aye, you were that way from a child," said Lady Cadogan, grimacing. "You never learn."

"Do you think to convince me you will not manage without me in London, ma'am? I promise you, I shall not believe such a faradiddle. You will enjoy yourself hugely, and I am persuaded that Eliza at least could not be in better hands then yours."

Lady Cadogan preened herself. "That is true," she said. "No one else could fire the girl off as well as I shall."

"But I do not wish to be fired off," said Eliza, pouting.

"I for one should like it above all things," put in Gwenyth. "You are a fool, Eliza, to wish to be stuck with that Bugg person."

"His name is Gwilym," said Eliza angrily, "and you are not to call him by that dreadful nickname again, Gwenyth, or I shall . . . I shall box your ears until they ring a full carillon, do you hear me?"

"Ydw," said the unrepentant Gwenyth.

"Speak English," pleaded Lady Cadogan.

Gwenyth grinned at her."Very well, but it seems a pity to say three words when one will do." She turned to Eliza. "I heard you, Eliza, perfectly. Is there anything else you wish to say to me?"

"Meri," begged Eliza, "only let me have five minutes alone with her."

"No, my dear. A lady does not indulge in physical violence."

"Oh, what a plumper. Why, you kicked Joss and pushed him into the river the week before he left only because he refused to let you ride his black Thunder. And you nearly scratched Nest's eyes out the time she told Papa you had been climbing the mountain alone again."

"That was different," said Meriel with grave dignity. "I do not like tale-bearers."

"You didn't like what Joss did when he hauled himself out of the river, either," said Gwenyth with a chuckle. "I was only seven then, but I remember."

"I don't," said Davy. "What did he do?"

"He put her straight across his knee and thrashed her soundly, and when she complained to Papa, he said it was no more than she deserved and that she was lucky he didn't repeat Joss's lesson."

Meriel chuckled at the memory. "I don't know whether I was angrier at the thrashing or the fact that Joss was still soaking wet when he caught me," she said. "I was as soggy as he was when he was done, and Papa scolded me dreadfully for coming into his presence in such a bedraggled condition."

The others laughed with her then, and the conversation turned safely to the subject of the next day's journey and the three days they would spend in Barmouth before the coastal packet sailed. As Meriel went upstairs later that evening, she felt a tightening in her throat. This would be the first time she had left Merionethshire since her single unsuccessful Season in London seven years before, and her feelings were mixed. There was sadness at the leaving, but underlying it was an undeniable sense of excitement. Adventure lay ahead. For once, she could almost imagine herself as the heroine in one of Eliza's idiotish books. Shaking her head at such foolishness, she turned her thoughts firmly to last-minute details that must be attended to before their departure.

2

Two carriages were required to transport the Traherne party to Barmouth. The ladies and young Master Davy occupied the first, a large and lumbering traveling coach with the Earl of Tallyn's crest emblazoned upon the door, while two abigails, Mr. Glendower, Marwyn, and piles of luggage occupied the second. The journey began early in the morning, and Davy, being the youngest, found himself occupying the forward, rear-facing seat between the younger two of his three sisters. In the short space of time it took the two carriages to reach the outskirts of Dolgellau, a scattering of neat stone houses and narrow streets at the confluence of the Wnion and Mawddach rivers, his squirming and stretching to see the passing countryside had begun to annoy them both.

"Do, for heaven's sake, stop wriggling!" exclaimed Eliza.

"I want to see," was his simple response. "Why are there so many people about at such an early hour?"

"Because Dolgellau is a market town, of course," responded Gwenyth loftily. "Don't you know anything? Sit still."

"There's a man with a pig on his shoulder!"

"Davy, sit back where you belong," commanded Eliza. "You are crushing my dress. Really, Meri, cannot you make him be still?"

Meriel smiled. "We have a half-day's journey before us, so the three of you will have to settle yourselves as best you can. Perhaps if one of you were to exchange seats with him, you would all be more comfortable."

"Well, I shall not," said Gwenyth firmly, "for I wish to look out also. Besides, if I sit in the middle I shall more than likely be sick."

"That's true enough," said Eliza with a sigh. "Very well, Davy, you may sit here. But don't scramble over me like a puppy, for heaven's sake," she added hastily. "If you will stand up a little, perhaps I can slide under you."

This feat was accomplished, and Davy was soon happily engaged in peering out at the passing populace, his button nose pressed against the glass. "Dolgellau is a very important town, is it not?" he said a moment later as the coach passed the Golden Lion, a bustling inn that had been nearly as famous in the days of the Tudors as it was now, and lumbered over the cobbles toward Saint Mary's church with its distinctive oak pillars and tall spiked steeple.

Gwenyth snorted. "Only wait until you see London, Mr. Know-all. Then you will think Dolgellau quite paltry."

Meriel chuckled at Davy's wide-eyed expression. "London is a much larger city, you see, but Dolgellau is certainly important to Wales, for besides being a marketing town, it is also a manufacturing center."

"Indeed," put in Lady Cadogan. "Do you recall from your lessons with Mr. Glendower just what is manufactured here, Davy?"

The boy nodded without taking his eyes from the view. "Flannel. He told me that the wool from our sheep is used for that purpose. Oh, look, we are coming to a bridge."

Once over the ancient stone bridge crossing the Wnion, it was but a short distance to the Barmouth Road, which wound through a dark and gloomy vale to the village of Llanelltyd, then beyond through the mountains, following the course of the River Mawddach. Both road and river were hemmed in by rocky cliffs and steep banks hung with plantations of larch trees. To their left, kingfishers dove into the river, which flowed swiftly as it carved its way through the rock, its tumbling, rushing progress audible even over the noise of the carriage wheels. It seemed to Meriel, who had traveled the route several times before, that each curve brought a new and more magnificent burst of scenery to view, so she could not be surprised that her small brother continued to peer from his window without any sign of incipient boredom. She exchanged an amused glance with Lady Cadogan.

"I daresay we are all looking forward to a change," that lady said, smiling.

"Indeed, ma'am."

" 'Tis early days yet, of course, but I daresay we shall not find Barmouth thin of company."

"Who will be there, do you think?" demanded Gwenyth.

Meriel leaned back, settling herself more comfortably against the squabs, as the conversation drifted on between her sisters and Lady Cadogan. It did not much matter to her who might be in Barmouth, so long as the Earl of Uxbridge was there with the papers he had promised to obtain for her. The three days they would pass waiting for the packet boat that would carry them south along the rugged coast would go quickly enough. For herself, she would have been content to remain two more days at Plas Tallyn, but she had let the weight of the others' arguments persuade her to depart early enough to enjoy several days at the seaside resort. Her senses stirred only when she thought ahead to her journey into France. Despite the peace, she could not help thinking that adventure, perhaps even danger, lay ahead. Tiny thrills raced up her spine at the thought.

The river alongside which they traveled began to widen considerably, and within the hour they reached the head of the Mawddach estuary, a broad, somewhat boggy arm of Cardigan Bay. Two more hours of winding road lay ahead, however, before they topped a rise and were able at last to look down upon the sea and the thriving little resort town that was their destination.

Despite the fact that Barmouth was the main port of Merionethshire, it was not a large town and was situated, Meriel thought, in one of the most undesirable places that could have been chosen for it. The golden beach that stretched for two miles on either side of it was pleasant enough, but while some of the picturesque houses had been built right upon the sand at the bottom of the huge rock cliff that entirely sheltered the town on the east, others occupied seemingly impossible positions at different elevations right upon the cliffside and were connected by a series of narrow, winding, entirely precipitous flights of stairs cut out of the rock.

"Goodness," Davy breathed, gripping the doorframe with white knuckles and struggling to lean forward enough to see out the window as the carriage began the steep descent toward the sea.

Eliza had closed her eyes as the carriage lurched over the rise, but Gwenyth peered from her window, craning her neck to see what lay ahead, her eyes sparkling with excitement. "Only look," she said, grinning. "I daresay that the people in some of those houses might almost cure their bacon by simply hanging it out the window over their neighbors' chimneys."

Meriel, bracing herself against the increasing incline and hoping the coachmen knew their business, smiled at her sister's comment. Certainly the houses were curious ones, looking as though they ought to slide into one another or topple into the sea at any moment. She had spent the summer here more than once as a child, however, and knew they were quite solidly built.

Since their stay this time would be a short one, she had arranged for them to put up at the most comfortable of several inns located at the bottom of the cliff where the road—the only road in Barmouth—ran between the cliffside and the quay. Instead of watching the steep, winding road ahead, she turned her attention to the wide, curving bay, where afternoon sunlight sparkled on green water and where at least fifty boats of assorted sizes rested at anchor.

Within the hour they were settled in their rooms at the lovely old inn and Mrs. Lewis, the proprietress, had begun to serve a light luncheon in their private sitting room. The rest of the afternoon was spent exploring the town and the quayside, and by suppertime Lady Cadogan had discovered that not only were the Earl and Countess of Uxbridge in residence at their home just north of the village, but that a number of her other acquaintances were in Barmouth as well. Thus, it was not surprising that the following morning found the Traherne ladies happily engaged in poring over a number of invitations that had been delivered to their sitting room with their breakfast trays.

"A boating party!" exclaimed Gwenyth, reading over Meriel's shoulder. "Oh, may I go too, Meri? Please?"

"You will only be sick," said Eliza calmly.

"I shan't!"

Meriel glanced up at her youngest sister. "I daresay you would be, you know, but the question will not arise—or not so far as that party is concerned, at any event—for it is not to be until Saturday and by then, you know, we will be aboard the packet. Half these invitations are for events that take place after our departure, I'm afraid."

"Not this one," said Lady Cadogan with a broad smile. "Only look, Meriel, my love. The Countess of Uxbridge desires our presence at a dinner party Thursday evening. How very kind of her, to be sure."

"Indeed," Meriel agreed, "though perhaps we ought to call at Uxbridge Hall earlier to obtain my passport and the letters his lordship promised."

"Am I included in her ladyship's invitation?" Eliza asked, her casual tone belied by the spark of excitement in her eyes.

Lady Cadogan twinkled back at her. "Certainly you are, my dear. It will be the perfect way to begin your come-out, for I daresay it will not be an extremely large party, since her ladyship is but lately delivered of her second son. Uxbridge, you know, is a distinguished military officer with the highest connections. Moreover, he is a most delightful and obliging gentleman, for you know he must have had to go to Aberystwyth in order to procure your sister's passport, there being no customs office in Barmouth, or anywhere else in Merioneth that I know about. Her ladyship, Meriel, mentions that he will have your documents for you Thursday evening, by the by, so we need not exert ourselves before that." She turned back to Eliza. "Lady Uxbridge, you will find, is as delightful as her husband, though, to be sure, she is a daughter of the Earl and Countess of Jersey, of whom you have often heard me speak. Caroline is a little like her mother, I'm afraid, but of course, such behavior is not at all odd in a *young* woman. You will wear your white muslin with the lavender silk sash, my dear."

After that everything else seemed a trifle flat to the younger ladies, for Gwenyth was nearly as excited about Eliza's first dinner party as Eliza was, and neither of them could think that Lady Cadogan or Meriel would enjoy the soiree to which they had been invited that evening nearly as much as they would the countess's dinner party. Indeed, the hours seemed to drag until at last it was time for Eliza to be handed into the carriage behind her aunt and elder sister. Less than twenty minutes later, the three ladies found themselves upon the threshold of a charmingly appointed rose-and-cream drawing room, hearing their names announced by a stately butler to the Earl and Countess of Uxbridge and their guests.

Meriel noted that there were some twenty persons present in the room, and as she made her curtsy to the gallant earl and his pretty, bright-eyed countess, she spared thought for little other than whether her slim sea-green skirt would trip her up or not, but as she raised her head to smile at her hosts, her glance encountered that of a tall gentleman to the earl's right. Something, perhaps the fact that he was staring directly, even appraisingly, at her, or, more likely, the casual boredom in his eyes, arrested her gaze. She could not seem to look away.

The gentleman was an inch or two over six feet tall, with thick, curling golden-brown hair and dark hazel eyes. His broad shoulders threatened to split the seams of his dark, form-hugging coat, and his thighs, beneath cream-colored satin breeches, bulged with solid, well-developed muscles.

It was not until she heard her host's low chuckle that she realized where her gaze had wandered, and Meriel's cheeks were flushed when she jerked her attention back to the earl.

"May I present Sir Antony Davies to your notice, Lady Meriel?" that gentleman inquired suavely.

" 'Tis a pleasure to make your acquaintance, my lady," said Sir Antony in soft, clipped tones.

Meriel murmured that the pleasure was hers, whereupon Lord Uxbridge said cheerfully, "Sir Antony is in Merioneth on business, ma'am, though he generally, I regret to say, resides in London. Lady Meriel, too, is a transient visitor, Tony. She departs on Saturday's morning tide for the French coast." He smiled at Meriel. "I have your passport, money, and several letters of introduction, including one to Lord Whitworth, the British ambassador in Paris, and will see that you receive them before you leave tonight. As per Lady Cadogan's instructions, your passport lists one Gladys Peat as your servant. I don't mind telling you," he added, "that I wish I might have added a footman or two, as well, for I cannot approve of your traveling without male escort, but I daresay your aunt has already told you what I wrote to her on that head, so I shall say no more."

Meriel, still flustered, listened while Uxbridge presented Lady Cadogan and Eliza, and then was presented in turn to another gentleman, who had also been standing, albeit unnoticed by herself, with Sir Antony and Uxbridge.

Mr. George Murray had little to recommend him in such company, for he was quite unlike any of the other gentlemen in the room. Indeed, Meriel thought, after exchanging but the merest of pleasantries with him, that he must be one of the officers lately serving under Uxbridge, for despite an intelligence of eye, he had more the manner of a common foot soldier than of a gentleman. He was of no more than medium height and was dressed neatly but with little elegance. His speech was undistinguished, and although she noted that the earl and several other gentlemen with whom she was slightly acquainted treated Mr. Murray with marked respect, she was grateful to find that not he but Sir Antony Davies had been partnered with her for dinner. Mr. Murray was, in fact, seated across the table from Lady Cadogan, who was at Sir Antony's right hand, so politeness would preclude their even having to converse with him. Not, she decided after some moments of silence, that Sir Antony's conversation was particularly stimulating.

"I believe his lordship said you reside in London, sir," she said at last as an opening gambit.

"A splendid place, London. Very civilized."

"Indeed, I have been there only once, but I found it a pleasant city."

"Do try some of this tripe, my lady. 'Tis remarkably well cooked."

"Is it indeed?"

"I shall have to inquire as to its making. My chef does not prepare it nearly so well as this."

"You provide your chef with recipes, sir?"

He glanced at her in surprise. "But of course. How should he otherwise know my preferences?"

Meriel hid a smile. "I daresay you are the sort of man who orders his boots polished with champagne, are you not?"

Hazel eyes glinted into hers, and Sir Antony's fork was suspended in space for a full three seconds before he lowered it to his plate. "You had that nonsense from Brummell, I daresay."

"The infamous Beau Brummell, sir? I know that he has made a name for himself by determining what shall and shall not be acceptable dress for gentlemen of taste. He has been described to me by friends who are so kind as to correspond occasionally with me from London, but I have never actually met him. At the risk of offending your sensibilities," she added confidingly, "I must confess that although their habits seem to have changed considerably since my sojourn in London, I am not generally drawn to dandies. Such preoccupation with appearance puts me off."

"One's appearance must necessarily be of some importance," he said, regarding her more closely than he had before, "but I do not, so far as I know, have my boots polished with champagne. I have recently acquired a new manservant, so I cannot presume to know all his secrets, but 'tis my firm belief that not even Brummell's man uses champagne."

"No, sir? But I was told—"

"My dear girl, you cannot have considered the matter," he said calmly. "Can you imagine what alcohol—

for that is what champagne is, after all—would do to good leather? A week of such polishing, and the leather would be utterly ruined."

Her eyes widened. "Why, that is true. Alcohol would dry it out, would it not?"

He nodded and returned his attention to his dinner.

Meriel turned back to her own plate, but although she scarcely heeded the gentleman seated upon her left, she found that she was uncommonly aware of Sir Antony's presence at her right hand. When a slight movement of his set her nerves atingle, she mentally scolded herself. He appeared, after all, to be nothing more than a lazy bon vivant, more interested in his dinner and the habits of his new manservant than in anything of importance. Still, when he turned his attention to Lady Cadogan, she found herself straining to overhear what they said to one another. It was no use, for his soft voice did not carry, and although she overheard her aunt's trilling laughter more than once, she could make out nothing of sense. A moment later, the gentleman on her left spoke to her and she had, perforce, to turn her attention to him. A half-hour passed before she was able to converse with Sir Antony again.

"Your aunt tells me," he said then, "that you travel alone into France. Is that not a somewhat unwise venture for a gently nurtured female?"

"Indeed not, sir. For one thing, I do not go alone. My maid, Gladys Peat—a most stalwart woman—accompanies me. For another, I am not so delicately nurtured as all that. I have grown up in what has been called the most rugged of all the Welsh districts, and I am accustomed to looking after myself and the rest of my family as well. Indeed, it is on my sister's behalf that I go to France. My youngest sister is to go to school in Rouen at Michaelmas if all goes according to plan. But I must first see the place for myself and interview the headmistress. 'Tis l'École de Bonté, which my aunt attended when she was a young girl—before the Revolution, you know."

"I see." He smiled at her then, and she found to her surprise that she was smiling back. Then, instead of arguing, as she had quite expected him to do, that it was not seemly for a young woman to travel abroad with only her maid, however stalwart, for company, he said, "Is it truly safe, do you think, to send your sister to France to school?"

Lady Cadogan's ears were clearly sharper than Meriel's, for she spoke up from his other hand. "Perfectly safe, Sir Antony, for we are at peace now, are we not? Moreover, where in England might a young lady acquire such a fine education for a mere eighteen pounds, fifteen shillings per annum?"

Davies settled back in his chair, and Meriel noted that his eyes were twinkling. "Where, indeed, ma'am? Is that figure inclusive? I must tell you I am something of an expert on school expenses, for I have a sister who must be much the same age as your niece, and the cost of her education has fallen to me."

Lady Cadogan frowned. "I believe the charge is a comprehensive one, sir, but I do not recall precisely."

"Neither French nor arithemetic is included," Meriel said. "I believe one pays a guinea extra for each. Oh, and another guinea if Gwenyth wishes to take wine instead of beer with her meals."

"That last," said Sir Antony, "would be a guinea well spent, would it not? Beer? Good Lord." But the hazel eyes were dancing now. "Is the drawing master thrown in for the comprehensive fee?"

"No, nor the music master either," she retorted. "They are three guineas more."

"But, Meriel dear, the comprehensive fee does include board, lodging, washing, and dancing," Lady Cadogan protested. "That is quite a lot, and nothing, you know, can compare with a good French education."

"I cannot agree, ma'am," said Sir Antony. "I believe a sound English education is better than what one can get anywhere else. I daresay that when you look more closely into this French school, you will discover that there are further charges for tea and sugar, pens and recreations, and no doubt for anything else the good mistresses can think up."

"Well, that is why I am going to see for myself," Meriel said matter-of-factly. "We don't know a soul in

Rouen. Our nearest relative is my sister in Paris, so before I can even consider sending Gwenyth, I must know that the school is in fact an excellent one and its mistresses completely trustworthy."

"If you desire to meet a trustworthy person in Rouen," said George Murray suddenly from across the table, "I believe I can help you, Lady Meriel."

She stared at him in amazement, realizing he had been attending quite openly to their conversation, but he was dearly unaware of having committed a social solecism. His very attitude confirmed her earlier belief that his background must be lacking in the social graces, but she couldn't bring herself to snub him. That, in fact, would be as much a breach of manners as his speaking across the table. Consequently she smiled."Can you, indeed, sir?"

"There is a priest," he said, somewhat diffidently now that he had her attention. "I will understand if you do not wish to make his aquaintance, for I know that much prejudice still exists, particularly in Wales, against those of the Catholic faith, but I met him some years ago through mutual friends, and we have corresponded whenever possible. Naturally, while the war was on, we were unable to write, but he remembers me well enough, and he must know nearly everyone in Rouen. If you like, I will give you a letter of introduction to him. He has mentioned the school, so I am certain he will be able to tell you a great deal about it."

"Thank you, sir," Meriel said. "I shall be most grateful for such a letter." She was amused a moment later to note that Sir Antony's attention was once again firmly riveted upon his dinner and that conversation around the table had become general, with a number of persons speaking across the board. Evidently Lady Uxbridge herself had encouraged others to follow Mr. Murray's example. Meriel watched that gentleman closely for some moments, but she could still discover nothing about him that warranted such a thought for his feelings from one so high in the instep as the countess was known to be.

After supper, when the ladies had retired to the elegant rose-and-cream drawing room, leaving the gentleman to their port, conversation turned rather quickly, Meriel thought, from the usual topics of family and children to the year-old peace treaty with France. Since she had heard little during the heavy Welsh winter about what was going forward, she listened carefully and soon discovered that feelings were mixed. Several persons in the Uxbridge drawing room had actually been in Paris the previous August to help celebrate Napoleon Bonaparte's assumption of the title of Life Consul.

"Such a charming man," said one plump baroness with a sigh.

Another, much thinner lady gasped at her. "Adelaide, have your wits gone begging? That dreadful man is responsible for the deaths of thousands of young Englishmen."

"Well, no doubt he is," the baroness admitted, frowning, "but I daresay he means well, you know."

"He cannot be trusted," said the thin lady.

"We had a letter from my mama only last month," put in Lady Uxbridge quickly as the baroness bristled, "informing us that yet another Frenchman has been found guilty of spying in London. Since that dreadful Joseph Fouché is no longer the French minister of police, and is indeed quite out of favor, why do you suppose there are still such persons abounding in this country? While he was at the helm, of course, one might expect anything of the French. But Bonaparte dismissed him. Moreover, we are at peace, are we not? It all seems prodigious odd to me."

"That's the French, when all is said and done," said the thin lady, as Meriel glanced quickly toward her sister, being grateful that it was Eliza and not Gwenyth who had accompanied them that night. Gwenyth, like their brother Jocelyn, would have taken immediate exception to the countess's casual notion that England and Wales were but one country.

"I daresay you know the French well," Lady Cadogan said, smiling gently at the thin woman. "I went to school in France myself, and I found any number of quite well-bred Frenchmen, who would no doubt be as appalled as any Englishman at the thought of spying on one's fellowman."

"Do we not send spies into France, then?" asked Eliza, who had been sitting quietly in a corner until now. "I should have thought we would if they send spies to our country."

"Goodness me!" exclaimed Lady Uxbridge, shaking her head. "Wherever can you have come by such a notion, I wonder."

Eliza flushed to the roots of her hair, and Meriel said quickly, "You cannot have thought carefully before you spoke, dear. Only think of how strongly the English believe in fair play. Surely you must realize that to spy, even upon one's enemy in wartime, simply is not done."

"Not by decent persons, surely," agreed a masculine voice from the doorway, and the ladies all turned quickly to discover that Uxbridge was leading the gentlemen in from the dining room. He chuckled, glancing over his shoulder to ascertain just how many of the others had overheard Meriel's comment. "Our womenfolk seem to be discussing a distressingly unfeminine subject, gentlemen."

His wife laughed. "Peace is certainly a feminine notion rather than a masculine one, sir, and that, I will have you know, is what we were discussing."

He moved to stand behind her chair. "And what, pray tell, does spying have to do with peace, Caroline, my dear?"

"Just what we were wondering ourselves," she informed him. "I was merely speaking of Mama's letter, the one where she mentioned the latest French spy, and young Lady Eliza wished to know if his English counterpart existed in France. I was happy to tell her he does not."

"Certainly not his counterpart," said Sir Antony, letting his gaze drift from one lady to another. "We have not had anyone since Sir Francis Walsingham during Elizabeth's reign, who has managed to create an information-gathering network equal to that of Joseph Fouché's. As you have noted, we are still discovering the remnants of Fouché's vast organization. However, ma'am, I hope no one is so foolish as to think that the English do not engage in any form of intelligence gathering, which is, after all, what spying is all about."

"Here now, man," protested the baroness's husband, "surely you won't have it that we stoop to such depths as those damned Frenchies—begging your pardon, ladies, but 'tis more than a man may stomach to hear such an accusation."

Sir Antony regarded him calmly. " 'Tis scarcely foolish to wish one's army to be prepared for what lies ahead, sir, when all it takes to accomplish the deed is a scout or two sent on ahead to look over the landscape and draw a map or two."

"Oh, that. Well, of course, we do that. Damned foolish not to, as you say. But those scouts are scarcely spies, sir. Brave soldiers, every one of them, wearing their uniforms as they ought to do. And when they're caught, by gad, as they too often are, they're civilly treated as prisoners of war, just as we treat theirs—when they turn up in uniform. When they don't, we hang 'em. Fair enough, I say. And not at all the same as a man's pretending to be what he ain't."

There was a small silence, after which a gentleman whose name Meriel did not know suggested that perhaps it wouldn't be such a bad idea as all that to send a spy or two to Paris to try what they could to discover what Bonaparte was about at the moment. "For, peace or no peace, if he ain't got designs for some new enterprise in the Levant, you may call me a Dutchman."

"Well, even if he has," said the baron, "surely you wouldn't ask an Englishman to poke and pry through the man's secret papers to find out? Dammit, man, it just ain't done."

"Even if it meant saving a regiment?" inquired Sir Antony gently.

Meriel turned with several others to stare at him, but his expression was enigmatic, and she could not tell for certain whether he was serious or merely trying to stir up a hornet's nest. Several gentlemen began then to speak at once, their voices increasing in volume until Uxbridge interrupted them with a laugh.

"My friends, we cannot determine Bonaparte's intentions by shouting about them in my wife's drawing room, I assure you. We must simply trust that our hard-won peace will continue and leave the details to such persons as Prime Minister Addington and his aides. Perhaps Miss Claversham," he added, nodding toward a blushing young lady in a white muslin dress, "will indulge us now by playing for a time upon the pianoforte."

Although Meriel saw one or two backs stiffen at the mention of the prime minister, giving her to believe that Mr. Addington was thought of no more highly here in Barmouth than Lady Cadogan had said he was in London, no one debated Uxbridge's right to put an end to such an improper discussion. Miss Claversham proved to be an accomplished pianist and had the good sense to begin with a soothing minuet, followed by several cheerful folk songs, so the mood of the company rapidly settled into one more appropriate to the occasion. Not another word was said about Napoleon Bonaparte or the Peace of Amiens, and Meriel's own thoughts soon turned to her sister Eliza, who, having quickly recovered from her embarrassment, was now responding in a quite unacceptable manner to the flirtations of a young sprig of fashion.

"Oh, pooh," that young lady said later in the coach when Meriel took her to task, "he was a perfectly harmless young man."

Tucking into her reticule the passport, several letters, and the comforting bundle of French money that Uxbridge had presented to her before their departure, Meriel said quietly, "I daresay you do not even know that young man's name."

"No, but it does not signify, for he said he would call upon us at the inn. Is he not the handsomest young man you ever laid your eyes upon, Meriel?"

"I quite thought Gwilym Dewsall was the handsomest young man of your acquaintance."

Eliza shrugged, glancing out at the street as the carriage drew up at the inn. "I daresay he was," she said casually.

3

Saturday's chill, damp dawn found the Trahernes at quayside ready to board the *Camden*, a coastal packet that would carry Meriel to Swansea and the others on to Bristol. A light fog covered Cardigan Bay, muffling the sounds of movement aboard as the gear for the twenty-three passengers boarding at Barmouth was quickly stowed.

"It looks like a ghost ship," said Gwenyth with a happy sigh as she watched Mr. Glendower and Marwyn giving rapid orders for the accommodation of their great pile of luggage.

"Don't be nonsensical," snapped Eliza, never at her best in the early morning. She shivered, drawing her heavy woolen cape closer about her shoulders. "It is a very small boat, is it not, Meri?"

"Pooh," said Davy. "Two masts and a jib is not small. You are just afraid it will sink, Eliza, but it will not. The *Camden* is a good stout English-built ship, Mr. Glower says."

"English?" Gwenyth looked at the vessel more disapprovingly. "Why can we not sail upon a Welsh ship, Meri?"

"Because this is the ship that sails to Bristol," Meriel said matter-of-factly before turning to her brother and adding in a sterner tone, "and you'd best not let Mr. Glendower hear you referring to him so disrespectfully, young man." Giving him no opportunity to compound his error, she tucked the heavy leather reticule containing her precious documents and a small but serviceable pistol more firmly under her arm, tugged her dark gray woolen cloak more snugly over her green traveling dress, and shifted her attention to Lady Cadogan. "Are you warm enough, ma'am? 'Tis a dreadful, damp chill in the air."

"Oh, don't trouble your head about me," said that lady cheerfully. "I shall do tolerably well just knowing we are leaving the winds of Wales behind us, not to mention all the cold and fury of a Welsh winter, which no one thought to remind me about before I decided to spend an entire year with you."

"Well, you might have remembered from your own youth, after all," Meriel said with a smile as they moved forward to follow the chaplain, Marwyn, and the stout young men who carried their gear up the gangplank.

"Indeed, I suppose 'twas not so long ago as that, but one does tend to forget how isolated Plas Tallyn is. Why, I had not heard the half of the London news we gleaned in Barmouth. Their being on the coast makes a great difference, does it not?"

Meriel agreed, looking over her shoulder to assure herself that Enid Broadman, who was Lady Cadogan's dresser, and Gladys Peat, her own maidservant, were following close upon their heels. They were indeed among the group of persons just behind their mistresses; however, it had not the sight of the two women that stopped Meriel in her tracks but that of a tall, broad-shouldered man emerging from a carriage a short distance from the foot of the gangplank.

"Gracious," said Lady Cadogan, following her astonished gaze, "is that not Sir Antony Davies, whom we met Thursday evening?"

"I wonder why he did not mention that he would be sailing with us," Meriel said before an impatient sound from a man just behind them on the gangplank recalled her to her senses. Apologizing briefly, she took Lady Cadogan gently by the elbow and urged her forward, quickly forgetting Sir Antony in the need to see to their belongings.

Mr. Glendower, having hurried on ahead, met them at

the entrance to their tiny cabin, situated just below the afterdeck. His long, thin, rabbitlike face creased with a broad smile. "I trust," he said, turning the smile directly upon Meriel, "that your ladyship will find the accommodations perfectly comfortable. Everything is neat as wax ma'am. Only look at how cunningly the young ladies' cots are built right into the inside wall, with doors that shut them off from the rest of the world."

"Into the bulkhead," corrected Lady Cadogan absently as she peered about the tiny cabin. "Ships' walls are called bulkheads, Mr. Glendower. Surely you know that." Ignoring his assurance that he did indeed know and had merely said "wall" in order that he would be understood by all his listeners, she gave a small sigh. "One always hopes one's accommodations will be larger. Ships have so little space."

Meriel could only agree with her. Though Mr. Glendower had referred to the small built-in bunks as accommodations for Eliza and Gwenyth, she realized gratefully that there were three such cubbyholes, built one atop the other. For although the larger bed, framed, curtained, and attached to the outer bulkhead beneath the tiny porthole, had been advertised as a double bed, she could see that it was no such thing. At best it was a foot wider than the closetlike bunks. She could not for a moment imagine getting any sleep if she had to share that bed with Lady Cadogan.

Mr. Glendower hovered expectantly, and she turned to him at last, saying, "This will do nicely, sir. I hope that you and Davy will be as comfortable."

"As to that, ma'am, it is doubtful. The great cabin does not provide much privacy, you know, but I did arrange for us each to have a separate bunk. I daresay I'd not sleep a wink with this young wriggler occupying the same bed."

Davy, whose interest had been claimed immediately by the little sleeping spaces that would be occupied by his sisters, turned at this moment to demand to know if his bed would also have doors upon it.

Mr. Glendower frowned at him. "You interrupt, sir. I was speaking to your sister."

"Yes, but you were talking about our beds. I wish to know will mine have doors like these, so that I can pretend I am in my own cave at night."

"Oh, Davy," said Eliza, chuckling, "one does not close the door at night. Only see how they may be hooked back against the wall. One would suffocate if they were closed."

"Our bunks have curtains upon them, however," Mr. Glendower said, "for some privacy is naturally required. And there will be hooks upon which you might hang your clothes, Davy, and a ladder to climb to reach your bunk, so I daresay it will be entirely to your liking. And of course the great cabin is, thankfully, reserved for gentlemen. You would not wish to be sleeping with the great unwashed, I'm thinking."

Meriel refrained from pointing out that the great unwashed generally chose other, less-expensive means of travel. Instead she tousled her little brother's hair and suggested that he go see for himself what his bed looked like.

"Yes, indeed," agreed Mr. Glendower with an arch look at her, "for I am persuaded your sisters and her ladyship must be wishing to examine their quarters without a pair of gentlemen looking over their shoulders. Come along with me, young man."

The small, stuffy cabin soon proving to be entirely too confining for four persons who wished to enjoy comfortable conversation, the ladies repaired above to the slightly larger ladies' saloon on the afterdeck, which had proper windows from which they could observe their departure. When they entered the room, they discovered two other women present, who nodded civilly and then returned to their conversation. A small stove, cold now, sat in the right-rear corner of the room. The only other furnishings were a deal table, a pair of chairs, and several banquettes under the windows, which began halfway back on each side and continued around the end, giving a view to the stern. This line of windows was interrupted midway by a second door that led to the railed aftergallery.

As Meriel moved to take her seat upon one of the

banquettes, her thoughts turned briefly to Marwyn, Gladys Peat, and Enid Broadman as she wondered what the servants' quarters might be like. The advertisement had said merely that they were clean. Would they have bunks, or hammocks like the crew members were said to have? She had little time to ponder the question, however, for as the ship caught the breeze in the bay and began to move more rapidly and with greater rocking motion away from the shore, Gwenyth turned suddenly from her position at the window and sank down upon the bench beneath it, one hand at her mouth, the other at her stomach. Her complexion was ashen.

Alarmed, Meriel moved quickly to her side. "Gwen?"

Eliza, turning toward them, regarded their younger sister with widening eyes. "I think she needs a basin, Meri. Oh, hurry!"

Looking rapidly around the saloon, Meriel saw nothing at first that would answer the purpose, but a moment later she strode to the black stove, snatched up and emptied the coal bucket beside it, and returned at once to her sister's side.

"Here, Gwen," she said. "It isn't Sèvres china, but it will do the trick."

Her gentle, teasing comment went unnoticed, for Gwenyth lurched gratefully toward the bucket and was violently sick. It was not long before Meriel realized that they could not stay where they were. Lady Cadogan had stepped out onto the aft gallery as soon as she recognized Gwenyth's distress, but the two other ladies who had been present when they entered the saloon had merely turned discreetly away. By the time Gwenyth pushed the bucket away and slumped miserably back upon the bench, both women were showing visible signs of distress themselves, and Meriel could scarcely blame them. She, too, felt rather sick.

Drawing a deep breath didn't help, for in the confines of the saloon there was little fresh air to be had, despite the fact that Lady Cadogan had left the door leading to the aft gallery ajar. When the other women moved quickly to join her ladyship, Eliza, looking toward Meriel, clearly hesitated on the verge of following their example.

"Go and get some air," Meriel told her gently, "but return as quickly as you can, for I do not wish to leave her alone, and I should like someone to send for Gladys Peat. Gwen must be taken to our cabin to rest."

Eliza nodded and turned away, but true to her word she was quickly back again. Meriel had moved the bucket with its disgusting contents away from Gwenyth, and now that she was certain the younger girl had no immediate need of it, she picked it up to carry it out on deck. At the far side of the aft rail, after glancing around to be certain the others were far enough away not to be offended, she emptied the bucket of its contents.

"If that stuff is what it appears to be, I'd fling the bucket overboard too," said a lazy masculine voice from behind her.

Turning quickly, she discovered Sir Antony moving toward her. His expression was calm, but the hazel eyes were twinkling, so she summoned up a smile. "I should like nothing more than to do as you suggest, sir, but the captain of this boat might object to my throwing his coal bucket away."

"So that's what it is," he said, lifting his quizzing glass to peer at the bucket as though it were some object of interest. "How practical you are, ma'am. I cannot think why you have been left to look after your needs alone in such a case, but I must hope that you are completely recovered from your indisposition."

"Oh, I am not indisposed, sir. 'Tis my youngest sister. She is not a good traveler at best, and I fear she is very ill now. Indeed, I must get her to our cabin and send someone to fetch my abigail, who was nursemaid to nearly all of us and will know precisely what is best for Gwenyth."

"Allow me to assist you, ma'am." He turned, looking forward along the rail; then, evidently catching someone's eye, he beckoned. A moment later a young, slender, dark-haired man detached himself from a group that had been leaning over the rail watching as the boat left the waters of the bay to attack the rougher coastal swells. "Peter Trent, my valet," said Sir Antony, regarding the approaching man. "Never far from my side. A most estimable fellow. Watches over my every need. Here, Trent, Lady Meriel has need of her tirewoman. Do see if you can find her."

"A pleasure to be of service," said the young man, bowing to Meriel. He looked up, revealing shrewd slate-gray eyes beneath straight, narrow brows. He wasn't so insolent as to regard her directly, but looked instead at a point just above her eyes as he inquired, "Her name, madam?"

"Gladys Peat, Mr. Trent. I shall be sincerely grateful if you can find her for me."

Trent nodded and began to turn away, but Sir Antony stopped him with a slight gesture, taking the bucket from Meriel's hand. "Take this away, Trent, and see that it is thoroughly cleaned before it is returned to its place in the ladies' saloon. What did you do with the coal, ma'am?"

Meriel found herself smiling at his matter-of-fact tone. "I dumped it onto the floor, sir," she said.

He nodded. "I daresay whoever attends to that bucket will see that the mess is cleaned up. I hope your sister recovers quickly."

"So do I, for I must tell you that with four of us sharing a tiny cabin, her continued indisposition will be most inconvenient."

"I should rather think so," he replied, much struck. "See here, ma'am, whatever were you about, to arrange for only one cabin for the four of you? In my experience, these cabins are deucedly small even for one."

"I do not not approve of extravagance, sir. We shall reach Swansea tomorrow, where I change to the Channel packet, while my aunt and sisters go on into Bristol aboard the *Camden*. For merely the one night it would be an unnecessary expense to order more than one cabin when each sleeps four or five persons."

"Nonsense," he said, but she could not imagine he meant to offend her, for his thoughts were clearly otherwhere. Frowning, he said, "See here, you cannot be comfortable with a sick child in a cabin with three other persons. 'Twould be astonishing an you were not all sick before the day is out. When Trent finds your maidservant, I will show you to my stateroom. You may safely leave the woman there with your sister."

"I could not, sir." But even as she said the words, Meriel was thinking of how uncomfortable it would be if Gwenyth continued to be sick, as indeed it was most likely she would be.

"Nonsense," he said again, more firmly. "As you pointed out, it will be only for the one night. I daresay I can rack up in the great cabin, for although I have been given to understand that all the staterooms are occupied, the boat does not seem to be filled to capacity."

"Oh, but it is two nights to Bristol, sir, and I greatly fear my little sister will be incapacitated the entire time. However, perhaps you mean there will be another cabin available after Swansea?"

"No, I leave the *Camden* at Swansea."

She cocked her head to one side, regarding him in surprise. "Are you not returning to London, then, sir?"

"No, Lady Meriel, I have formed the intention of visiting the French coast again." His expression was still calm, but his eyes were dancing again.

Meriel frowned. "You said nothing of such plans the other night, sir."

"Did I not? Perhaps I had not then realized that I wished to indulge myself with a period of foreign travel."

She believed she was beginning to understand his motives, but instead of being angered by her suspicions, she found that she was rather pleased. "Did you form this intention because I am traveling into France, sir?"

His eyelids drooped a little, hooding his expression. "You are very direct, ma'am. Are you offended?"

"Not at all, sir. Surely one must be flattered. However, I hope you have not formed an incorrect notion of my moral character, for I must assure you that I am not a woman of easy virtue."

"Dear me." Sir Antony raised his quizzing glass and regarded her through it curiously. "Whatever can I have said to stir such thoughts in your head, I wonder."

"Well," she said frankly, attempting to ignore the absurd way his eye was magnified by the quizzing glass, "my aunt warned me how it would be if I insisted upon traveling abroad with only my maid for escort, but I could not allow Mr. Glendower—her chaplain, you know, and no doubt a worthy man despite the fact that he is constantly ogling one—to accompany me. And as my elder brother is away, and I have no cousins upon whom I might call for assistance, there you are. I daresay you will agree with her, as Lord Uxbridge did, and say that, under the circumstances, I ought not to go at all."

"I will certainly say no such thing," he replied. "Nor can I believe you would be wiser to take the impertinent Mr. Glendower as your escort."

"Then you believe I am quite capable of looking after myself," she said, looking upon him favorably again.

He smiled. "As to that, ma'am, I cannot deny that if I were in any way responsible for your well-being I would forbid you to travel alone. No, no, don't poker up like that. You begin to look like a stuffy schoolmistress, which quite puts me off whatever it was I was going to say to you."

"You have no right to forbid me anything, sir," she said tartly.

"No, certainly not. Ah, here is Trent with your abigail, I believe. You will be wishing to see to your sister at once."

Much though she would have liked to continue their conversation, to be certain that Sir Antony quite understood that she would bow neither to his charm nor to his will, Meriel realized with a pang of conscience that she had been standing at the rail with him for an unconscionably long time. No doubt poor Eliza was feeling ill-used.

"You sent for me, my lady?" Gladys Peat, a buxom middle-aged woman with crisp brown curls set under a neat cap, regarded Sir Antony with a basilisk eye, drawing herself up and straightening her shoulders with a militant air.

Meriel, glancing up at the tall gentleman, saw that his lips twitched. Amused despite herself, she turned to her tirewoman. "Indeed, Gladys, Lady Gwenyth is ill and must be put to bed at once. Sir Antony here has most obligingly offered the use of his own cabin, where she will be a good deal more comfortable, I daresay, than in one of those tiny cubbyholes in ours."

"Yes, m'lady." Gladys' starched-up attitude disappeared in a swell of concern for Lady Gwenyth. " 'Tis a pity we've no laudanum by us. 'Twould be best an the poor lamb sleeps as much as she can."

"Sir," said Peter Trent, addressing his master, "I've some in my kit if Mrs. Peat would condescend to accept it."

Sir Antony bowed to Meriel. "As I said, ma'am, he sees to my every need."

" 'Tis not your need but Gwenyth's," she pointed out.

"Ah, but my need at present is to see to your needs," he said gently, "so you see . . ." He spread his hands, indicating that there was no more to be said, then turned to his man. "Attend to the matter at once, Trent."

The valet took himself off, and Meriel led the way back to Gwenyth's side. Her little sister looked no better than when she had left her, and Eliza looked considerably worse.

"Dear me, Eliza," Meriel said, "I hope you do not mean to be ill too. Auntie Wynne will go into flat despair."

Eliza managed a smile. "I shall be all right, I daresay, once Gwen is settled, although I must tell you, Meri, that if she is sick all night, I probably shall succumb too."

"Well, you need not trouble yourself, my dear, for Sir Antony—you do remember Sir Antony Davies, do you not?" When Eliza nodded, blushing delicately, Meriel continued, "Well, Sir Antony has most kindly given up his stateroom so that Gwen may be comfortable. Do you hear that, Gwen? You are to have a cabin all to yourself, and Gladys Peat to look after you for tonight, at least. If you are still unwell tomorrow, then you will have to make do with Broadman, for Gladys gets off the ship with me at Swansea, you know, but I daresay you will be right as a trivet by then."

Gwenyth smiled wanly but made no comment, and

Meriel could only be grateful when Sir Antony, having unceremoniously followed them into the ladies' saloon, now scooped the young girl up in his arms to carry her below. She could not think, looking at Gwenyth, that the child would have been able to walk the distance by herself, even supported by Gladys and one of her sisters.

Once below, Gwenyth was quickly tucked up in bed and dosed with the laudanum provided by Peter Trent.

"She'll do now, my lady," said Gladys Peat in a low voice. Then she turned toward Sir Antony, giving him a direct look. " 'Tis kind of you, sir, to put the child's needs afore yer own."

"Why did I have the feeling," Sir Antony asked as he escorted Meriel along the companionway a few moments later, "that I was being threatened rather than thanked just now?"

She chuckled, drawing her thoughts away from Gwenyth's predicament and looking up at the tall gentleman beside her. "Gladys doesn't hold with menfolk," she said.

"All menfolk?" His eyebrows arched comically.

"Nearly all. She was married years ago, but I don't think he can have amounted to much, and he died in circumstances that she refuses to discuss. My brothers and sisters and I, I regret to confess, have spent many a cheerful hour making up appalling adventures for him, though none of us ever met him."

"Has she no family?"

"A sister somewhere. She's mentioned her from time to time, but the sister is married, and they do not correspond. Her father was something of a brute, I believe, for though she has admitted having one, she always curls her lip when she speaks of him."

Sir Antony shook his head. "She is certainly not what I have been accustomed to in ladies' maids," he said.

"Are you accustomed to so many, then, sir?" Meriel inquired demurely.

His eyes danced. "Enough, ma'am, to have discovered that they have a habit of getting damnably in my way, and I've a strong notion that your Gladys Peat has just served notice of an intention to be the worst of such nuisances that I've yet encountered."

"Surely she would not forget her place, Sir Antony."

"Poppycock," he retorted. "Her attitude back there—in my own bedchamber, might I remind you—was that of a haughty dowager thanking a minion of the lowest extreme for a slight service. It was not that of a maidservant knowing her place."

Meriel smiled up at him sweetly. "I am persuaded, sir, that she will soon learn she has no need to protect me from a gentleman so kind and considerate as yourself."

The sound emitting from the tall gentleman's throat just then was certainly a snort, but she chose to ignore it, thanking him again for his kind offices on Gwenyth's behalf and excusing herself to look in upon Eliza, who had repaired to their own cabin to rest. Since by this time they had reached the door to that cabin, Sir Antony was left with nothing to do but bow and wish her well.

Meriel discovered that Eliza was not resting at all but was seated at a small desk near the head of the curtained bed, primping while she regarded her lovely reflection in a hand mirror. As Meriel entered, the younger girl turned, the fingers of her free hand still entwined in one honey-colored ringlet.

"Oh, Meriel, how is Gwenyth?"

"She will do. Gladys is with her now."

Eliza nodded, returning her attention to the mirror and peering closely at her face.

"Have you got a spot forming or something?" Meriel inquired.

"No, thank heaven." The younger girl straightened, setting the mirror down with a sigh. "I say, Meri, do you not think Mr. Trent is very handsome?"

"Good gracious, Eliza, he is a manservant."

"I know," Eliza replied, "but do you think him handsome?"

"He is well enough, I suppose," Meriel said, racking her memory for a vision of Sir Antony's valet and finding it difficult to remember what he looked like. "Really, dear, you must cease this foolish tendency to regard every gentleman you meet in some idiotishly romantical light." Her gaze shifted to a slim leather-bound volume lying open, facedown, upon the bed, its gilt lettering gleaming brightly.

Though she said nothing, her tact went unnoticed, for Eliza's gaze had followed hers, and the younger girl said tartly, "I know you cannot approve of the books I read, Meri, but there is truly no harm in them, and I do not imagine myself to be one of the heroines, regardless of what you and Auntie Wynne believe."

Meriel sighed. "I trust you have better sense than most of your heroines have, Eliza. Now you had best begin preparing for dinner, however. I believe they mean to serve it shortly after noon in the dining cabin."

The dining cabin was situated between the ladies' saloon and the great cabin on the upper deck and was scarcely large enough to contain more than half the full allotment of passengers the ship might carry. Upon this particular occasion, however, Meriel, Lady Cadogan, and Eliza found no more than three other persons waiting to share the meal with them.

"I do not see the two ladies we met earlier in the saloon," Meriel said to Lady Cadogan once they were seated at the long table occupying the center of the room.

"No doubt they have succumbed to seasickness," that lady said. "It generally overcomes half the passengers or more on any voyage, you know. And the worst time is just after the ship sets sail."

"I trust you do not mean to be sick, ma'am."

"Oh, no, I rarely feel any discomfort of that nature." She looked up just then and smiled brightly. "Good afternoon, Sir Antony. Will you not join us?"

"Indeed, my lady, if you will allow me," said the tall gentleman, bowing. Meriel smiled at him thinking how gracefully he moved for one so large and so broad. He returned her smile, then nodded to Eliza, sitting silently beside her aunt. "You are looking particularly charming, Lady Eliza. That shade of pink makes your cheeks look like fresh roses."

The color in her cheeks darkening noticeably, Eliza thanked him prettily for the compliment, then would have relapsed into embarrassed silence had he not exerted himself to put her at her ease. Within moments she was chatting with him as naturally as she might have conversed with a favorite uncle.

Meriel, watching them, suddenly encountered Sir Antony's twinkling gaze. Smiling at him, she decided he was really quite a pleasant gentleman, not nearly so dull as his earlier languid manner might have led one to believe.

4

Bidding farewell to the *Camden* at Swansea proved to be more difficult than Meriel had anticipated it would be, particularly since her youngest sister was still feeling sadly pulled. So accustomed had she become to looking after the younger members of her family that it was hard to let them go on to Bristol and London without her. Although Lady Cadogan remained cheerfully optimistic and Mr. Glendower was confident that Meriel need not concern herself with their well-being, Meriel could not help feeling pulled in one direction by her duty to Eliza, Gwenyth, and Davy, and in another by her need to have a look at l'École de Bonté and her duty to her sister Nest.

Thus it was, as she boarded the Channel packet *Albion*, that she looked wistfully over her shoulder to watch the *Camden* make its way slowly up the Bristol Channel. A few moments later, however, her mood lightened as she turned her thoughts toward France, and when she found herself alone with Gladys Peat in her new cabin, she asked that lady a question it hadn't occurred to her to ask before.

"Gladys, do you by chance speak any French?"

"French, my lady? Now, why on earth would a God-fearin' woman like m'self want to go speakin' a heathenish tongue like them Frenchies speak? And Britain at war with them as she has been. I should think shame t' myself an I did, ma'am."

"Well, I don't speak it either," Meriel said, smiling

over her shoulder as she allowed Gladys to help her off with her dark wool hooded cloak, "but I expect we shall find plenty of people who speak English. All the French people I met in London certainly did so, and André—the Comte de Prévenu, that is—must have spoken it, or Nest would never have understood that he wished to marry her. No doubt she has learned to speak French now after being so long in Paris, but Papa never held with ladies learning languages. He'd have been as pleased to have us speak naught but English when all was said and done, but that would not do for Mama, of course."

"That it wouldn't, m'lady. Your mam was a true Welshwoman, she was, and bound t' see all 'er chicks speaking the Welsh."

There was a tap at the door just then, and Gladys turned away to see who was there. Opening the door, she discovered Sir Antony, who smiled lazily when the sturdy tirewoman stiffened in disapproval.

"Good day to you, Mrs. Peat. I have come to assure myself that you and your charge are well-situated. Has her ladyship everything she requires?"

Meriel stepped forward. "She has, indeed, sir," she said. "How kind of you to inquire."

"I thought perhaps you might care to stroll about on deck, ma'am. The captain informs me that the nearer we sail to Land's End, the rougher the passage will be. Within an hour or so I daresay it will not be safe to stand by the railing, you know, and I did not think you would care to venture outside the ladies' saloon without an escort."

"I daresay that wouldn't have stopped me," she told him, smiling, "but I should enjoy a stroll, to be sure. Wait just one moment until I put my cloak back on and collect my muff for I am persuaded the air has not grown warmer in the past half-hour."

A few moments later they were at the railing, and Meriel, both hands lightly clasped in her large fur muff, leaned over to watch the waves that rolled toward them from the open sea beyond the distant Cornish shoreline. As each new swell caught them, the *Albion* rocked, then surged forward again. White foam boiled and tumbled along her waterline as her prow broke through the deep blue water, and there was a rushing sound that seemed to echo the sighing of the wind in the sails. For a moment the only other sounds were the creaking of the rigging and the screech of herring gulls overhead. Meriel drew a long, satisfied breath, enjoying the salty tang in the air.

"You like the sea?" He was looking down at her, though not, for once, through his quizzing glass. Nonetheless, he had returned to that languidness of manner which she deplored, and she had an impish wish to startle him.

"I should like to be a pirate," she said airily. "Women make very good pirates, I daresay. I have read that there use to be any number of them, like Ann Bonny and Mary Read."

He turned to look out over the water again, so she could not see his expression, but to her annoyance his voice was as mild as ever. "I believe they were none of them particularly apt at their trade, you know," he said. "Even the two you mention were captured by a British warship and tried for their crimes."

"And then hanged, I daresay. How very romantic." Shoving her hands deeper into the warmth of her muff, she managed a sigh much like one she thought Eliza might produce at such a moment.

He shot her an oblique glance, and she returned the look innocently, wondering if he would now react with more spirit. When she noted the twinkle in his hazel eyes, she did not know whether to be irritated or merely frustrated by it. His tone was still even when he said, "They were not executed, you know, although I believe they were indeed sentenced to death. No doubt their sex protected them in the end, but I doubt that their lives were at all romantic. Piracy has always sounded to me to be little more than boredom alternating with hard work and physical danger."

"Indeed, sir, you would prefer the comforts of a London drawing room, I daresay."

He appeared to give the matter some consideration, then said, "Do you know, it occurs to me that during the Season at least, a London drawing room often produces that same mixture of boredom, hard work, and physical danger."

She chuckled. "I should be most surprised to hear that you ever so much as wrinkled your neckcloth through hard work or danger in any drawing room, Sir Antony."

"Well, you would be out then, for when I was a halfling, I daresay I worked as hard as any at storming the beauteous citadels of the day, and I was more than once involved in a bout of fisticuffs over one dashing lady or another."

"Why have you never married, sir?"

He did look at her then, directly, and she was pleased to note a glint of surprise in the hazel eyes. "Has no one ever told you, my lady, that one should not ask such questions?"

"Of course. Personal questions are impertinent, ill-bred, and unbecoming," she said in a singsong voice as though she were repeating a lesson. "My papa was used constantly to lecture me about the necessity of learning to bend to society's rules. But I have never understood why one ought not to ask about the things one wishes most to know. And it is the oddest thing, sir, but when someone tells me I must not do something because there is a rule against doing it, I instantly develop a compulsion to do that very thing."

"Dear me, but you have never murdered anyone, have you?"

She grinned appreciatively. "No, of course not. I do not mean laws or even truly important rules, only the arbitrary social sort that accomplish little other than to interfere with my comfort or my pleasure."

"But you have had the charge of your sisters and brother for some time now, I believe," he said gently. "Surely you insist upon their obeying certain rules."

"I try not to make my rules entirely arbitrary, however. My father was quite a dictator within our family, you see, and I believe that is one reason my sister Nest married her Frenchman and my brother Jocelyn went to America."

"I see. They both fled the parental hand?"

"In a manner of speaking. Joss was caught up in a kind

of 'Wales for the Welsh and freedom for all' sort of thing, you see, and my father thought his actions a betrayal of all the Trahernes had stood for over the centuries. Marrying a Welshwoman, as Papa did, was one thing. Fighting for the Welsh cause—or indeed any cause that was not in support of the crown—was another. My sister Nest, of course, distressed him nearly as much by marrying a Frenchman, the Comte de Prévenu. Marrying an émigré was acceptable, particularly since André's family, the Depuissants, happened to be among those fortunate few who got out with their wealth intact, but agreeing to return with André when Napoleon Bonaparte granted amnesty to his family was another matter altogether."

"I suppose your father thought your sister ought to have convinced her husband to remain in England," Sir Antony said.

"Certainly, or better than that, to have come home to Wales to live with the family. But of course André would never agree to such a thing. He had strong feelings for his own country, and Bonaparte was agreeable to returning the Depuissant estates. Nest says he wanted strong noble supporters, and while the Depuissants are not particularly friendly toward him, they have made themselves useful from time to time. And, she says, he rather likes rubbing shoulders with the *beau monde*."

"Yes, I have heard that said too. Your sister's husband was fortunate. To have returned to France with his title and fortune intact argues more than a little family power, and most noble families of that type ceased to exist under the Terror, you know."

She smiled up at him. "That is perfectly true, of course, but André's parents—indeed, a good many of his family members—came to this country at the very beginning of the troubles to escape any difficulty. Then—and Nest says it is because they did manage to keep the greater part of their wealth—they were quickly restored to power when Bonaparte became leader of France, and they have held that position easily since then." She paused, frowning slightly. 'Until now, that is. André's good fortune seems to have ended, however, for he has been clapped into prison by Napoleon Bonaparte."

"What happened?" Sir Antony asked gently.

"I don't know. My sister is an admirably regular correspondent now that we are at peace, but precision of language is not one of her talents, I fear."

"Shatterbrained?"

His tone was so bland that Meriel nearly replied in the affirmative before she realized how impertinent the question was. She looked at him, her eyes alight with merriment. "To agree with you would scarcely become me, sir. Let me say rather that Nest is more interested in her social activities than she is in the political scene."

"But surely she is concerned with her husband's fate?"

"I have no doubt of that, which is why I am persuaded he can be in little real danger. Still, I intend to see for myself how matters stand with them."

"You know," Sir Antony said then in a more serious tone than she had yet heard from him, "those who know about such things are not altogether certain that this period of peace will last. If de Prévenu is no longer in favor with the First Consul, it might behoove your sister to think about leaving France while she still may."

Meriel frowned thoughtfully. "Until we reached Barmouth," she said, "I knew little about the current political situation. Clearly, persons like Lord Uxbridge and others of his ilk believe this peace of ours is an uneasy one. Still, there were others present who insisted that it is to Bonaparte's benefit as well as to England's to let the peace continue, and Nest insists that the mood in Paris is one of gaiety and pleasure. Surely that would not be the case if a recurrence of war is in the offing."

"No doubt," replied Sir Antony, pulling a gold watch from his waistcoat pocket. "I believe they will be serving dinner shortly, ma'am. Do you dine in the dining cabin?"

"No," she said, "for Gladys Peat will have it that it would not be at all the thing, even if she were to accompany me there, which she has no wish to do. My supper will be served on a tray in my cabin."

"In that event, perhaps I should escort you below."

She didn't see him again until later that afternoon, but having spent two full hours in her cabin, she once again felt the need for fresh air, and despite the fact that the little ship had begun to pitch rather alarmingly in the meanwhile, she wrapped herself well in her long dark gray woolen cloak, arranged its fur-trimmed hood carefully over her curls, and with fur muff in hand, made her way topside once more. It had been her intention merely to seek out the ladies' saloon, where she might find a book or a magazine to read. However, once she put her head above the deck, she discovered that the sky had darkened ominously and a fierce wind screamed through the rigging, cracking the sails like whips against their stout masts.

The sight of churning black water below and rolling black clouds overhead was an awesome one, and the wind as well as the unpredictable motion of the ship made movement difficult. Meriel found it necessary to slip her muff onto her left arm in order that she might cling to the bulwark wherever she could find a handhold. Her skirts whipped about her legs, her hood flew back, and her hair was blown loose as she flung herself from bulwark to railing, gripping the brass as tightly as she was able and pressing her hips forward. Instead of fear, however, Meriel felt only exhilaration as she pitted her strength against that of the wind. Carefully, hand over hand, she made her way forward, feeling one moment the same euphoria she experienced whenever she approached the summit of Cader Idris, and the next of a sudden spine-chilling fear that she would be flung headfirst straight down into the roiling sea. By the time she had made her way far enough along the railing so that she could see the open ocean ahead, she was worn out and would have liked very much to be able to sit down upon the bench attached to the bulwark, but she knew that to do so would be extremely foolish. There were no handholds, and she would most likely slide straight off onto the forward decking.

Behind her and overhead, the wind's roar was punctuated by the bustling and shouting of sailors as they leapt to obey orders bellowed at them by the boatswain, but no one paid her the slightest heed, and she was able to enjoy her view undisturbed. The swells beneath the little ship had grown to look like mountains and no longer broke neatly beneath the prow. Instead, the ship crashed sickeningly from one wave to the next, sending a wall of spray soaring to either side. Before long, she realized she was getting soaked, but despite the wind and the water, her cloak kept her warm enough and she had no desire to go below. Turning her face up, she exposed her cheeks enthusiastically to the needlelike sting of spray.

"Good God, what are you about?" The question roared in her left ear, startling her, before she had any notion that she was no longer alone. As she turned toward the voice, a powerful arm enveloped her shoulders and a firm masculine hand clamped the railing near her own. "Have you any notion how dangerous it is to be standing here like this?" Sir Antony demanded, his voice still loud enough in her ear to make her wince.

"Sir," she said, looking up into the face so near her own, "there is no need to shout. I can hear you perfectly well."

"I feel like shouting," he retorted, although he lowered his voice to a rumble. "You are sure to be blown overboard if you stand here. I cannot think what all those sailors are about not to have warned you."

"They are about their business, sir," she said tartly, "as you should be."

"Don't be childish," he said. "You must come inside at once."

"I shall not. I am quite safe here, and I am enjoying the wind and the excitement of the gathering storm. Only look, sir, there is a bolt of lightning. I daresay we are in for quite a tempest."

"No doubt, ma'am." He regarded the top of her head through narrowed eyes. "I should have expected such weather to have frightened you."

"Nonsense, sir, I am Welsh. Did such weather distress me, I should have spent the whole of my life in a distressed condition. One bolt of lightning will not send me running for cover. I have stood near the summit of Cader Idris—a mountain nearly three thousand feet high, I'll have you know—and watched much worse storms gather than this promises to be."

"So you climb mountains, do you? Somehow I am not

surprised." There was amusement in his voice now, and she looked back at him.

"Of course, I do. I have not been raised to be such a fragile honey as your London girls, you know."

"I begin to believe you, ma'am."

The ship pitched more sharply than ever just then, and his powerful arm instantly clamped her body to the railing. She was sure her ribs would be bruised, but she did not protest. Indeed, the thought that he wished to protect her was a warming one. A moment later, when the ship crashed down into the next trough and began to climb an even steeper wall of water, she made no further protest to his repeated insistence that they make their way to a safer position. She quickly discovered that the decision to leave the railing and the actual accomplishment of that feat were two entirely different matters, and when they had finally reached the comparative safety of the ladies' saloon, she sank down upon a banquette with a sigh of relief, tossing her muff onto the floor.

"That is quite ruined, I daresay. You were indeed in the right of it, sir. I remained outside longer than I ought to have done. You need not stay with me, however. I am quite content to remain here for a time."

He was braced against the bulkhead, watching her settle herself as gracefully as though she had little regard for the pitching deck beneath their feet. His eyes, glinting at first with what might have been anger in a more emotional man, softened as she spoke. Now it could be seen that he was amused.

"Where would you have me go, ma'am?"

"Why, to the great cabin, of course, or to your own. You ought not to remain here, sir."

He glanced around the empty cabin. "There is no one else here to be offended, and I've no wish to venture outside again at the moment. Already my neckcloth is limp and my boots have lost their polish. Moreover, not only is the sea attempting to swamp this craft, but I believe it is coming on to rain."

Glancing out the widow behind the banquette, she saw that he was right. Still, the thought of being alone with him in the saloon was an unnerving one. "Where do you suppose everyone else is?" she asked.

"Where is the estimable Mrs. Peat?" he countered.

"Laid down upon her cot. She managed to eat her dinner, but she felt queasy afterward."

"Then I surmise that most of our fellow passengers are in a similiar condition. I do not feel the ills of the sea, and I see that you do not either."

"No, of course not. 'Tis too exciting to waste one's time being ill."

"Then I suggest that we while away our time with a deck of cards, if one might be found in this saloon. Do you play piquet, ma'am?"

"Yes, of course, but I daresay there will be no cards," she replied.

"I hope you are not a gamester," he said a moment later, having lifted the bench top of one of the banquettes to reveal several packs of cards in a chest, along with a chessboard and a backgammon board.

They spent the stormy afternoon at the deal table, playing for vast mythical fortunes, and Meriel enjoyed herself very much. Sir Antony, despite an occasional remark that told her he was still in a fret over his neckcloth and boots, proved to be an amiable companion. She soon lost her nervousness, and having remembered that he had never told her why he had not married, she asked him again.

He shrugged but there was a gleam of laughter in his eyes. "Until now, I never gave the matter much thought, I suppose. What I cannot understand, however, is how it is that you have been left upon the shelf, my dear."

She grinned at him. "Turn about, sir? I promise you, I don't mind at all. I simply have never had either the time or the inclination to look about me for a husband. Oh, to be sure, I had a Season in London. Papa took me there, and my Aunt Cadogan did everything one might expect to launch me. I enjoyed myself tremendously, I assure you."

"In that case, I find it a good deal harder to understand how you come to find yourself still enjoying the single state," he said, picking up the hand he had just dealt himself and sorting through his cards.

Meriel discarded three, drew her replacement cards, then continued, " 'Tis not so difficult as you might think, sir. I simply met no gentleman that Season whom I could imagine climbing my mountain with me. And, of course, I expected to have a second Season in London the following year. Only as luck would have it, that was when Joss took it into his head to go to America. Papa was like a bear with a sore head as a result, and Mama was ill and so distressed that it was clearly my duty to remain at home with her. Nest had turned seventeen, so I persuaded Papa to take her to London while I stayed to look after Mama and the estate, as well. We have an excellent steward, of course, but there are still decisions to be made from time to time."

"And your father left you to make them?" Sir Antony asked, discarding two cards.

She smiled. "Only because he thought there would be none to be made in the few short months he would be away, I promise you. But I was interested, and our steward was willing to teach me, which was fortunate, as matters turned out. Nest married, and I never did go back to London. Then Papa and Mama died in the typhus epidemic and I was left with the children."

"My poor dear." Sir Antony leaned toward her as though he would comfort her, placing one of his large hands upon her forearm where it rested upon the table.

"I declare a *quart*, sir," she said, smiling. "You must not be thinking me a martyr to circumstance, you know. I promise you I love my home and my family. 'Tis my duty to look after them, and so I must, but 'tis not an unpleasant duty at all."

His hand gripped her arm more tightly, but he did not return her smile. Instead his lips pressed firmly against one another as though he restrained himself from speaking forcefully. A moment later the look was gone, as he said, "Your *quart*'s no good."

"Then I declare four queens." He nodded, and she led. As they played, she found herself telling him more about Plas Tallyn, and it was not until she retired to her cabin to prepare for supper that she realized that although she had told him much about herself, he had told her very little beyond the fact that he had been born in Shropshire and still had family there.

She discovered that Gladys Peat had yielded to seasickness. The older woman was not violently ill as Gwenyth had been, but she insisted that if she were to rise from her bed she would be.

" 'Tis not like me t' be givin' in like this, Miss Meriel. I beg you'll forgive me."

"Of course, Gladys. You must stay right where you are. I shall manage nicely, I assure you."

"Well, you'll be right here the night, so at least I may keep my eye upon you, but just where have you been all the afternoon, if I might be so bold as to inquire?"

"In the ladies' saloon," Meriel returned glibly. "I daresay I shall return there after I have eaten my supper, so that you may rest."

"That you'll not, m'lady. 'Tisn't fittin'. Like as not, there won't be a soul up there, and for all you think you can take care of yourself, you won't be safe there alone, and so I tell you."

Feeling her temper stir at these sharp words, Meriel forced herself to hold her tongue. It would not do to be at outs with Gladys Peat, and this was no time to remind her of her position. Having known her mistress from birth, Gladys was not one who might be counted upon to submit tamely to her displeasure. Indeed, Meriel knew full well that the only reason Lady Cadogan had not put up more of a fuss when she had declared her intention of traveling into France was that Gladys might be depended upon not only to protect her mistress but also to make a push to curb her more outrageous starts. Consequently Meriel bit her tongue and set herself to making her companion more comfortable.

By the time Meriel's supper was served by a cheerful young sailor who informed them that quite three-quarters of the passengers had refused their meals, Gladys had recovered sufficiently to sit up in her cot, but she declined interest in food. Meriel did persuade her to take a cup of tea and poured one out for herself. She said nothing further about going topside again, and Gladys clearly believed that she had reconciled herself to remaining safely below.

She had done nothing of the kind, however, and when she noted at last that her protectress had finally drifted into a deep sleep, Meriel closed the magazine she had been attempting to read by the light of the lantern swinging from a hook above her chair, and moved to peer out the tiny porthole above her bed. There were stars overhead and a bright three-quarter moon. The clouds had gone, and although the wind still blew strongly enough to send the little ship skimming through the water, the alarming pitching and tossing had declined to a mere rolling, sliding motion. Surely there could be no harm in going above for a breath of air.

On the thought, she collected her cloak and a pair of gloves. A few moments later she emerged from the companionway onto the upper deck to discover that it was indeed much calmer than it had been earlier, and she decided the ship must by now have made its way past that tip of Cornwall known as Land's End, into the generally calmer waters of the Channel. The roughest part of their journey no doubt lay behind them.

Drawing a deep breath of the crisp night air, she fixed her gaze upon the silvery path made across the sea by the moon's reflection. How beautiful it was. Except for the noise of the boat's passage through the water and the soughing of the wind in the rigging overhead, there was only silence, as though she was quite certain that there must be sailors somewhere on the deck or in the rigging, she could see no one when she looked about her. Then, just as she turned back to the sea, she caught a glimpse of movement near the forward bulwark. A moment later, there was nothing to see. Whoever it was had simply melted into the shadows. She stood very still, watching.

The wind died just then. A door opened from the great cabin, and a large shadowy figure emerged. In the instant before the wind picked up again and the sound was swallowed by the rattle and clink of the rigging and the slap of sails against masts, Meriel heard a tuneful whistling that she had heard before. That very afternoon, over his cards, whenever he had been about to play a winning card, Sir Antony had begun to whistle that selfsame air.

She had time to feel only the smallest twinge of alarm before the figure she had noticed earlier loomed out of the shadows behind him. She saw an arm raised, and then, before she could cry out, there was a sickening thud, and Sir Antony crumpled to the deck.

Without a thought for her own safety, Meriel cried out, but her cry was whipped away by the gathering wind, and the assailant paid her no heed. Furious and frightened now, and wishing she had not left her pistol behind in her reticule, she gathered her skirts in her left hand and with only the lightest touch of the right upon the rail to steady her steps, she ran toward the others, her heart in her throat at the thought that she might well be witnessing a murder.

"You there!" she shrieked. "Stop that at once." She could not see clearly enough to make out the man's features or even his shape, but she could see that he had bent over Sir Antony and had turned him onto his back. Sir Antony, unconscious or—God forbid— dead, lay like a stone. She had no weapon at all, and although the attacker had glanced up when she shrieked at him, he appeared to believe that she represented no danger for him, for he continued with what he was doing.

His seeming lack of concern infuriated her more. "Help!" she shouted again, hoping some crew member might hear her. But she was near enough now to see that the man was searching Sir Antony's pockets. "Robber!" she cried. "Thief! Oh, help me!" She was nearly upon him now, and could see that the man was masked. He raised his hand then, and she saw that he meant to hit Sir Antony again. "No, you shan't!" she screamed, launching herself at him without a second thought and feeling his taut body move back just as she hit him and fell to the deck. She grabbed for his feet, hoping somehow to keep him from getting away, but he eluded her, and the ship's movement pitched her toward the railing instead. Terrified lest she be flung overboard, she began scrabbling for a handhold, any handhold, when a foot crunched bruisingly into her side, and she realized the robber had not fled after all. He was trying to push her into the sea.

Sir Antony groaned, and hard upon that welcome sound came the piercing note of a boatswain's whistle. She could hear men shouting now, behind her, and the pressure of the foot against her side eased at once. Meriel could hear the attacker's running footsteps fading toward the bow as several men came toward her from the afterdeck. Breathless now, she tried to shout a warning that he was getting away, but she could not make the words come. A moment later, a rough hand gripped her upper arm and pulled her to a sitting position. Feeling dizzy and holding her free hand to her aching side, she looked up into an anxious young seaman's grizzled face.

5

"What's this, then?" the sailor demanded.

"Never mind me," Meriel said, looking toward the shadows of the bulwark, where Sir Antony was groaning more audibly now and beginning to move. "See to Sir Antony. I fear he has been grievously injured."

"Injured, is he?" The sailor helped her to her feet as he spoke over his shoulder to one of his mates. "See to 'im, lad. These landlubbers. Tripped over 'is own shiny boots, no doubt."

"He did nothing of the kind," Meriel snapped indignantly. "He was assaulted. Someone was waiting for him in the shadows there and hit him over the head as he emerged from the great cabin. I should think you would have a better care for your passengers."

The sailor looked perplexed. "Hit? Now, who would do a thing like that?"

"What's going on here?" A stout man wearing a jacket with a gold braid at the shoulders appeared out of the shadows. "What the devil's the meaning of this, Brand?"

The sailor straightened abruptly, saluting. "Beggin' yer pardon, sir, but the gennelmun done tripped 'n' 'it 'is 'ead, I'm thinkin'."

"You haven't thought at all," declared Meriel, standing easily now, her indignation making her forget her bruises. "That is Sir Antony Davies, Captain, if you are indeed the captain of this vessel. He was attacked by someone who hit him over the head and attempted to steal his purse. Indeed, he may well have stolen it, for he was certainly searching his pockets when I stopped him."

"When *you* stopped him?" The captain stared at her, but even in the dim light cast by the moon and stars, her authoritative demeanor caused him to change his tone to a more respectful one as he continued, "Begging your pardon, ma'am. Jeremiah Baggett at your command. I am certainly the captain of this vessel and must apologize for any inconvenience you have suffered. As you see, my men are this minute attending to Sir Antony, and I will see if there be a doctor aboard, thought I daresay there ain't. In my experience there never is when one is needed. I've told m' superiors time and again that we ought to provide a sawbones for every sailing, but they turn a deaf ear. Howsomever, did you indeed say that you stopped the assailant?"

"Of course I did," Meriel said, watching with a disapproving eye as two sailors attempted to lift Sir Antony and carry him into the great cabin. " 'Twould be better to take him into the ladies' saloon, would it not? I daresay there are fewer if any persons in there, and he may be made more comfortable."

The captain didn't argue but rapped out the necessary orders to his men. The saloon, when they reached it, was dark and quite empty, and Sir Antony was laid gently upon a banquette. "Fetch a blanket," ordered the captain, moving to examine the victim as several lanterns were lit. Meriel moved quickly to his side, drawing off her cloak.

"Here, sir, cover him with this until they bring blankets. He must not take a chill." As the light brightened above Sir Antony, she discovered a disconcerting fact. "Gracious me, his head is bleeding."

"Aye, so it is," agreed the captain, peering with matter-of-fact interest at the sluggish flow of blood from the side of Sir Antony's skull. He felt the area surrounding the wound and gave it as his opinion that Sir Antony's head weren't broke, merely dented. "He'll do, ma'am. See, he be coming round right enough."

Sir Antony did indeed choose that moment to open his eyes. For a moment it seemed that he had difficulty making them focus properly, for he peered at Meriel as though he were certain his senses must be deceiving him. Then his gaze shifted to the captain and beyond to the sailor, Brand, who had remained behind when the others departed.

"What's toward?" he inquired.

"You are supposed to say, 'Where am I?' " Meriel told him with a teasing smile. "That is what persons hit upon the head are said always to say when they come to their senses."

"Have I been hit on the head?" He reached up curiously, and winced when his fingers made contact with the wound. Looking at those fingers a moment later, he said in an offended tone, "Dear me, Captain, will you oblige me with a handkerchief before I get this stuff all over my coat." The captain, with a wry grimace, obliged him, and sir Antony's gaze shifted once again to Meriel. "My lady, what brings you here? I am persuaded you ought to be tucked up in your own cabin by now."

"Don't scold her, sir," the captain said, chuckling. "Like as not, she saved your hide, and at considerable risk to her own, I might add."

"Did she?" He glanced enigmatically at Meriel. "Might one inquire as to what transpired? I fear I have no memory of the incident."

"Not likely you would," the captain told him, "since your attacker came from behind. M'lady here saw the fella try to bash your brains out, and by what I can make of what she and my men have told me, she flung herself straight at him without a thought for the consequences. No doubt her methods were a bit rough and ready, but they answered well enough till 'e tried sendin' 'er t' Davy Jones's locker. Fortunately, my men arrived on the scene, having heard her cry out for help. She's afeard the feller took your purse, howsomever."

Returning the captain's handkerchief, Sir Antony reached awkwardly into his coat pocket and extracted his purse. "Doesn't seem to have taken a thing," he said, frowning. "Not a very efficient thief."

Captain Baggett shook his head, perplexed. "Can't

think who it was attacked you, sir. Wouldn't have thought we had any ruffians aboard, this trip."

Sir Antony's eyes, once again fixed upon Meriel, narrowed ominously, and she felt a surge of apprehension before she saw that he had relaxed again, and was able to tell herself that he had merely felt a quite reasonable annoyance with his assailant. There was no cause to think he was angry with her.

"His head must be bandaged at once, Captain," she said quietly when Sir Antony made no further comment.

"My men will be along shortly, ma'am, with the wherewithal. If I might make so bold, I'd suggest you go below before they return. Brand will accompany you to be certain you arrive safely. But before you go, perhaps you might tell me if you can identify Sir Antony's attacker."

"No," she said. "I cannot. He was larger than I am and I believe some few inches shorter than Sir Antony, but even that may have been a trick of posture or poor lighting. His face was masked." Brand stirred behind her, and she glanced at him, then turned firmly back to the captain. "I appreciate your concern for me, sir, but I prefer to see Sir Antony settled before I go."

"You'd be wise to go below at once, however," Sir Antony said gently.

Encountering an implacable glint in his eyes that she had never seen there before, she forbore to argue, telling herself it would do him no good to exert himself in unnecessary conversation. With a reluctant smile she said to the captain, "You will see that he has every care, sir?"

"We will, m'lady. We'll have him tucked up and in the care of his own man in the twinkling of a bedpost." He helped her don her cloak. "You go along with Brand there, and don't concern yourself further with this nasty business. I'll post a guard to be sure Sir Antony reaches the French coast safe and sound."

She thanked him and allowed young Brand to escort her below, where she discovered that Gladys Peat had awakened and was determined to read her a sound scold for her foolishness in leaving the cabin. Meriel listened only until her patience wore thin. Then, coolly reminding her protectress that she was well enough able to look after herself, she said good night and prepared for bed.

The following morning she learned that Sir Antony had passed a comfortable night and was much recovered, and by late afternoon when he finally emerged from his cabin, she was able to see for herself that he was quite restored to his customary good health. The wind was still high, so the crossing was taking less time than usual, but it was tedious because the high winds made for rough passage, and once again Meriel found herself with little companionship. Thus it was with unmixed delight that she greeted Sir Antony's invitation to take supper with him in the dining cabin that evening.

His invitation included Gladys Peat, and that lady would no doubt have accompanied them even had it meant her death to do so, but Meriel would not allow it. The unremittent heaving of the vessel had kept Mrs. Peat tied to her bunk, and her mistress could not believe that rising from it for no other purpose than to look after herself would do Gladys any good.

"There is no need," she repeated firmly when her abigail protested. "I am persuaded that I shall be as safe in Sir Antony's charge as in your own."

"But it will look so particular, m'lady—you dining privately with a gentleman. None of 'em—not even that Sir Antony—may be trusted to keep the line. You mark my words."

"No doubt, but I am no green girl, you know, and while I should not dream of dining privately with him in London or even Barmouth, there can be no good reason to refuse his invitation here. No one knows me, for one thing, and the dining cabin is quite a public place, for another. 'Tis not as though I will be dining *tête-à-tête* with him in his stateroom, after all."

Gladys clutched at her ample breast with a gasp. "I should hope not, indeed, Miss Meriel. The very idea!"

Meriel grinned at her. "There now, you see, things might be worse. Rest well, Gladys."

"I'll not rest till you return, Miss Meri, as you ought to know, and I'll thank you not to go jauntering about on deck tonight, either, miss."

"Oh, no," Meriel replied with a laugh. "I daresay Sir Antony will be as opposed to such a course as you are and will see me safely restored to you directly we have finished our repast."

A few moments later she found herself greeting the gentleman much as she would have greeted an old friend. During the course of the past days she had discovered him to be a man of great personal warmth despite that occasional languidness of manner that made her wish to stir him up, and she enjoyed talking with him, for he made no secret of the fact that he liked her. Indeed, she did not think she would be enlarging upon the truth to believe his feelings toward her were deepening rather quickly. Being a gentleman, of course, he kept his emotions under firm control, never allowing himself more than a warm look or a teasing smile by way of flirtation. And she enjoyed flirting with him, though she hoped her feelings went no further than that. More than once she had reminded herself that she was a good deal too old for romance and too busy in the general way of things for more than a mild dalliance. It was pleasant, nonetheless, to have someone to chat with during the tedious voyage.

That evening, when Sir Antony guided her to a private table with room for just the two of them against the dining-cabin bulkhead, she said nothing, merely casting a glance at the long table in the center of the room, where three women with their husbands and three other, unattached gentlemen were seated. No doubt, she decided, the rest of the passengers were laid up like Gladys Peat with the dreadful seasickness.

She took her seat, smoothing the slim skirt of her gray silk low-cut evening dress and handing him her lavender wool shawl.

"This room is warmer than I had anticipated," she said, smiling up at him.

"Whenever one has several bodies in a small space, the temperature rises, I believe," he replied, draping the shawl carefully across the back of her chair and taking his seat opposite her. "One must hope, however, that the heat will not wilt this shirt of mine."

He wore a coat of dark green superfine, a scarlet

brocade waistcoat, and cream-colored pantaloons, and looked much cooler, she thought, than she felt. "Your man must have starched your shirt very well, sir, for you look as crisp as a lettuce leaf."

"But not as damp, surely?"

She chuckled at his plaintive tone. "I must tell you, Sir Antony, that Gladys disapproves strongly of my coming here alone, but I see by your seating arrangement that you did not expect her to accompany me."

He grinned. "I heard that she was still indisposed and was convinced that you would not allow her to overexert herself on your behalf."

"I took a chance, however, for you must know she rang a rare peal over me for leaving our cabin last night, and I had no wish for another scold."

His expression grew serious, and he regarded her almost sternly. "You deserved a scold last night, did you not? What you did was very dangerous."

She tossed her head and forced a saucy smile to her lips, though she was conscious of a wish that he would not look at her so. "Fine words, sir, when I very likely saved your life."

"The luck was with us both, my dear," he replied gently, "and so we will say no more. Here is the steward with our supper."

In Meriel's experience men did not drop such matters so lightly, so she regarded Sir Antony skeptically, thinking it was only the steward's arrival that stopped him from reading her a lecture. But when he smiled at her, she decided he truly had put the matter behind them, and she was able to turn her attention to her meal with good appetite. They chatted easily together, and she found herself telling him more about life at Plas Tallyn. "I confess," she said after a time, "that when I am there, I yearn to experience the gaiety of London at least occasionally, but once I leave, a dreadful homesickness overtakes me almost at once. I have not the same freedom of movement and decision elsewhere, you see."

"You are scarcely hemmed about my guardians, my lady, even here."

"You don't approve of the fact that I travel with only my maid."

"I didn't say that."

"Oh, but you did, sir," she reminded him. "You said that if I were your sister you would not allow it."

"But you are not, and your own brothers do not seem to be in a position to stop you from doing whatever pleases you."

"Well, Davy is too young, of course, but I daresay that even if Joss were here, he would not interfere with me."

"Does he exert no authority over you, then?"

Remembering the incident with Black Thunder, she was betrayed into an impish grin. "He has indeed exerted a certain amount of authority upon occasion, sir, but with little effect, I fear. That is not to say that he could not force me to obey him an he took the effort to do so, but I have never been particularly submissive to his will."

Sir Antony's eyes twinkled. "I have no difficulty believing that."

After a time the conversation turned to France. Since Sir Antony had traveled in that country several times in the past, Meriel took the opportunity to ask his advice about certain matters, including the best way of dealing with French innkeepers.

"For you must know, sir, that I speak practically no French—only such phrases as one learns in one London Season—and I should like to know what service one might expect and what vails one must be prepared to dispense."

"Indeed, ma'am, but I believe you would do better to hire a courier to attend to such matters. A woman traveling alone will not command the same courtesy, I fear."

"Oh, I am accustomed to dealing with fractious servants," she assured him. "I have been in charge of our estates for several years now, and I doubt there breathes a Frenchman who could be any more recalcitrant than an irate Welsh servant."

He chuckled again, but then his expression turned serious. "Have you kept up at all with the news from France, ma'am?"

She frowned. "Not consistently. I learned much in

Barmouth that I did not know before, for example, and you yourself suggested when we were discussing my sister Nest that the peace is not so solid as we had believed."

"That is to put the matter delicately." He glanced up at the steward, who stood ready to serve their second course, nodded for him to get on with it, and held his tongue until they were alone again. Then he said quietly, "Addington is a fool, you know. He has recently sent Bonaparte a virtual ultimatum demanding that he adhere to the treaty."

"I did not know that," she admitted, "but I did hear Uxbridge say that the French have been fitting out new military expeditions. He would have it that Napoleon Bonaparte has used the peace merely to tighten his grip on Germany, Italy, Holland, and Switzerland. I daresay that is why Mr. Addington is angry. But we have not held to our part of the bargain either."

"You refer to Malta?"

"Indeed, sir. Mr. Murray and Lord Uxbridge commented upon the fact that Britain has declined to evacuate the island. Was that not also part of the treaty?"

He shrugged. "It would be foolish to give up Malta before there is a true peace on the Continent."

"Well, to hold it and demand that Bonaparte keep to the letter of the treaty does not seem fair to me."

"War is often not fair."

"But this is peace, and we ought to be doing our possible to see that it remains so."

He brushed a hand across his forehead, and she was instantly solicitous. "I ought not to be pressing you so, Sir Antony. Does your head ache again?"

"Like the devil," he said, "but it passes. Let us talk of something else. Tell me more about your brother Jocelyn. Is he a hothead?"

She chuckled. "Sometimes, I suppose. The whole of Merioneth was a hotbed of controversy some years back, what with the Calvinists opposing the established church, and the Republicans embracing the principles of the French and American revolutions. Joss was in the thick of the latter group. He said"—here she glanced up at Sir Antony from beneath her lashes—"that if France could but win time to reunite once the civil war had run its course, all would be well."

Sir Antony's lips twitched as she had been sure they would. "Perhaps your brother and his friends were unaware of the particular course that 'civil war' was taking."

"Oh, no, although Joss did say once that to call it the Terror was to refine too much upon the matter, that the turmoil was merely part of God's purpose—a sort of cleansing. He had that from some Calvinist friend of his, I expect. He said also that it was not the duty of the English to curse the French but to look to themselves, lest the judgment fall next upon them. He said the English must learn to read the Signs of the Times."

"Good heavens, what a young cawker he must have been. Did he say all this to your esteemed parent?"

Meriel bit her lower lip. "He did. And then when a number of his particular friends decided to go to America to join family or friends who were already there, Joss announced that he would like to go too. I daresay nothing further would have come of it if Papa hadn't been such a sapskull as to forbid him to do anything of the sort. The next thing we knew, he was gone."

"And you haven't heard from him since."

She shook her head. "He was never much of a correspondent. To tell the truth, I should not be in the least surprised to look up from my tatting one day to see him striding into the drawing room without having had so much as a scribble to warn us of his coming."

"Dear me, is there no end to your talents?"

She tilted her head. "My talents, sir?"

"Tatting?"

She laughed. "Well, I do know how, but I confess he would be more like to find me mending a sofa leg or shouting at my bailiff—his bailiff, that is," she corrected herself conscientiously.

He nodded, his eyes alight with amusement. A moment of silence fell, and Meriel could think of nothing intelligent to say to break it. Indeed, she could not seem to take her eyes from Sir Antony's mouth. His lips were slightly parted, and she could see the glint of his even white teeth behind them. Nibbling her own lower lip nervously, she tried to look away, but her gaze encountered his and she went perfectly still, stunned by the deep tenderness she read behind the laughter in his eyes.

She smiled back uncertainly, then looked quickly away to see if anyone had noted the impropriety of that silent interchange. To her astonishment, she discovered that all the other passengers had departed. They were alone in the dining cabin. Her cheeks flushed with color.

"Is something amiss?"

"No," she said, not looking at him. "Only we ought perhaps to leave, sir. The hour grows late."

He said nothing for a long moment, and she could feel her cheeks growing warmer than ever. She knew he was watching her, and the knowledge stirred emotions she could not name. Even to swallow was difficult. If she were to look up, to meet his gaze again, she knew she would begin to giggle in the manner of a nervous schoolgirl, or worse. Foolishness, she told herself. But the telling changed nothing. The warmth in her cheeks increased, and a fluttering sensation stirred deep within her breast. No doubt, she mused, her heart had grown weary of its present location and was attempting to shift itself to a new one.

With a tremendous effort she cleared her throat and raised her eyes to stare at a point just beyond his right shoulder. "M-my maid will begin to wonder what has become of me, sir."

He laid his napkin upon the white tablecloth. "Then we must return. It would be thoughtless of us to distress Mrs. Peat."

His tone was even, and there was nothing in the words themselves to startle her, so why, she wondered, did it seem as though his breath had caressed her bare skin? She forced her gaze to meet his at last and found that he was still regarding her with that unexpected tenderness in his eyes and a smile hovering upon his lips. She swallowed, still watching him, then jumped when he scraped his chair back and got to his feet. Her gaze remained fixed, so she suddenly had a fine view of the bottom pearl button of his scarlet waistcoat. Then he moved to assist her from her chair, and she took a firm grip on her nerves. When he draped her shawl across her shoulders, she was able to thank him in a nearly steady voice.

Though they hurried along the open deck to the companionway, the chilly air was enough to make her shiver violently and be grateful for his protective arm round her shoulders. But once in the companionway, Sir Antony did not release her. Instead, finding the corridor empty, he pulled her around to face him.

"You ought to have brought a cloak, my lady."

"Indeed, sir, you are right," she said, staring at his broad chest.

"I am always right, my dear." His voice came from low in his throat, almost as though he purred, she thought, and the sound set her nerves atingle again. It was too dark in the corridor to read the expression in his eyes now, but she didn't need to do so. She could feel it, and she was not surprised at all when he tilted her chin up with one firm hand and bent to kiss her full upon her rosy lips. A moment later, her eyes wide with wonder, she found herself in her own cabin face-to-face with a disapproving Gladys Peat.

Meriel was on deck with a number of other passengers before dawn the following morning, as the *Albion* approached the French cliffs. The moon was still up, and its silvery rays lit the high, chalky coast in a ghostly manner. Towers of two lighthouses glittered on the headlands nearby, and presently a long seawall became visible. Rounding its end, the *Albion* shot into smooth water, entering the little port at Le Havre between artificial stoneworks, on one of which sat a low, massive, circular tower.

"They say that Julius Caesar built that tower," murmured a familiar voice at her side. She looked up and smiled at Sir Antony.

No sooner had they drawn up at the wharf than a small army of male and female customs officers swarmed aboard the little ship. In the cacophony that followed, Meriel discovered that not only was every piece of luggage to be opened in search of contraband but that the agents expected to search her person and Gladys Peat's as well.

Drawing herself to her full height, she informed the female who had painstakingly conveyed this information to her that she would do no such thing.

"*Qu'est-ce qui se passe*?" Sir Antony's attention had been momentarily diverted, but he turned away from the agent to whom he had been speaking and addressed the female agent now expostulating with Meriel. The woman fell upon him in relief, babbling explanations in her own tongue, to which he responded with astonishing rapid-fire fluency. Some moments later, he smiled at the woman, pressed something into her hand, then nodded and turned to Meriel. "There is no longer any difficulty. You may go ashore with Mademoiselle Douane, and she will take you to the passport registry, where you must obtain a French passport. Do not allow them to take your British passport, however."

Meriel regarded the female agent dubiously, then glanced at Sir Antony. "You are not coming?"

"I must see to matters here. I'll be sure that your luggage gets ashore as soon as possible, and Mademoiselle Douane has promised to expedite matters in town. You may rely upon her, I assure you." He turned away then in response to a low-voiced murmur from Peter Trent, who had appeared as though by magic at his elbow. "I must go now."

Feeling somewhat bereft, Meriel watched him walk away, but Mademoiselle Douane proved to be helpful, and the formalities at the passport registry were speedily accomplished. The customs officer was even kind enough to help her hire a chaise for the journey to Rouen, and so efficient was she that they passed the turnpike gate on the outskirts of Le Havre before ten o'clock. Thus the afternoon was not too far advanced before they were settled into a tiny, dusty chamber under the eaves and above the taproom of the Sabot d'Or, a large, respectable hostelry in Rouen on the main road near the great stone bridge spanning the River Seine.

"Gracious, m'lady," Gladys said in disapproving tones when she saw the room, " 'tis none too clean, and dreadful noisy. That filthy window there looks right out upon the street, and what with all the hawkers, and carts and carriages rattling by, the din will never let us sleep."

"You heard the landlord, Gladys. 'Tis all he has available, so we must make the best of it. Now, bustle about, because I mean to visit Père Leclerc as quickly as possible."

"A papist," said Gladys, shaking her head. "What be you thinking of, Miss Meriel, to beg assistance from such a one?"

But Meriel merely laughed at her, and within the hour a hired gig set them down before a tiny stone cottage adjoining an exquisite Gothic church that backed upon the river. The path leading to the cottage entrance through a squeaking wicket gate was flagged, and Meriel and Gladys made their way carefully, for the stones tilted at crazy angles that threatened to trip the unwary.

The door was opened to them by a small, wiry, neatly attired man with thinning cinnamon-sugar hair and a stoic expression. Speaking slowly, Meriel announced their errand, whereupon the man bowed and silently led the way to a tiny parlor overstuffed with furniture of every imaginable sort. Then, informing them in passable English that they would enjoy a cordial, he departed.

Meriel looked at Gladys, her eyes twinkling. "Gracious me, what a good thing we needn't wear panniers anymore. I daresay even one petticoat would impede progress through this room."

"Indeed, my'lady, but everything is as neat as wax."

The cordial, when it was presented, had a fruity flavor, and Meriel liked it very much, but she suspected that it might be heady stuff and sipped cautiously. She was glad, when her host appeared, to get it upon the table and leave it there.

The priest proved to be an elderly gentleman with a neat white fringe encircling his otherwise bald and shining pate. His cassock draped gently over his round stomach, and he carried his hands folded at his waist, which was girded with a long rope sash of twisted gray cording. His smile was gentle, and his voice when he greeted her was low-pitched and melodious.

"Good evening, *mademoiselle*. I trust Fernand has seen

to your wishes." His English was precise, overlaid with a delightful Gallic accent.

Meriel rose gracefully to her feet and curtsied. "Good evening, sir. I have brought a letter from your friend Mr. Murray, who thought you would be able to help me." She extracted the letter carefully from her leather reticule and handed it to him.

"*Merci, mademoiselle.* Be seated, please." He waved her back to her chair, nodded at Gladys Peat, then took his seat upon a straight-backed chair that looked as though it had served the inhabitants of the cottage since the days of Julius Caesar. "You permit?" He gestured toward the letter, and she nodded, watching in fascination as he removed the seal with great care and unfolded Mr. Murray's letter. Despite these careful movements, however, he scanned the missive rapidly, and when he had finished, he looked up with a smile. "It will be my pleasure to assist you, *mademoiselle.* I know the . . . how you say?" He tapped his head, frowning briefly before his brow cleared and he went on, "Ah, yes, I know the headmistress, Mademoiselle Lecolier, well and can recommend l'Ecole de Bonté without reservation. What do you wish to know precisely?"

She explained, asked a number of questions, and received reassuring responses. In less than twenty minutes she rose to her feet, held out her hand, and said, "I thank you most sincerely, sir. Just knowing that you think so highly of Mademoiselle Lecolier and her staff will make my visit to the school tomorrow a pleasant one. I have not been quite easy in my mind, you see, about allowing Gwenyth to attend a school so far from home. She knows no one here, although our sister, the Comtesse de Prévenu, is no farther away than Paris."

"Ah, *la comtesse de joyeuse*, the merry countess, she is your sister, *mademoiselle*?"

Meriel smiled. "Is that how she is called here? It is a most appropriate name for her, I think. Yes, indeed, she was the Lady Nest Traherne before her marriage to the *comte*. You know her?"

"Not to say 'know,' *mademoiselle*, but I hear delightful tales of her. She is well-loved in Paris, you know. It is a great pity that the *comte* has offended, but *la comtesse*, she sees the bright side of everything. She goes her merry way, they say."

"So I am told," Meriel said dryly. "She writes that all is well despite her husband's imprisonment, but I must see for myself if that is the truth of the matter."

"You go to Paris, *mademoiselle*?"

"Indeed, sir, as soon as my business here is done." She extended her hand. "Thank you again for your kindness."

He nodded, smiling but abstracted, no doubt having dismissed her already and returned his thoughts to his religious duties. Within moments Meriel and Gladys Peat were back in the hired carriage, and less than a quarter-hour later they were set down once again at the Sabot d'Or. Inside, as they moved toward the stairway, the fat innkeeper stepped forward to meet them, much, Meriel thought, as though he had been awaiting their return.

"*S'il vous plaît, madame*," he said, bowing so low his dark curls threatened to sweep the floor, "*je vous en pris*."

"What is it?" Meriel asked.

"What ails the man, m'lady?" Gladys demanded at the same time. "He looks fit to bust himself."

The innkeeper straightened, then bobbed again before saying obsequiously in careful English, "I regret, *madame*, that you were put into the wrong chamber. Had we but known that you travel with the English milord, such an error would never have been permitted."

6

Meriel stared at the fat little innkeeper. "We have been moved to another bedchamber?" When he nodded fervently, she said, "But you insisted that there *were* no others."

"A mistake, *madame.*" He wrung his hands. "My wife, it was my wife who made the error. Please, *madame*, you will not be dismayed. I insist—"

"Good afternoon, Lady Meriel."

The greeting came from the top of the narrow stairway, and Meriel looked up to discover Sir Antony Davies on the point of descending. He was dressed exquisitely in cream-colored breeches, top boots, a perfectly cut coat of chestnut superfine, and a somewhat startling green brocade waistcoat embroidered all over with bright yellow flowers. He had hesitated on the second step from the top, his quizzing glass poised before his right eye, and he peered down at them now as though they were interesting but foreign specimens. She could not say she was surprised to see him. No other English milord would be likely to have claimed acquaintance with them.

"Good afternoon, Sir Antony," she said wryly. "You told this man we were traveling with you?"

He shrugged. "He may have received such an impression. Are you vexed with me, ma'am?"

"Not if you have acquired a better chamber for us than the one we had," she said, keeping her tone light with an effort. She was vexed but she would not show her feelings before the landlord. She turned to him now. "Where is the new room, if you please?"

"I show you, *madame*. At once, *madame*."

"One moment," Sir Antony said gently, descending the stairs with his usual languid air. "Have you been to visit the headmistress at l'École de Bonté already, my lady?"

"No, sir, we merely called upon one Père Leclerc, a priest who is acquainted with Mr. George Murray. You will recall, sir, that Mr. Murray kindly offered to provide me with an introduction to him, saying that he would have information about the school."

"And was Leclerc helpful?"

"Indeed, sir, he assured me that the school is an excellent one, and I quite look forward to making the acquaintance of Mademoiselle Lecolier." She glanced at the innkeeper, who was looking from one to the other of them with a puzzled frown as though he were attempting to keep up with the conversation.

Sir Antony had reached the ground floor by this time and stood quite close to her, looking down with a twinkle lurking deep in his hazel eyes. "You know, ma'am, I believe my sister would truly benefit from a French education. Perhaps you will not object if I accompany you to the school tomorrow."

She gazed at him steadily. "I have no objection to your company, sir, though you must forgive me if I take leave to doubt you mean to send your sister here to continue her studies."

"Must I?" he inquired blandly. "Ah, but here is the good Santerre awaiting your pleasure. Oh, and I have taken the liberty," he added in that same bland tone, "of ordering supper in the private parlor later. I do hope you and Mrs. Peat will join me."

Meriel was suddenly aware of a leaping mixture of emotions in her breast. Annoyance vied with pleasure, and there was a sense of pressure as well. Her first inclination was to snub him, but as she stared into those innocent eyes, she could not bring herself to believe that Sir Antony really meant to manipulate her actions. He was merely being kind. One could not snub such a man. Consequently she smiled and nodded.

"You are most considerate, sir."

"Oh, no," he replied. "I merely dislike dining alone."

She chuckled and made ready to follow the landlord. Halfway up the stairs, she looked back over her shoulder, expecting to discover Sir Antony still standing at the foot of the stairway watching them. To her disappointment, he had already disappeared into the taproom.

The new bedchamber, located at the rear of the inn, away from the noise and bustle of the street, was far more pleasant than their former quarters. Even Gladys Peat exclaimed her pleasure. Meriel smiled at her enthusiasm, but when the older lady pointed out that despite the many faults undeniably possessed by all gentlemen, a lady generally did better to have one arranging things for her when traveling in Foreign Parts, she took instant exception.

"Had I realized there were other rooms available, that foolish innkeeper would never have fobbed us off with the one he gave us," she declared stoutly.

"Perhaps, m'lady, but the fact is that he took advantage of your good nature, and 'twas Sir Antony who mended the matter in a trice." She sniffed. "He took a great deal upon himself that he ought not to have taken, of course. But that be always the way with them, which only goes to show."

What it went to show, Meriel had no desire to know, so she turned her attention to preparing herself for supper, which proved to be an entirely pleasant meal. There was nothing in Sir Antony's behavior to unsettle her. Although he seemed more alert than usual, as though he were watching her carefully, perhaps even as though he feared he might have vexed her despite her assurances to the contrary, his conversation was as benign as ever.

If she was disappointed not to observe the look of tenderness she had seen the night before, she told herself it was just as well. She had her family duties to occupy her mind and could not be thinking of other, more fanciful matters. Firmly directing her thoughts to such questions as she might wish to ask Mademoiselle Lecolier upon the morrow, she ruthlessly abandoned Sir Antony to exchanging commonplaces with Gladys Peat.

The following day, when Meriel was ready to depart for the school, she discovered that Sir Antony had been awaiting her pleasure for some time in the coffee room. Smiling, she informed him that she would be ready in a trice, just as soon as she sent round for the gig she had hired the previous day.

"There is a carriage awaiting us at the door, ma'am," he said gently.

"Really, sir, you take too much upon yourself."

"Not at all," he returned smoothly. "I had thought it decided between us that we would go along to the school together, so I arranged for a carriage comfortable enough to carry three. That gig you hired has room for only two."

There was nothing to say to that, so she gathered her dignity without a further word, ignoring a grimace from Gladys Peat that as much as told her that that lady had known precisely how it would be, and stepped outside and into the carriage.

It was a far cleaner and more comfortable vehicle than the one that had carried them to Père Leclerc's cottage the previous day, and without a thought she closed her eyes and leaned back against silken squabs with a sigh of pleasure. Then, when the coach body shifted to accommodate Sir Antony's weight as he moved onto the seat facing hers, she opened her eyes and straightened self-consciously, finding it difficult to meet his twinkling gaze.

Gladys sat stiffly beside her, saying not a word, but the journey was a swift one, for the school was located a mere two streets from the inn. Soon they found themselves in a refreshingly neat office facing a lady of some sixty years, whose elegant dress and perfect posture impressed Meriel the minute the woman stepped forward to introduce herself.

"I wrote to you, *mademoiselle,* to tell you I was considering placing my youngest sister, Gwenyth, in your school."

"Indeed, my lady," said the headmistress in nearly

unaccented English, "I remember well. You wish now to see the school, yes?"

"Yes, thank you, and to make certain inquiries. This gentleman is Sir Antony Davies, who is interested in your school on behalf of his younger sister."

The headmistress nodded, indicated that they should take their seats, then spread her hands as though to say she welcomed whatever questions they might have. For the next half-hour Meriel was regaled with the virtues and merits of l'École de Bonté, and the tour that followed showed her a well-managed boarding school so efficiently run that she could only be impressed. The extra fees, although they proved to be as numerous as Sir Antony had foretold they would be, were still reasonable and well within the limits she had set for herself. Thus, it was with surprise that she heard herself saying, once they had returned to Mademoiselle's office, that she would give the matter her full consideration and let Mademoiselle know as soon as she had come to a decision. Had she been asked why she was equivocating, she would have been hard pressed to give a sensible answer. She knew only that when she opened her mouth to say that Gwenyth would be delighted with the school, those were not the words that issued forth. Fortunately, no one questioned her. Back in the hired carriage, both Sir Antony and Gladys Peat were silent on the subject.

The next morning when she descended the stairs to find that the post chaise she had hired to carry her to Paris was standing ready in the innyard, she was scarcely surprised to discover Sir Antony standing near it, booted and spurred, wearing buckskin breeches and a dark coat. He had formed the intention, he told her casually, of traveling on that day.

She had taken his measure by now. "To Paris, sir?" she inquired, raising an eyebrow in gentle mockery.

"Why, yes, ma'am." Taking the reins from the groom who led a large bay gelding into the yard, he handed the boy a douceur before turning back to Meriel with a tiny smile upon his lips. "Surely I mentioned earlier that such was my intention."

She chuckled. "No more, sir, than you informed me

that you meant to take up residence in whatever inn we chose for ourselves in Rouen, but I ought to have realized that you would do so. Do you have no faith in my ability to look after myself?"

If she had thought to startle him into admitting a wish to look after her, she had missed her mark. He did indeed look faintly shocked by her candor, but that was the extent of it. "Nonsense, my lady. I should never dream of setting myself in judgment over your activities. 'Tis merely that our ways seem to converge, and I prefer company to the lack of it."

She shook her head, not believing a word he said, but she was unable to deny the warm feeling that spread through her at the thought that once again he was exerting himself on her behalf. She had not the least doubt that he meant to see that her journey to Paris was a comfortable one, and she had to confess—to herself if to no one else—that she felt the safer for his presence. She had not thought before what it would be like to travel with only a pair of French-speaking postilions, but as she glanced at them now, mounting the near-side horses, she was grateful for Sir Antony's presence. Without further discussion, therefore, she laid her hand upon his arm, preparing to accept his assistance into the chaise.

"*Mademoiselle!*"

Turning abruptly, she saw the elderly priest hurrying toward them across the innyard, his skirts caught up in one hand, presenting to her view a pair of surprisingly skinny legs and shabby black boots beneath. He was nearly breathless when he reached them.

"What is it, sir?" she asked, smiling at him.

Taking a moment to regain his customary poise, the cleric nodded at her, returning her smile. At last, taking a deep breath and patting his heaving chest, he said, "You depart for Paris, yes?"

"Yes."

He nodded again. "I have been thinking and thinking, *mademoiselle,* about your concerns for your sister, the merry countess, and I believe I have devised a way to ease those concerns if indeed they may be eased."

"And how is that, sir?"

"I have a friend, *mademoiselle.* Once he thought to take holy orders, but he discovered he had not the calling. We were boys together, no? Now he is a *personnage,* a man of consequence. Indeed, *mademoiselle,* he serves the First Consul as a member of his ministry. But he is not like so many others, you see. He is a man of great kindness, a man I am certain will hear your concerns and reply to them honestly. Moreover, I believe he is already acquainted with the Comtesse de Prévenu."

He paused to take another breath, and Meriel stared at him, digesting what he had said to her. "Do you mean that your friend would tell me if my sister is in danger? He would warn us if she is meant to follow her husband to prison?"

"Indeed, *mademoiselle,* I believe he would do such a thing. Moreover, I believe he will be able to allay your concerns with regard to the so estimable Comte de Prévenu. That family, you know, *mademoiselle*—the Depuissant family—is a most powerful one, one of the first of the great families to return to power after the Terror. Through the many amnesties, they have regained nearly everything they once held, and I believe Napoleon merely imprisoned André Depuissant, the young *comte,* as a way of reminding the family that it is the First Consul who holds the ultimate power to determine their fate. Still, it is my belief that he will not wish to set himself against them for long. My friend will know the truth of all this."

"His name, *mon père?*"

"Alexandre Deguise. He is what we call a *sous-ministre d'état,* a deputy minister, I believe you English would call him." He reached into the folds of his cassock and handed her a folded letter sealed with green wax. "You will present to him this letter, *mademoiselle,* and he will assist you. Of this I am certain."

"Thank you, sir, you have been very good." She glanced at the letter, noting that there was no address on the outside of it. Committing the name Alexandre Deguise to memory, she tucked the folded paper into her heavy leather reticule along with her passports, other letters of introduction, and the little pistol, thanked the priest again for his thoughtfulness, and allowed Sir Antony at last to assist her into the chaise.

Peter Trent emerged from the inn at that moment and hurried toward them. "I beg your pardon, Sir Antony, for my tardiness, but your decision to change your dress at the last minute necessitated some repacking, you know. Everything is in readiness now, however, and your trunks may be loaded into the coach in a trice."

Sir Antony glanced at him. "Follow at your leisure, Trent, but without dalliance. I daresay we'll make Paris by evening. I shall put up at the embassy with Lord Whitworth."

Trent nodded, clearly relieved that he would not be expected to reach the capital before his master, and turned away toward the second coach.

Within moments they were off and soon rattled over the stone bridge. The road now ran alongside the River Seine, and was heavily rutted in places, and dusty, but it was not in the least impassable and the postilions seemed to think the ruts were nothing about which to concern themselves. At first Meriel put up with the bouncing and jolting, having no wish other than to reach Paris and her sister Nest as soon as possible, but after some fifteen minutes of tooth-rattling progress, she let down the window and shouted at the rear postilion to slow the pace. At first he ignored her, seeming unable to hear or understand, but Sir Antony rode up alongside him and leaned over to speak in his ear. Immediately the postilion shouted to his mate and the pace slowed considerably.

"Thank you," Meriel said, smiling, when Sir Antony dropped back again to ride beside the chaise. "I daresay they do not feel the pace as we do, and of course they are accustomed to passing vehicles on the wrong side of the road, but I must confess that every time one flies past to the left, it startles me, especially since the postboys are mounted on the same side they would be at home. Why is that, do you suppose?"

"I haven't the least idea," he replied, grinning back at her. They continued to converse in this amiable fashion for a time, but despite the slower pace, conversation was difficult because of the dust and the rocking of the chaise, so Meriel soon put up the window again and settled back against the squabs. Gladys Peat was dozing, and despite the magnificence of the great river flowing past, some fifty yards to their left, Meriel soon grew bored with staring at the passing countryside and closed her eyes as well. She wakened again when they stopped to change teams and refresh themselves at Elbeuf.

The pace was swift again after the change, the postboys seeming to take energy from the fresh mounts beneath them, but it was not long before the condition of the road forced them to slow down. They passed through the villages of Gallon and Vernon, each time catching only occasional glimpses of the river until they were on the open road again.

Meriel was just thinking to herself that Sir Antony would be right and they would make Paris before nightfall when with a loud, crunching smash the chaise lurched sideways and bounced to a sickening halt. Fortunately the postboys were alert, so the horses were not injured, but the wheel had not merely come off. It was broken, and as Meriel clambered from the chaise, she saw at once that the damage would not be easily mended.

Sir Antony took immediate charge of the situation, much to her relief, for she felt she could trust him implicitly to deal with the repairs that must be made. Consequently she made no demur when he suggested that she would prefer to walk to the next village, a place with the charming name of Mantes-de-Jolie, rather than await another carriage.

"We have got well ahead of Trent and the other coach, you know," he said, smiling, "and while I would offer the use of my horse, you will not wish to leave Mrs. Peat behind. Moreover, while I daresay the old fellow might be persuaded to carry one lady, he would certainly balk at two. It would be more sensible for me to ride on ahead, arrange accommodations for the night, and send back a repair party."

"Accommodations for the night! Oh, surely the wheel can be fixed before then," Meriel protested.

" 'Twould be best an we don't expect it," he said. "In my experience, even the simplest of repairs often takes a day or two. I'll see to it we're not kept longer than the one night, but more than that I hesitate to promise. Do you object to the walk?"

"No, of course not," she replied, forcing herself to reply calmly. "Having had no exercise in nearly a week, I quite look forward to it, I assure you." He nodded as though he had expected her to say no less, but when she saw that his eyes gleamed with a look she could not interpret, she turned away to speak to Gladys. "You will not mind a brisk walk, will you?"

Gladys Peat shook her head. "Not me, m'lady. 'Tis a joy to be shut o' that bounder, I can tell you. How people can tolerate long journeys in one of them things is more than I can understand. How far be the village?"

Meriel glanced up at Sir Antony. "Well, sir?"

He peered along the roadway as though measuring the distance in his mind's eye, then said thoughtfully, "I daresay no more than two or three miles at most. I'll more than likely meet you on my way back. Would you prefer that I bring a couple of mounts or another carriage with me?"

But she declined. "I truly shall enjoy the walk, sir, and it would not suit me to mount a horse in this rig." She gestured downward at her forest-green traveling gown. "The skirt is not so slim as an evening dress would be, but 'tis slim enough to make it unseemly for me to attempt to mount a horse."

Nodding, he turned the bay gelding and within moments was lost to sight around a bend in the road. Meriel and Gladys set off, enjoying the crisp air and bright sunlight. For a short time they left the dusty road to walk along the river, and Meriel found it difficult to remember that she was in a country other than her own, but they soon returned to the roadway, not wishing to miss Sir Antony. He met them on the outskirts of the tiny village with the information that he had hired bedchambers as well as a private parlor for their use at the Cheval Vert in the Rue des Arbres, the village's only side street.

"Everything else is filled to the rafters," he said. "There's been more than one carriage accident, for one thing. Though the ruts are certainly a menace to any traveler, they must be a boon to the local wheelwright."

"When can he fix our chaise?" Meriel demanded.

"Well, at first he said a week."

"A *week*!"

"Yes, but I have prevailed upon him to do his possible to see us on the road again by late tomorrow morning. You will find the inn quite comfortable."

"No doubt your precious wheelwright is in league with the village innkeepers," Meriel snapped, her annoyance at the delay surfacing with a vengeance, "for I should think that replacing a wheel would be a simple enough operation not to require hour upon hour of delay."

He looked down at her, his expression unchanged. "Why, so it would be, ma'am, if we were at home and had our own people about us. Or even if it had been a clean break. But it was not a clean break and part of the axletree was damaged as well. Moreover, the wheelwright quite properly insists that others must come before us. He will send men to bring the chaise into the village—not an easy task, I daresay, and certainly not one with which I wish to concern myself—"

"No, for you would soil your breeches, no doubt," she declared waspishly.

"No doubt," he agreed, regarding her thoughtfully and rather sternly. "Your walk seems to have tired you, Lady Meriel. Perhaps I ought to have ordered up a carriage for you after all."

Sharp words of denial leapt to her lips before she realized that he was rebuking her for her bad temper. She was not accustomed to reprimand, certainly not from anyone beyond her own family, and even more certainly not delivered in such even tones. Thus, her own hot words hovered for some seconds upon her tongue before she swallowed them. But swallow them she did, and once she had regained a semblance of her composure, she grimaced self-deprecatingly.

"I have not even thanked you for coming to our aid, have I? 'Tis not as if you are responsible for us, after all."

"You would scarcely have expected me to leave you sitting in the road, now, would you?"

"Certainly not, sir." She smiled a little, glad to hear the teasing note in his voice once more.

"That's better," he said approvingly. "Walk straight to the center of the village, ma'am, and turn to your left at the only intersection you will find. The inn is as near to the river as it can be without being in it."

Then, giving spur to his mount, he was gone, and she turned to find Gladys Peat looking at her rather strangely.

"What is it, Gladys?"

The older woman recovered rapidly. " 'Tis naught, Miss Meriel, only that I disremember ever seein' you come down off your high ropes so sudden as that afore."

"Well, I was in the wrong, surely."

"That never stopped you other times."

Meriel's eyes narrowed. "That will do, Gladys. Kindly remember your place." She smiled mischievously. "And I will endeavor to remember mine."

That brought a dry chuckle from her companion, and harmony was restored. The inn proved to be small but charming, boasting a small garden that backed directly upon the river. From their bedchamber window they could watch boats traveling up and down, and there was very little noise. Certainly much less noise than they would have suffered in a hostelry smack upon the Paris road. Supper that evening was served in the private parlor Sir Antony had hired for their comfort, and afterward she and Gladys Peat retired once again to their bedchamber, both feeling the effects of a long day.

Meriel was certain she would fall asleep the moment her head touched the pillow, but perversely that touch had the exact opposite effect, bringing her wide-awake. Soon she heard the gentle, rhythmic snoring of her companion, but an hour later she was no nearer to slumber herself. She heard noises from the taproom now, so silent was the rest of the world. Indeed, she was so conscious of every creak and whisper that she believed she could even hear carriage wheels from time to time on the Paris road.

Silver light streamed in through a gap in the window curtains, giving her to realize that the moon had risen, and she got up at last, shivering in the chill, to peek out at the moonlit landscape. Below the garden the river looked like a wide sparkling ribbon, empty of traffic now, glimmering magically as moonlight skipped across ripples of water stirred by a faint breeze.

Perhaps, she thought, a stroll in the garden would relax her so that she might sleep. Glancing at her snoring companion, she decided quickly that whether such an outing would relax her or not, it would certainly be an adventure. On that thought she moved quickly to find a wool frock and her heavy hooded cloak. Slipping these on along with a pair of walking boots, and remembering her nocturnal experience aboard the *Albion*, she removed her pistol from her reticule and dropped it into the pocket of her cloak. She was ready now, she assured herself, to meet anything.

She had explored a bit and found the door into the garden earlier, so she moved confidently along the corridor to the rear stairway. Not a soul did she meet, nor did she hear anything but the steady cadence of masculine voices from the taproom. Several minutes later she was breathing the chilly night air, looking out at the river over the low hedge at the bottom of the garden. The Seine was not a wild river like the Dovey, the Wnion, or the Mawddach back home. There were no tall, rugged cliffs to be seen, only low rolling countryside. But the river's movement was swift, and the lapping of its waters along the shore was soothing to the nerves, while the glitter of moonlight on its ripples gave one to think of fairies and little people, rather than worries over the right school for one sister or possible danger to another. A breeze stirred leaves in the shrubbery, making them whisper as though they told secrets to one another. Overhead, a cloud drifted across the moon, sending sooty shadows darting from shrub to tree in the little garden, shadows that lightened, then disappeared when the cloud moved on.

The noise and occasional laughter from the taproom increased briefly before a door slammed in the distance, muffling the noise again. Meriel lifted her head, listening, wondering if someone else had taken it into his head to visit the garden. No one had. She was quite alone.

After a time, however, she realized that the air had grown colder, and much as she was enjoying her peace and solitude, she knew she would be unwise to linger long enough to catch a chill. Thus she gathered the folds of her cloak more closely about her and made her way back to the inn.

Stepping carefully, in hopes that her movements might not be overheard by anyone else, she made her way up the narrow stairway, emerging at last upon the small landing and the corridor that led past Sir Antony's bedchamber to her own, and beyond that to the main staircase, where a single lamp glimmered softly. As she drew a long breath, pleased that she had got out and returned with no one else being the wiser, she heard a small click as of a latch being disengaged. Halting, her breath trapped in her throat, she watched with trepidation as the door to Sir Antony's room began slowly to open inward. So slowly did it move, in fact, that with scarcely a thought to her own safety she reached into the deep pocket of her cloak and extracted her pistol as a man's head and right shoulder began to precede the rest of his body through the doorway.

7

Standing perfectly still, Meriel watched as the thief—for what else he could be, she could not imagine—peered cautiously down the corridor toward the main stairway. Then, as his head began to turn toward her, she stiffened, waiting for him to catch sight of her. When he did, he started, then went still. Since the only light in the corridor was behind him, she was unable to make out his features, but she could see enough to know that he was neither Sir Antony nor his valet. She tightened her grip on the pistol as he began to withdraw into the bedchamber again.

"Hold where you are," she said sharply, "unless you wish to feel a ball in your shoulder."

He hesitated, then said in a drawling and decidedly English voice, "I daresay you wouldn't hit within a yard of my shoulder, ma'am, but I'd as lief you not raise the countryside by discharging that weapon."

"I hope you will not be so foolish as to act upon that belief," she said dryly. "I have been able to shoot since the age of eight and I would engage to blow the pips out of a playing card at any reasonable distance. As for raising the countryside, I have no more desire than you to do that; however, I do feel that we ought to raise Sir Antony, don't you? No, perhaps you do not," she went on in a musing tone when he remained silent. "Since you no doubt have several of his belongings in your pockets, I can well believe that you might not at all wish to disturb him. How fortunate you are that both Sir Antony and Trent are sound sleepers."

"Fortune has naught to do with it, ma'am," the would-be thief said, an odd note of amusement entering his voice. "I trust it will not disconcert you to learn that neither Sir Antony nor Trent—whoever they may be—is within. I do not enter rooms which contain persons when I can avoid doing so. 'Tis much more pleasant not to be interrupted at one's work, don't you know."

"I daresay." His information was not particularly welcome. Her own bedchamber lay but two doors along the corridor, and to be sure, Gladys Peat slept within, but Meriel knew from experience that only a trumpet sounded in that woman's ear would stir her from her slumber. She could scarcely order the felon below. Just the thought brought a vision to her mind of the uproar that would be caused were she to parade him into the taproom at gunpoint.

He seemed to comprehend her dilemma. "A standoff, ma'am? Surely you would be wisest to let me depart in peace. Oh, damnation," he added cryptically and with a sigh of resignation.

Even as she wondered what possessed him to speak so, the sound of footsteps drifted to her from the main stairway. A moment later, by light of the lantern at the end of the corridor, she recognized Peter Trent's lean figure and breathed a sigh of relief.

"Mr. Trent," she called in a low tone, returning her gaze quickly to the thief, "is Sir Antony below?"

"Aye, he is that," Trent muttered on a note of surprise. "What's toward, then?"

"Fetch him at once, if you please," she said, still keeping her voice down in hopes that she would not waken anyone who might be sleeping nearby. "Say nothing to alarm anyone else, but tell him the matter is urgent."

"I say, is that a gun you've got there?"

"Certainly it is. Now, don't stand gaping. Go, man."

"But you oughtn't to be handling a weapon, ma'am. Surely you ought to give it over to me." He stepped quickly toward her.

"Don't be nonsensical. Do you expect me to go into the taproom and hale your master forth?"

Trent halted, clearly realizing that he could expect no such thing. For her to enter a taproom full of men would be unthinkable. "But you could send one of the servants—"

"For goodness' sake, you idiotish man, don't stand blathering at me. Go and fetch your master at once." He fled, and to Meriel's surprise her captive chuckled. She glared at him. "I daresay you will be laughing out of the other side of your face in a few minutes, fellow. Sir Antony Davies is not a man to be trifled with."

"But I was not laughing at Sir Antony, though I doubt you've any need of his assistance. The way you sent that fellow scuttling gives me to believe that sharp tongue of yours would be a match for anything, ma'am."

But Meriel was listening for sounds of Sir Antony's arrival and paid his impertinence no more heed than it deserved. She had no doubt of her ability to manage the situation, of course, but Sir Antony was large, after all, and sufficiently powerful-looking to deter the thief from attempting anything foolish. After some moments, when she still had heard no sound of approaching footsteps, she said calmly, "You had better step out of that doorway, I suppose. I should dislike hurting you more than necessary if you try to escape before he arrives, but there is a great deal of shadow there, and I might misfire."

"In that event, I shall be happy to accommodate you, ma'am. I've no wish to be killed."

"I doubt it would be so bad as that," she said thoughtfully, "but I might cripple you if I aimed for your shoulder and caught your elbow instead. Do not move quickly, fellow."

Raising his hands to shoulder height, he stepped carefully away from the dark doorway, and Meriel discovered that he was a slender man of medium height. That was all she could see, however, for he was outlined now from behind by the glow of the lantern.

"Move nearer the wall," she commanded. "You block my view."

"Very well," he said, complying, "but you have not long to wait. I hear men on the stairway."

She heard them too, the moment he spoke, and the relief she felt was profound. In a moment she could safely turn the situation over to Sir Antony and then the thief would get his due.

Even as the thought passed through her mind, she saw Sir Antony's large form appear at the end of the passage with the ubiquitous Trent close behind him. Gesturing for the valet to remain by the stairway, Sir Antony strode toward her, moving more quickly than was his custom.

"What goes on here?" he demanded harshly, not bothering to keep his voice down.

To Meriel's astonishment, the thief turned his back on her to face the approaching man directly. "I fear," he said blandly, "that this lady has interrupted me at my work, sir."

Sir Antony stopped and peered at the man for a long moment. Then he straightened and said grimly, "Interrupted you, fellow? How might that be?"

"Why, I was just stepping into the corridor, you see, having accomplished a good night's work, when this excellent woman pointed her pistol at me and told me the jig was up. Frightened me witless, I can tell you."

Sir Antony ignored the fellow's light tone and pushed past him to stare at Meriel. "Pistol? What the devil are you doing with that thing, my lady?"

"My lady?" The thief had turned too, clearly surprised to hear her title.

Meriel kept her attention focused upon Sir Antony, conscious of a strong wish that he would direct his displeasure where it belonged, rather than toward herself. For some reason she could not fathom, his nearness made her feel more vulnerable than she had felt when she was alone in the dim corridor with the thief. Forcing an even tone, she lifted her chin and said, "Of course I carry a pistol. I should be foolish not to look to my own protection, traveling alone as I do. I much regret the fact that I did not think to provide myself with it that night on deck, but I thought myself safe aboard the ship, you see. Had I not been such a goose, your assailant would not have got off so freely."

Sir Antony drew a long breath, and Meriel had an

uncomfortable notion that he was restraining himself from saying more to her. Instead, he turned back to the would-be thief, allowing her to recover her poise and to note with surprise that the other man was staring at her with a respect bordering upon awe.

"You, fellow, what have you to say for yourself?" Sir Antony demanded.

"Why, only that I have been rolled up, sir, horse, foot, and guns," said the thief with a grin. He reached into his pockets, retrieving an enameled snuffbox, a diamond cravat pin, two rings, and several other objects, which he held out in the clear expectation that Sir Antony would take them from him.

Sir Antony stared at the booty. "Good Lord, man, you would steal the diamond pin my mother gave to me? I ought to throttle you for that alone."

"I beg you will do no such thing," the thief said, chastened for the first time. "I could scarcely know there was sentimental value to such a trinket, and am, moreover, returning it to your keeping. Surely, you will not bear a grudge."

"Sir Antony," said Meriel indignantly, "I trust you will send your man, Trent, for the *gendarmes*. This fellow must be taken into custody at once."

"Oh, ma'am," said the thief, turning to her, "surely, you would not cast a fellow Englishman to the terrors of the dreaded French *gendarmerie.*"

"I am not English, I am thankful to say, but Welsh, so you may expect no such silly sentiment out of me. Well, Sir Antony?"

Sir Antony cleared his throat, but when he spoke it was in his customary lazy tone. "My dear Lady Meriel, I cannot think it will serve any great purpose to turn this poor fellow over to the French. If we were in England, of course, I should have not the slightest hesitation in calling for the constable. But it would be a cruel thing to do here in France, where we know not what the punishment might be."

"Considering that the value of what you hold in your hand would ensure his being hanged in England," she retorted, "I cannot think what the French might do that could be worse."

"Ah, but that is the matter in a nutshell," Sir Antony said gently. "We do not know. Moreover, we should undoubtedly have to delay our departure in order to stand witness, you know."

"Oh, for heaven's sake, you treat this matter too lightly, sir. Why, I practically risked my life to capture this house-breaker, and now I daresay you will turn him loose and perhaps even reward him for providing you with a night's entertainment."

"As to the risk you took, ma'am," Sir Antony countered, a sterner note entering his voice, "be sure that we will discuss it in greater detail before we are any of us very much older. However, our discussion can certainly hold till morning, and I believe we can trust Mr. . . . I did not catch your name, fellow . . ."

"Carruthers," the man said, bowing. "Roger Carruthers, at your service." He had been watching them both closely, and now he added, "I must tell you, sir, that I am filled with gratitude by your understanding, and—"

"Stubble it," said Sir Antony rudely. He turned away long enough to beckon to Trent, still guarding the stairway, then turned back to Meriel. "I will escort you to your chamber, Lady Meriel."

"But he will get away," she protested.

"No, he will await my pleasure," returned Sir Antony placidly.

To be sure, the thief showed no inclination to move from where he stood, merely watching them as though they were characters in an interesting play. Then, as Sir Antony led her away, Meriel was astonished to hear Carruthers bid her a cheerful good night.

"He is the most impudent fellow," she said to her escort in an undertone when they reached her door. "I have never met anyone like him."

"It is to be hoped that you do not meet many thieves," he said evenly.

"You are vexed with me, are you not, sir? But really, it was most fortunate that I came along when I did, or he would have got away with your valuables." She regarded him hopefully from under her lashes.

"How did you happen to come along, my lady? You ought to have been sound asleep in your bed."

She glanced down the corridor to see that Trent was watching Carruthers closely. When she looked back, she discovered that Sir Antony had not taken his eyes from her. Feeling suddenly ill-at-ease again, she attempted a light tone and succeeded merely in sounding defensive when she said, "I could not sleep, so I went for a stroll in the garden." Even in the dim light of the corridor, she could see his jaw tighten ominously and so she hurried on, "It was quite lovely and peaceful outside. The moon was bright, and there wasn't a soul to be seen anywhere. Even the river was deserted. But it soon grew too cold for comfort, you know, so I came back inside. Just when I reached the top of the rear stairway I saw him emerging from your room. At first I thought it must be you or your man, but the movements were so stealthy that I soon changed my mind and reached for my pistol."

"And Mr. Carruthers simply obeyed when you told him to halt?" Sir Antony sounded politely disbelieving.

"Well, at first I think he meant to make a run for it," she admitted, "but once I had drawn his attention to the fact that I was armed, he grew more compliant."

"I see." He looked at her again, long enough and sternly enough to set her knees to quivering. Then he said gently, "You have not the least notion of what danger you might have been in, have you?"

"Fiddlesticks, I was in no danger," Meriel said, recovering her courage at this slight on her capabilities. "I am quite expert with a pistol, sir, so I had no fear that he might harm me. He might have got away. I don't deny that, for I had no wish to kill him, but that is the worst that would have happened."

Sir Antony said nothing. He merely stood silently gazing down at her for another long moment. Finally he nodded in an abstracted way and wished her good night. "Do be sure to lock your door," he added as he turned away.

Feeling more ruffled by this odd treatment than if he

had read her a sharp scold, Meriel stepped abruptly into her bedchamber and threw the bolt with a loud snap, noting as she did so that Gladys Peat did not so much as alter the rhythm of her snoring.

As she prepared once again for bed, she thought back over the events of the previous half-hour and decided the whole incident was a peculiar one. The thief had the manners of a gentleman, for one thing, and a very impudent gentleman at that, making him unlike any thief she had ever imagined. And Sir Antony, instead of showing irate indignation over the felonious invasion of his bedchamber, had taken the matter lightly for the most part. Indeed, if he had been disturbed, it had been by her involvement and nothing more. He had been as startled as Peter Trent to learn that she possessed a pistol, and she was quite certain he had little faith in her ability to use it properly. No doubt that accounted for his strange attitude. His stubborn belief that the thief might have harmed her had simply kept him from reacting as she had expected him to react to the theft itself.

As to why his displeasure had unsettled her so, she had not the slightest notion. Perhaps it was no more than that she had been unaccustomed of late to being criticized by others. On the other hand, she could not recall that her father's angriest tirade had ever had the power to set her knees to quivering, and Sir Antony had done the thing with no more than a look. Then, too, it was odd that one sort of look from the man could make her feel as though he had caressed her, while another made her feel as though he had stripped away all her defenses.

She spent another twenty minutes dwelling upon these thoughts and others like them before she finally fell asleep, and as a result, when Gladys Peat attempted to awaken her the following morning, the task proved to be a difficult one.

"Come now, my lady, 'tis nigh on to ten o'clock. They serve breakfast only until eleven in this establishment, and I for one be hungry. Get up now, do!"

Meriel curled into a tighter knot beneath her eiderdown quilt and groaned, "Go away."

"That I'll not, miss. Just you rouse yourself or it's the cold water I'll be getting, and that's a fact."

Her mistress chuckled and peeped out from beneath the thick quilt, her eyes still bleary with sleep but twinkling nonetheless. "I believe you would, Gladys, though the last time you did so, I was fourteen and the temperature was near zero in my bedchamber because Papa was indulging in one of his fits of economy and refused to allow a fire to be kindled there. I declared it was too cold to get up, and you said you'd just see about that and threw a wet towel right under my bedcovers. I am persuaded they heard my screeches all the way to Dolgellau. 'Tis a wonder I didn't catch my death."

"Not you, m'lady. Never sick a day in your life."

"No, that's true enough," Meriel agreed, stretching languorously. "Stoke that fire up a bit, will you? Just thinking of that cold towel has given me gooseflesh."

Gladys moved to obey her but looked sternly back over her shoulder even as she stooped at the hearth. "Don't you be dallyin', now, Miss Meriel. Sir Antony says the chaise will be ready afore noon, and I have no wish to be a-wastin' time here that might be spent with Lady Nest."

"Madame de Prévenu," Meriel corrected with an impish gleam in her eye. "Do you know that until only three years ago some people still called her Citizeness de Prévenu? The title lingered from the Revolution you know, but Nest wrote that it was the oddest thing to hear. Napoleon Bonaparte, of course, prefers titles to the lack of them, as people have learned over the years."

"First Consul for life, they call him now," Gladys said with a sniff, ignoring her mistress's correction of Nest's title as she generally did. "Settin' himself up to be king, like as not, and him without a drop of royal blood in him. 'Tis a crime, and no mistake, m'lady."

"They say he is charming, however," Meriel pointed out. "I wonder if we shall meet him. Nest says even people of consequence pay gigantic bribes in order to be invited to one of his receptions."

"Bribes to him? Well, if that don't—"

"No, no, of course not," Meriel replied, laughing. "To his aides, of course, to be put upon the lists for the receptions, to receive invitations. He doesn't make out the lists, you know, any more than their majesties do for their drawing rooms and levees."

"Well, I hope you'll be doin' no such godless thing, Miss Meriel." Gladys got to her feet, brushing her hands together to remove any ashes that might have clung to them. "Are you gettin' up now, miss?"

"Yes, yes, don't do anything absurd, for heaven's sake. I am sure I am quite as anxious to be gone from this place as you are yourself. If you will see that our breakfast is ordered in the coffee room, I shall endeavor to wash my face and hands and get into my dress."

"Sir Antony has seen to all that, m'lady, as you might have trusted him to do. We breakfast in that same parlor we supped in last evening. And you'll be needin' me to do up them buttons at the back of your gown, unless you be wishful of wearin' something other than your traveling dress."

Meriel sighed. "I am very tired of that dress," she admitted. "I daresay I shall never wear dark green again. However, it is far more practical in all this dust than anything else would be."

"Indeed, m'lady, and I have brushed it out so it don't show a speck of dust from yesterday."

"Oh, I'm sure you have, Gladys." Impulsively Meriel got up and gave the woman a hug. "I don't know what I should do without you, you know. You have always taken such good care of me."

"There, now, Miss Meriel, have done. Why, people would stare to see you hug your maid." But Gladys' stern features relaxed noticeably, and Meriel took no notice of the reproof.

"Is there no hot water?" she asked instead, feeling the tepid water in the basin.

"Aye, there was," said her handmaiden with a glint in her eyes. "Until it took me all of thirty minutes to waken your ladyship. *And* it took the best part of an hour to get these heathen Frenchies to provide it, so I'm thinkin' you'd best make do with what you've got."

"Yes, Gladys," said her mistress meekly, hiding a smile

as she added with a long sigh, "I suppose I shall manage well enough."

"And we'll have none of your dramatics either, miss."

"No, Gladys."

She dressed quickly and within the half-hour found herself in the private parlor, seated across from Mrs. Peat, indulging in a large, delicious breakfast. Sir Antony, having eaten earlier, sat in a large overstuffed chair near the only window, reading a newspaper.

"Is that an English paper, sir?"

He glanced up at her. "No, 'tis French."

"I daresay you read French well, then."

"Tolerably."

"What does it say?"

"A number of things. Are you enjoying your breakfast?"

"Yes, thank you." She saw that he had turned his attention back to the newspaper, and remembering her father's harsh attitude toward anyone who dared to interrupt his reading, she hesitated to speak again, particularly in view of the way they had parted the night before. After some moments with no sound in the room other than the clinking of silver against china and the rustle of the paper as he turned a page, however, she could stand it no longer. "Is there news of Napoleon Bonaparte?"

"Merely that he is presently in Boulogne," he said briefly. Then, after a pause, he looked up with a smile. " 'Tis abominably rude of me to continue reading, I daresay."

"Oh, no, I do not mind in the least," she said mendaciously, relieved to see him smile, "only I wondered if there was any news that might affect us, you know."

"Not a great deal, except Addington seems to have issued another ultimatum to the French with regard to releasing those countries we discussed the other day from what he calls the French bondage. 'Tis foolish of him, I fear. He will accomplish little more than to annoy Bonaparte."

"And if he becomes annoyed?"

Sir Antony shrugged. "The man is unpredictable."

"But surely he has some sort of policy he follows, which makes it possible to judge what he must do."

He looked at her in amusement. "You seem to know a deal about such things."

"No, only my papa and Joss often argued about what they called 'English policy,' so I assumed that France had something similar."

He chuckled. "Not Bonaparte. In point of fact, I daresay that is one of his biggest problems, that he has no policy to speak of. He merely wishes to rule all Europe. That Peace of Amiens is not much at all, you know. He gave England no trade agreement—not that he had to do so, of course, since he was actually the victor of that round, but it would have made peace more of a possibility."

"We have peace," she reminded him.

"Ah, yes, so we do." He nodded. "I have not yet heard the First Consul admit being satisfied with what he's got, however."

They chatted in this vein for some minutes, and Meriel was impressed that Sir Antony did not mock her interest as her father and Jocelyn—and, indeed, most other gentlemen of her acquaintance—had done. Ladies simply were not expected to be interested in anything they chanced to read in a newspaper other than royal and social news. But when she had the chance, Meriel liked to read the political news, even the dispatches. However, those newspapers that did find their way to Plas Tallyn were generally weeks old, so she rarely was able to discuss current news. It was with some disappointment, therefore, that she received the information, relayed by a footman, that her chaise had been repaired and was standing in the innyard awaiting her pleasure.

It was but a matter of twenty minutes before they were ready to depart, and to Meriel's surprise, another gentleman stood with Sir Antony in the yard when she emerged from the inn. His back was toward her, but he was slender, of medium height, and there was something familiar about him. Not until he turned toward her and grinned did she recognize him, however.

"Merciful heavens!" she exclaimed under her breath.

"What is it, m'lady?" Gladys inquired behind her.

"That man with Sir Antony is a thief. I . . ." She hesitated, not wishing to admit to Gladys that she had stepped out the previous evening, but then, realizing there was no other way, she went on, "I caught him stealing from Sir Antony last night."

Mr. Carruthers' grin had widened, and she was sure he knew just what she was telling Gladys, but her maid's astonishment could not be ignored. "Just what do you mean, miss, you stopped him? You was safe and snug in your bed, you was."

"Well, I stepped out for a breath of air, and when I returned, I surprised him creeping out of Sir Antony's room."

"Miss Meriel!"

"I know, 'twas very bad of me, but indeed I came to no harm, and I had my pistol by me, so I had no compunction about stopping him. Fortunately, Sir Antony was just below in the taproom, and came upstairs before I had to think what to do with my capture. But how dare that man accost us in the yard in this fashion!"

Striding forward to demand an explanation of such impertinence, Meriel realized that Sir Antony had moved nearer to Mr. Carruthers. Furthermore, he was smiling, if not so broadly as his companion, then certainly quite cheerfully. She came to a halt before them, her eyes glittering with indignation.

"What are you doing here?" she demanded of Carruthers.

"Why, I have decided to ride on to Paris, and since that is also your destination, ma'am, Sir Antony has most kindly invited me to join your party."

"This is not Sir Antony's party, and he has no business to be inviting anyone to join it," she said angrily. "Moreover, I have no wish to be seen in company with a common thief."

"Oh, not common, surely," Mr. Carruthers protested. "I steal only from the best people, as you must have realized, my lady. Indeed, I am most profoundly sorry if I gave you a fright. I would never have stepped into the corridor at that moment if you had but made the smallest noise to announce your presence."

"No doubt that is true enough," she agreed dryly.

Sir Antony chuckled, then clapped Carruthers on the back. "My lady, this fellow has promised to mend his ways and I believe he means to do so. I cannot think there is real harm in him, and he would not be safe traveling alone, for a solitary traveler must always be at the mercy of any rogue he might meet."

"I daresay Mr. Carruthers can look after himself."

"But," said Sir Antony gently, "I should prefer to look after Mr. Carruthers. Who knows where next he will turn up if we do not keep him safely under our eye."

There was certainly something to be said for that, Meriel thought, although she could not believe Carruthers would be so foolish as to twice mark Sir Antony or the rest of them for his activities. If she were left to decide for herself, she would still call out the nearest constable. So it was with some disgust that she climbed into the chaise, turning a cold shoulder to both Sir Antony and his new protégé.

8

The distance from the village of Mantes-de-Jolie to Paris was less than thirty miles, but the road remained rutted and difficult to negotiate in places, so even though they changed teams wherever they could do so, their progress was slower than Meriel would have liked. To add to their difficulties, it came on to drizzle before they had reached Saint Germain. What had been a bright blue sky at noon changed within two hours to dismal gray. It was a spring rain and not a particularly chilly one, but neither Meriel nor Gladys Peat could long remain comfortable while they watched the two riders hunched in their saddles with only their turned-up collars for protection from the elements. After less than fifteen minutes of this, Meriel let down the window and shouted for them to come into the chaise.

"No need for that," Sir Antony shouted back. " 'Tis little more than a heavy fog. We shan't drown."

"Don't be foolish, sir," she retorted sharply. "I don't wish to be responsible for your death from inflammation of the lung."

"If the postboys can tolerate it, we can."

"The postboys, in case you have not taken note of the fact, carry sensible bright yellow oilskins in their saddle pouches and have long since donned them. Do stop being ridiculous, sir, and come in out of the rain."

"I'm agreeable, sure enough," shouted Carruthers, laughing.

A grimace crossed her face before she could stop it. She had little desire to share the close confines of the chaise with the thief. Nevertheless, she could not demand that he ride alone in the misty rain. Swallowing her annoyance, she shouted to the postboys to halt the chaise, and commanded that both men tie their horses to the rear and come inside at once.

"This is most kind of you," said Carruthers, making himself as comfortable as possible on the forward seat, which, unlike its English counterpart, was little more than a hard, narrow bench. "We'd have been drenched within the hour."

She nodded, saying nothing, but was amused rather than otherwise when he continued chatting as though she had replied to him quite civilly. He talked of the weather and of the probable gaiety of Paris in the spring. Then he went on to ask questions about London, confessing that he had been absent from that city for nearly a year. When Meriel informed him in polite but unencouraging tones that she had not seen London in rather longer than that, Sir Antony spoke up at last, saying that he could no doubt provide Mr. Carruthers with town gossip that was, if not the latest, at least more recent than a year old.

He sounded amused, Meriel thought, which was strange, since he was clearly uncomfortable, perched as he was upon a seat which was far too narrow for a man of his size. He had leaned into his corner, and as he talked, he continued to shift from time to time as though he searched unsuccessfully for comfort.

Meriel recognized a number of names as the two gentlemen chatted. What surprised her was not so much that she knew the same people as Sir Antony but that Carruthers also seemed to know them. Then, as she pondered the matter, she decided that, to be successful, a thief must certainly know who possessed those objects most worthy of his attention.

Nevertheless, long before they reached the last turnpike, on the bustling outskirts of Paris, she had been drawn adroitly into the conversation and found herself laughing and talking with both gentlemen as though she had known them forever. She had become accustomed to chatting with Sir Antony in such a fashion, but it was astonishing to her that she could feel comfortable talking with a man like Carruthers. With even more amazement, however, did she hear herself suggesting, as they turned out of the narrow, cobbled Rue St. Honoré, between tall iron gates, into the courtyard of the magnificent Maison de Prévenu, that both Sir Antony and Mr. Carruthers must certainly step inside long enough to warm themselves before the fire and to meet her sister.

Even before they had descended from the chaise, the tall red doors of Maison de Prévenu had been flung wide and liveried servants hastened down the broad limestone steps to hold umbrellas over their heads and to help the postboys unload the trunks and portmanteaux strapped to the front and rear of the chaise. As they entered the vast two-story front hall to be greeted by a bowing dark-coated butler and several minions in jackets of pale blue over cream-colored breeches, Meriel heard a sudden rush of clicking heels on the marble floor, and almost before she had time to turn toward the sound, found herself enveloped in lavender-scented sea-green chiffon as her sister Nest flung her arms about her.

"Oh, Meri, I can scarcely credit that you are come at last," she cried, standing back again to look at her. Poised thus, she could be seen to resemble her younger sister only with regard to her fair complexion and light hair. Her face was rounder, as was her figure, for she was no longer as slim as Meriel remembered. Indeed, beneath the flowing yards of translucent green chiffon with which she had draped herself, it could be seen that she had grown rather buxom.

"My goodness, Nest!" Meriel exclaimed, looking her over in return. "You have changed beyond recognition, but 'tis most becoming."

Nest laughed merrily. "So dearest André tells me. He likes his women soft, he says, and he cannot deny that I have grown very soft indeed." She turned toward the two gentlemen, her eyes dancing. "But you have not introduced your handsome escorts, my dearest. Indeed, you did not even warn me that you would have an escort. I remember distinctly that you said you would be traveling with only dearest Gladys Peat—and how wonderful it is to see you again, Gladys," she added, diverted. "You must follow Michel, the blond one there, upstairs, and he will show you where I have put the Lady Meriel. Now then," she went on without pause, "who are these delightful gentlemen?"

Laughing, Meriel shook her head. "You do not change after all, Nest, but remain as wonderfully shatterbrained as ever. First you demand their names and then you chatter like a magpie so that no one else can put a word in edgeways. The large, rather lazy-looking gentleman is Sir Antony Davies, and I promise you, his demeanor owes nothing to exhaustion. 'Tis the way he always looks. He appointed himself our courier somewhere along the way and, in fact, has traveled with us since Barmouth. The other is Mr. Roger Carruthers. He is a—"

"An ardent admirer of your magnificent self, madam," interjected Mr. Carruthers, stepping forward with exquisite grace to kiss Nest's hand. As Meriel watched indignantly, he raised his head, retaining the still-slim little hand in his, and gazed into Nest's sparkling blue eyes. "You are as beautiful as I have heard, madam, and I confess I had believed such a thing must be impossible."

"Dear me, what a charming man," said Nest with a chuckle, withdrawing her hand from his at last with patent reluctance. "I daresay you have heard any number of things about me, sir, but I promise they are not *all* so true as that."

Even Sir Antony chuckled at these audacious words, and Nest turned to him at once, her smile wide upon her lips, displaying fine white teeth. The two front ones overlapped a tiny bit, but this flaw only added to the charm of her smile. "How do you do, Sir Antony?" she said demurely. " 'Tis a prodigious pleasure to make your acquaintance. I hope you and Mr. Carruthers will visit us often during your stay in Paris. Have you acquaintances here?"

"A few, madam. I shall be staying with Lord Whitworth, I believe."

"The British ambassador? Oh, that will be amusing for

you. Such a charming gentleman, if only he were not so dreadfully plagued by the necessity of adhering to English policy, poor man. He could have a deal more fun, I daresay, if he were not continually shoved into the awkward position of having to defend England's actions. I prefer to think of myself as French these days, I can tell you."

"But you are not English, anyway," Meriel pointed out, amused by her sister's uncharacteristic descent into political discussion.

"Well, I might as well be, for all the understanding these people have of the difference between the Welsh and the English. Of course there are some who realize the Welsh have been rebels since the beginning of the relationship between our two countries and who therefore think of us as kindred spirits—like the Americans, you know—but for the most part they think of me as English, do what I might to persuade them otherwise, and that, I promise you, can be embarrassing. But we should not be standing here in the hall. My *belle-mère* will scold me for running out to you like an underbred hoyden, but I could not wait. I no sooner heard the carriage wheels on the cobbles outside than I was up and in a dash to greet you. But now you must come upstairs to the salon and refresh yourselves."

But the gentlemen declined, Sir Antony declaring that since he had ordered his man to go straight on to the embassy, he must likewise stir himself to join him there, and Carruthers mentioning the need to find a place to rack up. When it looked to her as though her impulsive sister would invite him to spend the night at Miason de Prévenu, Meriel interrupted without a qualm for her poor manners, bidding both gentlemen adieu and assuring them that she and Madame de Prévenu would be happy to receive them if they should chance to be at home when either Sir Antony or Mr. Carruthers might call.

When the two men had gone, Nest looked at her sharply. "That was rude, Meri dear. Mr. Carruthers could certainly have stayed here with us, as you must know. There are any number of guest rooms, and if you are thinking it would not be the thing, that is only because you have not recalled to mind the fact that Madame Depuissant, my mother-in-law, is also in residence right now, as is André's brother, Pierre. So you see, it would be quite *convenable* for Mr. Carruthers to remain with us."

As she talked, she led the way up the broad carpeted stairs to a gallery and into a high-ceilinged salon decorated in bright shades of green and gold. Following behind her, Meriel paused on the threshold of this magnificent chamber to say tersely, "Nest, that man is no gentleman. He is a thief."

"What?" Nest turned in a swirl of green chiffon to face her. "Nonsense, Meri. What can you possibly mean?"

"I mean precisely what I say, as I always have done. He is a thief. He tried to steal Sir Antony's diamond pin and a number of other trinkets, which was how we chanced to become acquainted." She described the meeting briefly, then added, "I am mortified at the thought that I actually invited him into your house. I cannot think how I came to do such a thing."

Nest chuckled. "*Quelles sottises*! You needn't apologize for that. Indeed, 'tis most exciting, for I have never met a thief before. Do you hear, *belle-mère?*" she inquired, turning now with a flourish toward the plump black-garbed lady who was seated with her knitting upon a gilt chair near the cheerfully crackling fire. "We have entertained a thief in our front hall."

Meriel had not noticed the woman before, and realizing that she must be the dowager Comtesse de Prévenu, hurriedly dropped a curtsy. "How do you do, *madame?* I beg your pardon for chattering so. I did not realize anyone else was here."

The plump lady nodded, lowered the tangle of cheerful pink knitting to her spacious lap, and smiled graciously, then gestured to a matching chair on the opposite side of the green Aubusson hearth rug. "Seat yourself, *mademoiselle,*" she said in English. "There is no fault. I am well accustomed to my daughter-in-law's impulsiveness. Was yours a pleasant journey?"

"A trifle tedious, perhaps, but the company was pleasant." As Meriel took her seat, she noted gratefully that her sister had rung for refreshment, and she gave but half her mind to her exchange of amenities with the dowager as she listened for sounds that would herald the arrival of the tea tray. It came at last, however, and once she had taken the edge off her hunger with tea and delicious little iced cakes, she was able to pay closer heed to the older woman.

At first her impression was that Madame Elise, as that lady preferred to be addressed, was a cushiony white-haired gentlewoman whose greatest interest would be her knitting or perhaps her grandchildren. But then, when Meriel asked Nest what on earth she had meant by referring to the ambassador's duty to defend England's actions as a burden, she noted a shrewd gleam in Madame Elise's gray eyes.

Before she could think more about that look her attention was claimed by her sister, who said pettishly, "Well, of course one must expect the ambassador to say that England is doing right, but really, Meri, it *is* too bad, when everyone knows that England is the one pushing France to the brink of war."

"Oh, Nest, surely you know 'tis that Bonaparte creature who is at fault. He wants only to conquer the whole of Europe, that is all."

"He wishes to be called Napoleon, not Bonaparte, and he is not a creature," retorted Nest indignantly. "You have never seen him, after all, so you cannot know how handsome he is and how charming he can be. Otherwise, I protest, I should never forgive you for saying such things as that."

"Nest, for pity's sake, that man is naught but an upstart soldier playing the part of a king—Napoleon the First, I imagine he thinks himself. As for his being handsome, why, we have heard even in the north of Wales that the man is as plump as a puffin. And so charming is he, miss, that he has imprisoned your own husband!"

Nest hunched one plump shoulder. "Everyone says he will release André very soon, and as for his being naught but a soldier, I am sure his birth was perfectly respectable. He was not born into the first circles, perhaps, but only because his papa was Italian, and I am persuaded that no one regards his background at this present, in any event."

"Well, nevertheless, if the current situation is an uneasy one, it is not England's fault. Why, Napoleon has taken over Switzerland, Holland, and Belgium, and any number of other countries without yet being satisfied. He but hungers for more and more."

"His greatest wish," Nest retorted passionately, "is to *unify* Europe. Why, only a month past, he lost his temper completely because Lord Whitworth simply refused to cooperate in his attempt to bring peace to the Continent. In front of everyone who is anyone, Napoleon shouted that England is determined to make war on France, that they will drive him to do as they wish, but he also declared that although they will be the first to draw the sword, he will be the last to sheathe it. Oh, Meri, it was a magnificent speech. All who heard it talked of nothing else for weeks. At the end Napoleon bellowed, 'Woe to those who show no respect for treaties!' and stalked from the room. By the time he reached the street, however, those who saw him reported that he was perfectly composed, so great is his command over even his most violent emotions."

"Oh, Nest, how could you be so taken in?" Meriel demanded. "Mr. Carruthers and Sir Antony spoke of that same confrontation only this afternoon, and Sir Antony at least is very well-informed. You may believe it if he says that Napoleon's composure afterward only served to prove that the whole business was contrived from first to last in hopes that such a violent threat of war would force England to back down on her refusal to turn the island of Malta over to the French. In fact, as you must know, the opposite has occurred, and Britain has now made conditions that must be patently unacceptable to him, that France must evacuate Holland and Switzerland and consent to a ten-year occupation of Malta by English forces. *That* is scarcely what he can have hoped for."

"I daresay it is no more than he expected, however," Nest said, regaining her temper with an effort and speaking more temperately. "You do not understand, Meriel, for you hear only England's side of the matter. Once Napoleon's objective is attained, Europe will become a federation of free and sovereign states—"

"Under his rule," Meriel inserted dryly.

"True, but there is nothing wrong with that, for the federation will benefit from all the liberal principles of the French Revolution. The only obstacle to success is England, which for years has been directed by a greedy, reactionary government that never ceases to stir up war against poor France by means of bribery and intrigue. As long as France is obliged to defend herself against the attacks of first one, then another foolish hireling of Whitehall, certainly Napoleon must fluctuate his actions according to the requirements of the moment. You must admit, Meriel, that you cannot defend Mr. Addington's actions so easily as I defend Napoleon's."

Staring at Nest, as astonished by her glib tongue as by her attitude, Meriel scarcely knew what to reply. She had little wish to defend Prime Minister Addington, a man whose abilities she had scorned since his earliest days in office, but neither could she agree, after having heard Sir Antony's views on the subject, with her sister's notion of the relationship between England and France. Fortunately, Madame Elise chose this moment to remind them of her presence.

"*Mes enfants*," she said gently as she picked up her knitting needles and set them to a speedy, rhythmic clicking, "you do yourselves no good by these discussions. Friends—and certainly sisters—ought to leave the discussion of politics to those who can do some good by such discussion. *Bien sûr*, you are neither of you in a position to understand the other without long and arduous dispute. Instead you should be elated to find yourselves in each other's company and should be planning what first to do to celebrate your reunion after so much time."

Meriel bit her lower lip, then looked up at Nest, who was seated across from her near the dowager. A rueful smile began to tug at her lips, and she said contritely, "Papa always said we could argue about anything, but I daresay he never would have thought 'everything' could possibly include politics."

Nest replied with a chuckle. "To be sure. I daresay everyone back home would stare to hear me talk of such things, for although you always liked to know what went on in government circles, I am persuaded I never did so before in my life. But it is impossible to be a member of the Depuissant family without becoming aware of how things stand in the political arena. They are, all of them, involved to some extent. Why, even Mama Elise, you know, is a genius when it comes to inviting the right people to a dinner party. And with all the factions rampant in this town, that is no mean achievement, I can tell you, for we mix as much with the ministers of government as we do with the *beau monde de Paris*, as you will soon see."

"Have you," Meriel asked casually, "ever met a gentleman by name of Monsieur Alexandre Deguise?"

"Oh, to be sure," Nest replied. "Monsieur Deguise is a charming gentleman. Rather elderly and precise, you know, but a man quite at home at any social affair. How come you to know him, Meriel?"

"Oh, I do not, but I met an acquaintance of his in Rouen when I was looking into that school for Gwenyth, you know, and received a letter of introduction to him."

"Gwenyth in school in France," Nest said, laughing. "It is so difficult for me to credit such a thing. Why, I can scarcely imagine her any older than when I left. Let me see, she must have been but nine or ten then. Now she is a young lady, I daresay."

"Well, not a lady yet," Meriel said with a grin, "but she intends to become a lady of quality and entertain royalty at her soirees. Thus Auntie Wynne insists that she should have the benefits of a Continental education."

"Oh, how is Auntie Wynne?" Nest demanded. "Tell me all about her."

So Meriel launched into a lengthy description of family affairs, bringing her sister up-to-date on all the other members except, of course, their elder brother, Jocelyn. "For I tell you, Nest, I still have not had so much as the briefest note from him or from anyone else about him."

"Oh, he'll turn up when he's of a mind to do so," Nest replied comfortably. "Now, tell me more about Davy. He sounds the veriest imp." Tears glistened suddenly in her eyes. "Oh, Meri, four years is such a long time. How I wish you could have brought them all with you!"

"Well, you and André will simply have to visit Plas Tallyn."

"I think you'd be more like to see us in London," Nest told her with a twinkle. "André is not much of a traveler at best, and he would find Wales entirely too flat."

"If he does," Meriel said, laughing, "he will certainly be the first person to do so."

"Oh, Meri," Nest gurgled, shaking her head, "you know perfectly well that I meant he would be bored. No one could forget our magnificent mountains. But the social life at Plas Tallyn leaves a deal to be desired, and André does like his social life."

"He must like politics as well, or how came he to be imprisoned?"

"Oh, that." Nest shrugged and reached forward to the low table between them to refill her teacup. "He merely said something foolish, and it chanced to come to Napoleon's ears at a moment when he refused to be amused."

"What on earth did André say?"

Nest flushed slightly. "It doesn't bear repeating. Indeed, I am not certain myself what was said, for I wasn't present, and although I have heard any number of tales, I refuse to credit any of them."

"It is said," put in the dowager evenly, her tone at variance with the lightning movement of her knitting needles, "that my son cast aspersions upon Napoleon's faithfulness to family and country and that it was the first rather than the last that annoyed him. He is a great man for family, you know."

"I have heard that he approves of large families, certainly," Meriel said carefully, "and that he once said the greatest woman on earth would be the one who bore the most children. But I have also heard it said that he would keep women locked up within their homes, that he does not approve of their socializing at all, so I probably know as little about him as my sister says I do. Surely no man would be so foolish as all that."

"I daresay my son would agree with you upon that head, *mademoiselle,* but Napoleon does indeed have such notions. He believes that in no other way can a man be certain that his children are his own. And it was in a discussion of this matter that *mon cher* André made whatever comment it was that he made."

"Merciful heavens!"

"We will hope so," Nest said, grinning at her. "Napoleon Bonaparte does have an odd notion or two, but since he insists that he means to abide by the liberal policies so hard won by the Revolution, policies which gave Frenchwomen an influence they did not hold before, not to mention separate property rights, he cannot make too great a point of those notions. My money is my own here, Meri, which it would not be in England, you know, and Napoleon would like to change that. At our very own dinner table, he once said that women should stick to knitting." She smiled at the dowager, who only shook her head.

"He thinks you can knit?" Meriel said teasingly.

Nest chuckled. "He has never seen me do so, certainly, but he believes all women are born knowing such things. But he has never said they should not leave their houses, Meri, only that they should not do so without their husbands' consent or receive visitors of whom they do not approve." Her eyes twinkled. "A husband in this country attempting to control his wife to that extent would not get very far, I can tell you, and so I am sure André must have told him."

"But if that was all . . ."

"Oh, I daresay it was not. André speaks his mind always, and Napoleon is not one to brook opposition to any of his views, even such absurd ones as those."

"Then André may be in prison for a long time," Meriel said gently, "and surely you must also watch your behavior, my dear."

Nest laughed merrily, exchanging a droll look with her mother-in-law. "You must know, Meriel, that even Napoleon's own wife does not agree with him on such issues, and he has sufficient command of good manners to avoid pressing them when he has been invited to a dinner party. He may wish to instill such notions into a new generation of French men and women, but he is not so doltish as to belabor them where it will do him no good. I have nothing to fear from him, I assure you, other than perhaps a pinch in a dark corridor. As for André, if Napoleon were not at this moment in residence in Boulogne, looking to his latest collection of warships, I am persuaded that André would have been here to greet your arrival. But tell me more about the fascinating Sir Antony. Is he your latest flirt, Meri dear?"

9

Caught off guard, Meriel returned a quick and somewhat startled denial and quickly changed the subject to ask her sister whether she and Madame Elise meant to dine at home that evening.

"Oh, my goodness, no," responded Nest. "How dull that would be, even with you to bear us company, my dearest. We dine with Thérèse Cabarrus, the most fascinating creature. Her house is in the Faubourg Saint-Germain, and it will be swarming with people. She never considers whether there will be room to talk or whether so many guests will be suffocated, but you will be marvelously entertained, dearest. And 'tis a wonderful house."

Madame Cabarrus' house proved to be everything Nest promised it would be, and Meriel discovered, as well, that her sister was as much a social butterfly as ever. She did not even suffer the lack of a male escort, for her brother-in-law, Pierre, a cheerful young man who allowed few serious thoughts to disturb the tenor of his mind, was only too happy to accompany them. And once arrived, the merry countess soon gathered a court of masculine admirers to whom she quite unselfishly presented her sister.

Since Meriel knew that the Peace of Amiens had brought a rush of tourists to France from Britain, she was not surprised to discover that quite half of her companions hailed from that small island. What she was unprepared for, however, was the latest in French fashion. She had been astonished at their meeting by the translucence of her sister's layers of sea-green chiffon, but since there had indeed been several layers, only the outline of Nest's body had been visible beneath them. And when Meriel met Madame Elise and Nest in the vast front hall before setting forth for the evening, both were wearing long silk evening cloaks, so it was not until they reached the mansion in the Faubourg Saint-Germain that she was privileged to experience the full effect of such flimsy materials as were considered proper evening wear for the ladies of the French *beau monde*. The impact of the vision thus brought to her eye left her breathless.

Her first impression was that several of the statues in Thérèse Cabarrus' moonlit garden had suddenly sprung to life and ventured among the guests. Nest's attire, when she was divested of her cloak, was seen to be scandalously low-cut and daringly diaphanous, but nothing could have looked more like a "Diana" than Thérèse herself, who greeted her guests attired in nothing more than a light, transparent drapery, with no sleeves to her gown but only a gold chain twisted around the upper part of each slender arm, like a bracelet, and her neck entirely bare of ornament or fabric. She was remarkably pretty nonetheless, Meriel thought, with her hair dressed in a crescent-shaped arrangement like a goddess. Two of her particular friends, to whom she promptly introduced Meriel and the others, though a little plumper than their hostess, were attired in the same style but with their hair twisted into long snaky curls. Madame, their mother, who was introduced as a great friend of Madame Elise's, was, like that lady herself, entirely too much *en bon point* to pretend to a sylphlike appearance, but nevertheless, and unlike Madame Elise, she did not choose to add to her size by too much covering.

It seemed to Meriel, in fact, that every woman, were she seventeen or seventy, stood almost in a state of nature, for the Parisiennes seemed to prefer to cover themselves with cosmetics, particularly rouge, rather than with clothes. But their manners were universally captivating, and by the time the meal was over and the dinner guests had joined others in the cardroom or in the drawing room to play charades or enjoy conversation, she had been made to feel quite at home in their midst.

"Good evening," said a familiar voice at her shoulder before she had been fifteen minutes in the drawing room. "Whitworth mentioned that Thérèse is a particular friend of your sister's, so I hoped to find you here tonight."

She turned with an instant glow of pleasure to find Sir Antony looking down at her with his usual sleepy smile. "Good evening, sir," she said, regarding him with an appraising eye. He wore a purple velvet coat and a violet waistcoat, the wide cuffs of the former and the entire front expanse of the later embroidered all over with twining greenery. His collar was high-standing with small lapels, and she noted with approval that the shoulders of his coat required no padding. Likewise did she approve of the fact that he had not chosen to litter his person with a great deal of jewelry as the French exquisites did. He wore no more than his gold quizzing glass on its black silk ribbon, an amethyst stickpin in his cravat, a large gold signet ring on his right hand, and assorted fobs and seals upon his fob ribbon. His nether parts were encased in ecru satin breeches, clocked cream stockings, and neat black shoes. "You look as fine as fivepence, sir," Meriel told him, "but I must confess that I am disappointed to see that you don't wear gold earrings as the other gentlemen do. Such a charming affectation."

Sir Antony was betrayed into an ungentlemanly sound perilously akin to a snort, and his eyes narrowed as he scanned her face for some sign that she was hoaxing him.

Meriel was quite unable to retain her look of false innocence under this piercing stare. An involuntary chuckle gave her away.

"Puppies," said Sir Antony, glancing around. " 'Tis as though association with the Corsican has emasculated them all."

"Oh, surely you are too hard upon them, sir. My sister tells me that Mr. Bonaparte, who prefers to be called Napoleon in quite the royal manner, has charmed all the ladies in Paris."

"No doubt. But 'tis the men who concern me. Look at them."

She obeyed him and was forced to agree that they were by and large a mincing, dandified lot. Nonetheless, she found it difficult as the evening passed to condemn any of the gentlemen she met for anything more serious than a lack of interest in any but the lightest conversation. She attempted more than once to bring up the subject of the uneasy peace, but each time her listener, whoever he was, adroitly evaded the issue.

She did not meet Père Leclerc's friend Alexandre Deguise that night, nor for several nights after that, and when she did, it was at a musicale in the home of one of Madame Elise's friends. With people chatting on her every side, she could scarcely do more than introduce herself and mention that she had been given a letter of introduction to him from the priest in Rouen.

"I will do myself the singular honor to call upon you at Maison de Prévenu, *mademoiselle,*" said the elderly gray-haired gentleman with a courtly bow. And so he did, the following day, not long after Meriel and her sister had departed from the breakfast parlor. They were sitting companionably together in a charming sunlit chamber known to the inhabitants of the house as the ladies' boudoir when Monsieur Deguise's card was carried up on a silver tray by one of the blue-and-cream-clad footmen.

"*Merci*, Michel," said Meriel when he presented the card to her. She scanned it briefly, then looked at her sister with a smile. " 'Tis Monsieur Deguise," she said, "the gentleman I inquired about when first I arrived. I chanced to make his acquaintance briefly last evening at Madame de Poine's musicale, and he promised he would call. Show him into the downstairs drawing room, Michel, if you have not put him there already. When I have fetched Père Leclerc's letter, I shall go down to him at once."

"Not alone, you won't," said Nest, laughing at her as the footman departed. "That don't suit my notions of propriety one bit. You may have traveled across France with gentlemen dancing attendance, but you shan't entertain one in my drawing room without a proper chaperon, and so I tell you to your head."

"Fiddlesticks," retorted Meriel. "It has naught to do

with propriety and all to do with your insatiable curiosity, my girl. I am well able to deal with a gentleman old enough to be our grandfather without interference from you."

"Call it what you may," said Nest, still chuckling. "You run along and get your letter, and I shall reintroduce myself to your beau."

So it was that when Meriel descended to the ground-floor drawing room, it was to find her sister happily engrossed in conversation with the elderly deputy minister. Nest looked up with a wide grin.

"You find us out, my love. I have been flirting outrageously with your latest conquest, and I mean to cut you out with him before the week is out."

Meriel was a trifle dismayed by her sister's behavior, but she quickly realized that her visitor was only flattered. Smiling at him, she said, "You must think us quite without manners, sir. I am so pleased that you have honored us with a visit this morning. Here is the letter from Père Leclerc. It was kind of him to refer me to you."

"One can never have too many letters of introduction when one travels beyond one's own country, *mademoiselle*," Monsieur Deguise said in his low, rumbling voice. He straightened his neckcloth with a slight, expert gesture, lifted the seal, and began to read.

Remembering what the priest had promised to ask of him, Meriel suddenly wished her sister were elsewhere. After all, she could scarcely discuss her need to be assured of Nest's safety with Nest sitting right there. Not—from what she had seen of her sister since her arrival—unless she wished to have a basin of cold water emptied over her head at the first opportunity. She watched Monsieur Deguise with feelings of uneasiness, but she need not have worried.

When he had finished reading, he looked up at her, glanced at Nest, smiled, and returned his gaze to Meriel's anxious face. "I shall be most pleased to be of service to you in any way I possibly can, *mademoiselle.* I daresay we shall encounter one another from time to time, since it appears that we have friends in common. Thus, if there is ever anything you require, you have but to ask." He turned slightly toward Nest. "*Sans doute, madame,* you have a great concern for the fate of your husband?"

Nest shrugged, but the quick frown that had crossed her pretty face as he spoke belied the gesture, and she realized the fact at once. "You are too quick for me, *monsieur.* I do feel concern, despite the fact that I know in my heart that all will be well."

"I can tell you, *madame,* that your heart speaks truly. The First Consul has already tried the patience of the great and generous Depuissant family more than good sense should permit. The *comte*'s uncle, who is a man of resource and wealth, as you know, has already made some discomfiting demands and has refused to provide Napoleon with further funding for his armada at Boulogne until the *comte* has been released. It will not be more than a week or two at most. Only till Napoleon returns to Paris, I am convinced."

After that, Meriel was able to relax her own concerns. Surely if André was in a way toward being released from prison, Nest was in no danger so long as the uneasy peace continued. If war were to break out again, then there might be danger to them all, but Nest had been in France before while England was at war with her, and she had survived that. With a clear conscience, Meriel turned her full attention to enjoying Paris.

The Parisian spring was all that Mr. Carruthers had told her it would be. The boulevards which encircled the town were thickly planted with high branching trees, under which there seemed to be an eternal scene of festivity. All the best cafés, Meriel soon learned, were out-of-doors, and a thousand groups of happy-looking people could be seen at any time of day or night, sitting under blossoming arbors, quaffing lemonade, wine, cider, or beer, and conducting themselves with such cheerfulness and decorum that she found it a delight to watch them. Besides the usual evening parties that she might have taken part in in London as well as in Paris, she discovered in the weeks that followed that one of the favorite pastimes of the *beau monde de Paris* was to go "vagabondizing." Upon more than one occasion, but always under the escort of several gentlemen, she and Nest found themselves poking their noses into every haunt of the lower orders that they could find. There were cabarets full of dancers, "Theaters for the People," and entertainment booths on every major boulevard presenting conjurers, puppets, menageries, and the like.

"Music seems to be the very breath of Paris," she told her sister one evening as they strolled along a boulevard lined with tall trees and a number of these booths, from all of which a harmony of sound floated on the gentle breeze.

"Very poetic," said Nest, looking at her. "I believe you are becoming a romantic at last, Meri. Do you not think so, Mr. Carruthers?" she inquired of the gentleman strolling at her side.

"Nonsense," Meriel retorted before he could draw breath to speak. She had grown accustomed to seeing him often, because her sister flatly refused to see anything amiss in admitting an erstwhile—or so one hoped—thief to her drawing room, particularly when he was handsome and possessed of a charming impudence. Indeed, Nest seemed to have set Mr. Carruthers up as her latest flirt, making her sister wish more than ever that Napoleon would return from Boulogne and set the Comte de Prévenu free, so that he might take his pretty wife in hand.

A chuckle from the tall, sleepy-looking gentleman beside her made Meriel look up at him in pretty confusion. "Nest will be giving you and Mr. Carruthers quite an incorrect opinion of my nature, Sir Antony. I have no sensibility, and well she knows it. Moreover, though this sort of entertainment no doubt suits Mr. Carruthers down to the ground, I daresay you must disapprove of vagabondism quite as much as Papa or Joss would."

"You wrong me, Lady Meriel," said Sir Antony calmly.

She looked up at him again and this time surprised a look that she had often seen since their arrival in Paris. This time, however, there was an additional admiring warmth in his eyes that made her feel that her new Parisian gown of pale apricot muslin was quite unsuitable. She had had her doubts when Nest had insisted upon its purchase, but she had been unable to deny that it set off her charms as no other gown she had ever owned had done. Indeed, that it set them off too well was her concern at the moment. She blushed and, feeling the warmth spreading throughout her body, she was certain the blush spread from her Grecian topknot to her shell-pink toenails. The spring evening was balmy, and the only wrap she carried was a long scarf of lavender silk that she wore draped over her elbows. Suddenly she had an urge to wrap that scarf around her torso. She looked away, but that didn't help for she could feel his gaze upon her like an intimate caress.

It was disturbing, she thought, that she could remain so aware of Sir Antony without so much as looking at him. His presence seemed to vitalize the very atoms of the air around her, setting nerves atingle and making her feel more alive than she had ever felt before, except possibly when she stood atop her favorite mountain after the long, hard climb to reach the summit. Now so aware of him was she that her breasts swelled of their own accord, pressing hard against their light covering, their tips stirring as though he had touched them with his fingers. The warmth in her cheeks became painful. She didn't dare to look up.

Fortunately, Nest commented just then on the way the trees on either side of the boulevard met like an arch over the middle, and the moment passed. "And do you know, Meriel," she went on, happily unaware of any charged feelings in the air, "I do not believe Joss would disapprove of what we are doing in the slightest. He was always an adventurer, you know."

"Ah, yes, indeed, but he rarely invited us to go adventuring with him," Meriel pointed out, recovering her poise, but avoiding Sir Antony's eyes nevertheless. "His notion of adventuring was that it was famous sport for gentlemen and altogether unsuitable for ladies."

"Your brother sounds like a fine fellow," said Mr. Carruthers with a droll look.

"Oh, pooh, he was never so fusty as Meriel would have you believe," Nest told him, laughing. "And in

Paris, moreover, what we are doing is entirely *comme il faut*."

"Except to your Napoleon," Meriel said dryly, "who would keep women in their drawing rooms under the eyes of their husbands. No doubt he would believe both of us to be compromising our virtue by this delightful outing."

Nest grinned at her. "You are determined to find fault with Napoleon, but I shall not allow you to draw me into another argument. Not tonight, at any event."

Before that week was out, however, Meriel had written to Mademoiselle Lecolier to inform her that she had decided against enrolling Gwenyth in l'École de Bonté. As she sanded the final draft of her letter, she wondered why it had taken her so long to write. She knew now that she had realized long since that the political situation was entirely too unstable for her to contemplate sending her young sister into France. Even with Nest and the powerful Depuissant family at hand, Meriel knew she would not be easy. And England, as Sir Antony had said more than once, had many excellent schools.

Indeed, now she came to think upon the matter, she realized that she had nearly decided against l'École de Bonté before ever laying eyes upon the place. Certainly what she had seen there had had nothing to do with her decision. Anyone must be glad to send a child to Mademoiselle Lecolier, in confidence that the child would be prepared in the best way possible to take her place among the ladies of the *beau monde*. But not if the child might be trapped by war in France, far from her loving family.

Meriel knew that negotiations were still in progress between the two countries. She knew, too, that Napoleon's foreign minister, Prince Talleyrand, and his brother Joseph Bonaparte were both exerting themselves in the cause of peace. But since neither Napoleon nor the British cabinet seemed to have yielded so much as an inch, she could not be optimistic as to the probable outcome. And now that she had made her decision regarding l'École de Bonté and had discovered Nest to be as safe as one might expect and in momentary expectation of her husband's release, Meriel began to turn her thoughts toward her family in London. Whenever she had previously mentioned that she ought to be thinking of leaving, Nest had protested vehemently, and Meriel had allowed herself to be easily overborne, so that April had disappeared into May before anyone had any notion of how the weeks might have gone so quickly.

"You have shown me a whirlwind of activity," Meriel told her sister over breakfast one bright morning the second week of May. "I should not have been so busy even in London with the Season at its peak."

"No, indeed, dearest, and so I promised you it would be. But, alas, if I had had my way, all this activity would have resulted by now in your engagement to be married."

Meriel stared at her. "What on earth are you talking about? I have no wish to marry. Good heavens, Nest, I am nearly seven-and-twenty. My days of thinking about marriage are long since gone by."

"No woman is ever past the age of thinking about marriage," Nest told her, reaching for the toast rack, "and what's more, you have a perfectly eligible *parti* in Sir Antony. That man is head over ears in love with you, my dearest, as anyone with half an eye can see."

Meriel flushed. "You are all about in your head, Nest. I don't deny that we have enjoyed a most agreeable flirtation, but with the family to look after, I have no time for anything more than that, and I cannot believe Sir Antony, having reached his middle thirties without making a push toward matrimony, has given the slightest thought to it now."

"Only encourage the man a trifle and you will quickly see how wrong you are," Nest said, turning a stern eye upon her sister as she spread jam thickly upon her toast. "When he compliments you upon your gown, you immediately turn it into a compliment for me, saying that you would never have done so well on your own without my excellent advice. That is true, of course, but you need not say so. Why, it must put the poor man quite off his stride. Furthermore, whenever he casts sheep's eyes at you, as he does constantly, you turn the conversation to politics or to the weather, for pity's sake. Or else you simply draw another person, such as myself or Mr. Carruthers, into the conversation. Yes, and if you don't want Sir Antony—though why you shouldn't, I'm sure I cannot say—you might have Mr. Carruthers merely for the dropping of your handkerchief."

Meriel burst into a peal of laughter. "Mr. Carruthers! Really, Nest, just because he has made himself perfectly charming these past weeks and has been welcomed into your friends' homes as quickly as into your own does nothing to mitigate the fact that he is a common thief."

"Nonsense, there is nothing common about that man. He's a gentleman born, that one is. Perhaps he's been cast off by his own. Whatever it is, he's a deep one, that's all."

Meriel shook her head in exasperation. "I have no time for this idiotish conversation," she said, pouring herself more tea. "Nor do I have the time or the inclination to marry. I have an estate to look after, and I am responsible for two young women and one schoolboy. What on earth would you have me do with them if I should marry?"

This question appeared to be unanswerable. Nest's voice was hardly as firm as it had been before when she suggested, "Auntie Wynne?"

"Don't be absurd. You must remember what she is like. A delightful creature, and I am sure I value her as I should, but now that she has tasted London life again, she will not wish to return to Plas Tallyn. She is not even particularly fond of the children, you know, and it was only by promising her that they would behave themselves like paragons while I was away that I convinced her to look after them for this brief time. And you know as well as I do that the letter I received only two days since betokens an impatience for my return that I can no longer ignore. I daresay if Gwenyth or Davy has not got into a scrape, Eliza has found another unsuitable beau and fancies herself in love again." Meriel's tone by the last sentence had become rather abstract, for her thoughts, of their own accord, had returned to her sister's conviction regarding Sir Antony's flirtations. Surely Nest was wrong. She had little time to dwell upon the matter, however, for a footman entered just then, bearing a message upon his silver tray.

"Goodness," said Nest, "whoever would call at such an hour as this?"

"Read the note and see," suggested her sister with a twinkling look.

Nest opened the note and scanned it briefly. "*Mon Dieu*, Monsieur Deguise is below and insists that he must speak with us at once. I hope nothing has happened to imperil André's release. We were told only another day or so."

Meriel patted her hand, then folded her napkin and arose from her chair, smoothing the skirt of her russet linen morning dress. "Perhaps it is no more than news of the negotiations," she said calmly. "He has feared recently that they might fail, and he knows I have a keen interest in what transpires."

When the two ladies entered the ground-floor drawing room, Monsieur Deguise turned quickly from his contemplation of the empty fireplace and strode toward them with a haste that was quite unlike him.

"*Madame, mademoiselle, merci du bon Dieu*!"

"What is it, *monsieur?*" Meriel demanded. " 'Tis not something gone amiss with de Prévenu, surely?"

"No, no, *mademoiselle,* he will be free within the week. Napoleon is in Paris, he is angry, and he is in need of funds, so there is nothing to trouble you there. The news I bring is sufficiently bad, *bien sûr*. The talks, they have collapsed. Lord Whitworth leaves for England today."

"Good heavens, then the embassy is to be closed?"

"*Vraiment, mademoiselle. En effet*, you and your sister must prepare to depart from France at once."

Nest regarded him in dismay. "Depart from France? Don't be absurd, *monsieur.* I have no intention of departing, come what may, for I am part of a French family now, and they will protect me. Nor is there any reason for my sister to depart, for she is Welsh, not English, and will be in no danger."

"I cannot agree, *madame,*" he said, gazing at her quite seriously. "She has come into France on a British passport, for such is what is issued at all English ports." He glanced at Meriel, who nodded her head. Her passport was indeed a British one. "In such a case there is a record of her entry as a British citizen in the Le Havre passport registry. It is such registries as that one that the authorities will check, if worse comes to worst. Me, I know this."

"But that is absurd," Nest protested. "She is my sister. My husband's family will protect her."

Monsieur Deguise was not convinced, but he soon saw that to argue further would be an exercise in futility. Thus he took his departure, leaving the two sisters to discuss the morning's events at their leisure.

"You know, Nest," Meriel said when he had gone, "he was perfectly in the right of it. You ought to pack up and come home with me."

"No, I shan't do anything of the kind. Oh, Mama Elise," she exclaimed in relief when her mother-in-law chose that moment to enter the room, "Meri is afraid there is going to be war and says I must go home with her."

As always, Madame Elise carried her knitting with her. Today it was a shawl in bright shades of green and pink. She settled herself comfortably in a wide-lapped chair near the fireplace, arranged her knitting to her satisfaction, and then turned her attention to her impatient daughter-in-law.

"Your sister is a woman of excellent sense," she said then.

"Oh, no!" Nest cried. "You cannot mean to say that I must go with her. You cannot! My place is here with you, with André's family. I will not go."

"Of course you will not go, *ma chère*. I have said only that your sister shows the good sense, not that you must obey her. You have to obey no one but your husband, and he is not here yet to tell you what you must do."

"Then he is likewise not here to protect her," Meriel pointed out gently, "and I cannot think it wise under the circumstances to await his pleasure."

"I would not go even if he said I must," Nest said stubbornly, "but he would not say such a thing. I know he would not."

"No, I do not believe he would," said Madame Elise, smiling at her, then turning the smile upon Meriel. "It is a good thing that your sister loves my son so much, I think, *mademoiselle.* It would be good for you to find a man to love like that. But for now, you must think only of yourself and what you wish to do. I cannot promise that my family can protect you, but they will protect *ma chère* Nest. Her safety need not concern you."

Knowing that the Comte de Prévenu was still in prison despite the fact that three weeks had passed since her arrival did not give Meriel a strong opinion of the Depuissants' ability to protect their own, but she said nothing then. When Sir Antony arrived an hour later with the same news of the negotiations that Monsieur Deguise had brought them, however, she had no qualms about expressing her fears to him.

Nest had followed her into the drawing room to greet him, and Madame Elise arrived several minutes later. Thus it was that Meriel had to phrase her sentences carefully, but she had no fear that he would not take her meaning. Indeed, he understood her perfectly well.

"I agree that you would both be safer in England," he said firmly. "I have come to offer my services to escort you there."

"That is kind of you, sir," Nest told him, "but there is no need. As we are Welsh, not English, there is scarcely any reason for us to fear the onset of war between England and France. Anyone knows that the Welsh rarely side with the English on any matter."

"My dear madam," Sir Antony said patiently, "you complained to me in this very room not three weeks past that the French have great difficulty distinguishing Welsh from English. Moreover, while I feel sure that Napoleon might conceivably understand and appreciate such political and historic niceties, I am equally convinced that his minions will not. The mere fact that Lady Meriel is in France on a British passport and speaks English will preclude any further questions if the *gendarmerie* detain her. The sooner she is off French soil now, the better. With all pretense at negotiation ended, the next step, I assure you, will be a declaration of war by one side or the other."

"It will be the English who will declare war, sir. I

would stake my best bonnet against anything you would care to name."

He failed to convince her either that Napoleon would be the aggressor or that she or her sister would be in any danger regardless of who declared war upon whom, and although Meriel was certain he was right about the fact that she, at least, ought to depart from Paris as quickly as possible, she could not agree to leave until she had had time to make at least one further push to convince her sister to accompany her.

This Nest flatly refused to do, and when word came to them that evening confirming the fact that the Comte de Prévenue was to be released within the week, Meriel knew there was no argument at all that would change her sister's mind. As it happened, she had very little time to consider the matter, for they received another visit from Monsieur Deguise the very next day. His news was not good.

"*Mademoiselle,*" he said sadly, "I regret to inform you that King George the Third has this day declared war upon the sovereign state of France. Furthermore, Napoleon has given orders that all British tourists are to be detained for internment at Verdun. The arrests are to begin at once."

10

"There now, did I not tell you that the English would begin it?" inquired Nest smugly. "How fortunate that Sir Antony did not accept my wager, for he would look prodigious odd in my best bonnet."

Monsieur Deguise looked at her as though she had quite lost her mind, and even Meriel was distracted enough to tell her rather sharply to hold her tongue. "For did you not hear what else our kind friend has said?" she demanded. "British tourists are even at this moment being arrested."

"Oh, pooh," said Nest, unimpressed. "I keep telling you and telling you that you are perfectly safe here."

"Begging your pardon," Monsieur Deguise put in hurriedly, "but even the so-powerful family Depuissant will be unable to protect her from arrest. In effect, as I said to you before, the Lady Meriel entered France under a British passport, which is registered in Le Havre. Me, I tell you more, that there will be a little list, just as soon as someone gets to drawing it up."

"He is right," Meriel told her sister. "You may be able to help after I am arrested, but I'd as lief not have the experience if it can be avoided." Then she turned her attention back to Monsieur Deguise. "You have been most kind to warn me, *monsieur.* Or, when you say that no one can protect me from arrest, do you mean that such arrest is imminent and unavoidable?" The thought made her stomach clench, but Deguise hastened to reassure her.

"Oh, no, no, *mademoiselle,*" he said quickly. "I come but to warn you and to urge you to flee as quickly as you may arrange to do so. Your presence in this house is no secret, so it will not be long before someone comes, but I believe you will have sufficient time to pack a case or two."

Stepping to the bell-pull, she gave it a hearty yank, and when the footman appeared, she asked her sister to relay orders to Gladys Peat to begin packing. "Have him tell her to pack only what is necessary and to do it quickly."

When the young man nodded, appearing not the least disturbed by the odd orders, then made his bow and departed, Meriel turned back to Deguise. "What do you advise me to do, *monsieur?* Do I return the way I came?"

"Indeed, *mademoiselle,* I have given the matter much consideration. No doubt it would be simpler to find someone to take you across La Manche—that is, your Channel—from Calais, but I believe that way will be extremely crowded with other British tourists. You would be wiser to go by way of Dieppe or Le Havre, and I myself should choose the latter simply because you are familiar with the route and because you can resort to a water coach if the road should prove to be overlittered with the *gendarmerie.* Then, too, your friend and mine, *le bon père de Rouen*, will surely be willing to assist you. Therefore, my advice is certainly to go to him as quickly as you may, then accept his guidance from there."

"But how will she travel?" Nest demanded. "Surely there will be *gendarmes* and soldiers on every route, searching for British tourists. Her papers, as you have pointed out, will do her no good."

Monsieur Deguise smiled. "I have taken the liberty, *mademoiselle,* of bringing with me today such papers as I believe might be of greatest assistance." With a small, triumphant flourish, he extracted from his coat pocket a packet of foolscap papers which he presented to Meriel.

She unfolded them, thinking they would be all in French, but to her surprise, some were not, and with growing delight she rapidly scanned the contents. "Good gracious, *monsieur,* how came you by these?"

"Me, I have my methods, *mademoiselle,*" the elderly man said modestly, "and I am blessed with many friends."

"One of whom, at least, is American," she said dryly. "I am become Mary Travers, American citizen, Nest. Only look at these." She held the papers out to her sister, who took them eagerly.

"There is a separate passport here for Gladys Peat, too, in her own name," Nest noted with admiration, "saying that she too is American. Would it not have been simpler to provide them with French identities, *monsieur?*"

"Indeed," he replied with a twinkle, "a good deal simpler. However, unless your sister and her maid wish also to pose as mutes, I can imagine no way by which they might answer the simplest questions without exposing themselves. And me, I have an imagination of the most lively."

"Indeed, you have been very clever, *monsieur,*" Meriel said gratefully. "But I am persuaded that you must have taken a great personal risk on my behalf. 'Tis more than I deserve."

"Not at all. You were entrusted to my care, *mademoiselle.* Which reminds me," he added, reaching into yet another pocket. "I have here a letter explaining all to the good priest in Rouen. The possibility exists, you know, that today's news will not yet have reached him in detail, so I have explained the whole in my letter. Thus you will not have to waste precious time putting him in possession of the facts. How soon can you be prepared to depart, mademoiselle?"

Meriel refolded the precious documents and placed the letter neatly with them before replying. Then she said slowly, "I do not know. I daresay within the hour if I am pressed to do so."

"I should advise such a course most strenuously," he said.

"Wait, Meri," Nest protested, "you cannot leave so soon as that. Indeed, I still do not wish you to leave at all, but surely you would be better advised to discover what Sir Antony thinks of all this business before you act precipitately."

Monsieur Deguise made her a small bow. "I attempted

to find the good Sir Antony before coming to you, *madame,* but he has removed from the embassy, *naturellement*, and it is thought that he rode some distance yesterday with the ambassador's party toward Calais."

Meriel stared at him in dismay. "He has not left France, *monsieur,* surely."

"No, no, for one of the servants at the embassy informed my man that Sir Antony's effects were removed to a nearby hostelry. My people are searching now, but even if my information was correct, I do not know when he may be expected to return, or if he will even take such a risk to himself, and it is not safe for the Lady Meriel to await his pleasure."

"No, indeed," Meriel said, repressing her disappointment and wondering briefly at the same time if she had somehow grown to expect Sir Antony to look after her. She squared her shoulders. "I have no call upon Sir Antony, and I am persuaded he will have need to look to his own safety. There is no reason that he should concern himself with mine, for I am certainly well able to look after myself, as I have always done. Indeed, by the time the messenger finds him, I daresay I shall be quite a distance upon my way." She paused, her thoughts moving rapidly, then looked again at the round little deputy minister. "You have mentioned, *monsieur,* that many know of my presence in this house. Moreover, I recall now that I named Maison de Prévenu as my destination when I filled out all those forms in Le Havre, and again when we entered the city. Will not my sudden disappearance under such circumstances as these bring danger to my sister and her family?"

"That, too, I have considered, *mademoiselle,*" the little man said with pardonable pride. "It is my belief that once you are gone, the attention of the police and military may be diverted to other matters, for none will wish to annoy the so-powerful *famille* Depuissant, particularly now that the *comte* is to return to its bosom. Anyone inquiring after you may simply be informed that you have departed. A shrug, a spreading of hands, a claim to have no knowledge of your present whereabouts will no doubt prove to be sufficient. For myself, I shall engage to deal with the passport registry at Le Havre. This, most fortunately, comes within my purview as deputy minister. British tourist Lady Meriel Traherne shall be seen to have departed these shores before any arrest order was dispatched. So long as you are not detained upon the road, *mademoiselle,* there will be no—how you say? —untoward repercussions. You have but to reach the coast, to board a vessel friendly to your dilemma—a vessel of which I trust the good Leclerc shall have knowledge, for I do not—and all will march most satisfactorily."

Meriel shook her head, marveling. "You do too much, *monsieur*. Indeed, left to my own devices, I should not have known at all how to go on. You have all my admiration and a gratitude which knows no—"

"*Ça ne fait rien, mademoiselle*," he cut in with another of his courtly little bows. "It is I who am pleased to have been of service."

He left immediately, and Meriel hurried upstairs with Nest right behind her to discover Gladys Peat flinging clothing into two portmanteaux without regard for creases or for careful selection of garments.

"Good heavens, Gladys, have a care for my new dresses, if you please. We will leave anything that cannot be carried in the portmanteaux, for we have no notion of how quickly we may have to travel, and trunks may impede the swiftness of our progress, but that is no reason not to pack carefully."

"They say them Frenchies be arrestin' everyone from over the Channel," Gladys said grimly. "I'm not lookin' t' kick my heels for the greater part of this new war of theirs in some prison, Miss Meriel, and that's the nut with no bark on it."

"Well, we shan't have to do anything of the kind," Meriel told her loftily. "Monsieur Deguise has brought us false papers that will see us safely through. We shall simply be enjoying an adventure together. What a fortunate thing it was that Père Leclerc gave me that letter of introduction to him."

"Indeed, 'tis a fortunate thing that you became acquainted with the priest," Nest said, chuckling.

"Oh, I met him through yet another new acquaintance," Meriel told her, explaining about the Uxbridge supper party two nights before her departure from Barmouth and her meeting there with George Murray. "I had heard, of course, that one cannot have too many letters of introduction when one travels, but I certainly never thought that avoiding arrest was the reason for collecting so many of them."

Nest stayed only long enough to be certain that Meriel required nothing further before sallying forth to inform Madame Elise of her sister's imminent departure and to order a chaise for her transport. The chaise was at the door within the hour, a smaller version of the one that had carried her to Paris. It was bright yellow and drawn by a full team of strong-looking bays, under the management of a pair of postilions attired in yellow jackets and beaver hats.

The portmanteaux were quickly strapped to the front of the chaise and the two women assisted inside. Then the steps were put up, the door fastened shut, and the postilions quickly mounted. Meriel let down the window to wave good-bye to Nest, who stood beside the chaise with her mother-in-law, tears coursing down her cheeks.

"Try to write," Meriel told her.

"I shall, though I've not the slightest notion how letters may be carried to you," Nest replied, her words nearly drowned by her tears.

Just then a masculine shout punctuated by a clatter of hoofbeats on the cobbles sounded behind them in the courtyard, and Meriel, with a stirring of joyous excitement, turned to look out the opposite window toward the tall iron gates. Disappointment rose swiftly when she realized at once that the slender, medium-size gentleman galloping toward them was not the man she had hoped to see, but a certain stirring of familiarity made her peer at him more closely. Then, realizing the postilions had given their horses the office to start, she whisked her head swiftly round again and shouted at them to hold where they were.

Looking back toward the two women, she knew she had judged the matter correctly. Tears still streamed down her sister's face, but they were clearly now tears of joy. Madame Elise, too, was crying, her round countenance wreathed with smiles.

"André!" shrieked Nest, running forward to meet him.

"*Mon fils!*" cried Madame Elise, holding out her arms.

The young man threw himself from his saddle, flinging his reins to the cobbles in his haste, thus making it necessary for one of the Depuissant servants to leap to grab them before the overheated gelding took it into his head to dash off again. André Depuissant, Comte de Prévenu, with a broad grin on his handsome face, swept his wife into his arms and somehow managed to make room there, scant seconds later, for his mother as well.

Watching this scene, Meriel was conscious of a relaxing sensation deep within her breast and knew at once that despite all the assurances she had had to the contrary, she had continued to worry about her sister's safety if she remained behind. But Nest would now be safe. Of that she was certain.

A moment later, the *comte* realized that he had an interested audience and firmly disengaged himself to stride forward to greet Meriel.

"I was told of your visit to Maison de Prévenu," he said, grinning. "I must apologize for the regrettable fact that circumstances kept me from seeing personally to your comfort."

She chuckled, holding her hand out to him through the open window. "I am truly happy to see you safe at home again, André, but 'tis you who must forgive me for taking my departure just as you arrive. 'Tis the worst of bad manners, I fear, but quite unavoidable, as perhaps you know."

"Indeed, *belle soeur*, you must go, and quickly. I would provide outriders, but 'twould be to make your progress the more noticeable, and I am of the opinion that this must not be so. You have papers?"

"Indeed, sir, I am well-provided," she told him. "I go as an American lady."

"Then perhaps outriders would not be so bad an idea at that," he mused.

"No, no, sir, for to hire strangers would take too long, and to send men of your own would be too dangerous.

Either they would be recognized or one would let the cat out of the bag. 'Tis safer to go as I came."

"*Oui*, and that swiftly," he said, kissing her hand and releasing it as he stepped away from the chaise. "One last *adieu*," he said to his wife, drawing her forward again.

"Oh, Meri, do be careful," Nest said, her voice still laden with tears.

"Don't concern yourself," Meriel told her, smiling broadly. "I shall enjoy myself hugely, I promise you. I am a match for anyone who might seek to detain me."

The *comte* motioned for the postilions to be on their way, and the chaise lurched forward. Beside her, Gladys Peat gave a long sigh of satisfaction. "It gives me such a feel, Miss Meriel, to know that her ladyship will be safe now, and so I tell you."

"Why, Gladys, do you mean to say that you would trust a man to look after Nest more than you would trust Madame Elise?"

"He is head of that family, m'lady, and I believe I can trust him to look after his own, though he is a man, and a French one at that. I didn't approve of the Lady Nest's decision to marry him those many years past, and I don't doubt that, pretty as she was, she couldn't have found a perfectly respectable gentleman at home to marry her, but there's no gainsaying the fact that them two love each other, and there's a deal to be said for love when all is said and done." Coming to a halt at last, more for want of breath than for any other reason, Gladys crossed her arms across her plump bosom and gave a jerk of her head as though to underscore what she had said.

Meriel grinned at her. "There can be no doubt that they love each other, certainly," she said, settling into a more comfortable position and rearranging her skirts so they would become as little wrinkled as possible. The chaise was moving with commendable speed over the cobblestones, and she told herself it would be little time indeed before they reached Rouen and the safety of the priest's cottage.

As they passed through the city gates and came to the first turnpike, however, she realized that there were a number of hazards yet before her. A half-dozen soldiers stood ready beside the pike keeper, and although Nest had seen to it that the postilions were provided with a sufficient number of tickets to see them through every stage, even should it prove necessary for them to carry Meriel all the way to Le Havre, the waving of one of these from the window as they approached the pike did nothing to stir the keeper from his position inside his little shack. In consequence of his seeming dalliance, the chaise was forced to come to a complete halt.

"Remember, Gladys," Meriel said in a hasty undertone, "we are Americans. Say nothing to give us away."

"Not me, m'lady," muttered her handmaiden, looking warily toward the approaching soldiers.

There were two of them who had detached themselves from the others to attend to these travelers, and one yanked open the chaise door even as Meriel reached to let down the window. The impertinence of such an action was enough to stir her to anger.

"See here, my man," she said indignantly, "what are you about to treat two ladies so discourteously? Is this the French charm of which we hear spoken so often back home in"—she racked her brain swiftly, seeing once again before her mind's eye the papers Monsieur Deguise had given her—"in Boston?"

"*Ah les anglaises*," the soldier said, nodding with satisfaction.

"Not English," Meriel said firmly, "American." She repeated the word several times in haughty tones. In response the man beckoned to a second soldier, who came quickly to his side.

"There is a problem?" the second man said carefully. "You are English, *madame*. You must stop."

Meriel's temper flared dangerously and she repeated that she was certainly not English, as he and the other soldier so stupidly and offensively supposed, but American, and thus not a personage with whom to be trifled. As his mouth dropped open to beg her pardon for any offense and to attempt to explain his excellent reasons for stopping her chaise, Meriel reached into her leather reticule and, without disturbing her British passport or the little pistol that lay nestled beside it, extracted the identification papers Monsieur Deguise had given her. Waving these at the soldiers, she allowed herself to indulge in a small tirade, which was ignored by both men as the second carefully examined the papers.

"Idiotish man," she said at last, fearing that if he were to examine the papers too closely he would recognize their falsity, "we are in a hurry." She summoned up what little French she had learned. "*Nous dépechons, comprenez-vous? Les brigands*!"

The second man nodded, smiling now, and attempted to reassure her that with soldiers at every turnpike there would, for once, be few bandits at large to prey upon travelers. Then, to her surprise, he nodded to his compatriot and spoke to him swiftly. The other man promptly scribbled something upon a sheet of yellow paper and handed it to him. The English-speaking soldier, with a snappy bow, handed the paper in turn to Meriel and explained with painstaking care that he was providing her with a safe conduct.

As the chaise moved forward again a moment later, Gladys let out a long sigh of relief. "I declare, Miss Meriel, I was never nearer having a spasm in my life as when that dreadful man yanked open the door like he did. And I can tell you, when you started ripping up at him like a shrew, I felt my heart just leap into my mouth, I was that frightened. And what be that yellow paper he gave you, may I ask?"

Meriel chuckled. "Can you credit it, Gladys? 'Tis a safe conduct. If I understood him correctly, it will see us safely to Rouen. We have only to show it anytime we are stopped, which I daresay will be at every stage along the way."

And so it proved. Only twice did anyone seek to question her closely, and on both occasions, drawing on her experience at the first turnpike, Meriel carried the matter off with a high hand. Their progress, despite these successes, was still slow, due to the abominable condition of the road, and it was well after dark before they reached Rouen, their journey having taken them all of nine hours. Directing the postboys to the priest's cottage, Meriel hoped the elderly gentleman was not one who retired early to his bed.

But there was a light in the window of the stone cottage. Leaving Gladys with the postboys to wait, she descended unaided from the chaise and hurried up the flagged pathway to the front door, knocking imperatively. She had to wait only a moment before there was a small flurry of activity on the other side of the door and it was swung open by the priest's wiry middle-aged servant.

"Good evening, Fernand," Meriel said quickly. "Is the good father within?"

The man nodded silently and stood aside to allow her to enter. With only the slightest hesitation and a quick glance back at the chaise, where she knew Gladys Peat waited impatiently, Meriel stepped past him into the narrow hallway.

"There, *mademoiselle,*" the man said briefly, indicating the lighted parlor to the right of the door.

Entering the cluttered little room swiftly, Meriel discovered the priest ensconced in a deep wing chair near a crackling fire, a book in his hand and a glass of amber-colored liquid at his side. He looked up at her entrance, pushed his spectacles down on his nose in order to peer over them at her, then quickly set aside his book and came to his feet.

"*Mon Dieu, mademoiselle,* what brings you to us at such an hour?"

"'Father, I require your help. You must know that war has been declared again, but perhaps you do not know that Napoleon has ordered that all British tourists are to be interned at Verdun for the duration. Here, I bring you a letter from your friend Deputy Minister Deguise." She searched rapidly through her reticule, pushing the identity papers down in order to find the letter. A moment later she handed it to him. "He said it would explain all," she told him. "While you read it, perhaps I may send for my maidservant to come inside. She is terrified lest we should be stopped by the soldiers before we are able to reach the coast and safe passage across the Channel."

Having pushed his spectacles back into place, he was

already reading and responded with an uncharacteristically curt nod. Paying little heed to what she was certain was a reaction to the circumstances rather than to her request, Meriel turned calmly to the servant. "Will you attend to the postboys, if you please?" When the man nodded, she went on rapidly. "They have been paid for this distance and more, but I do not know what the good father will determine to be the best course of action for us, and I cannot think it is a good idea to leave them standing in the street while he decides."

"You will come to collect your maid, *mademoiselle?*" the servant inquired politely after a brief glance at his master.

"Yes, of course, if you like. I daresay she will feel the safer for my presence, even for so short a distance as the walk from the roadway into the cottage. You will attend to the rest?"

"As you say, *mademoiselle,*" he replied, bowing.

She hurried back out to the chaise and discovered Gladys Peat on the point of descending from it.

"Oh, m'lady, I'd no notion what to think. Where have you been this age?"

"Don't be foolish, Gladys, I've been gone less than five minutes. You are scarcely like to have been clapped into irons in such a small space of time. But do you come into the cottage now," she added hastily, seeing storm warnings on Mrs. Peat's round face. "There is a warm fire and no doubt Fernand will find you a cup of tea once he has seen to the disposal of our chaise."

"Lord, m'lady, you ain't sendin' them postboys off! Why, how be we gettin' to Loo Haver, may I ask?"

"I am merely seeing to it that the chaise don't stand where it is, Gladys," Meriel explained, hustling her maid toward the open door. "You must surely realize that a post chaise and four steaming horses standing outside a simple priest's door must draw unwanted attention. Such a sight cannot be a usual one anywhere but in Gretna Green."

They were inside now, and Gladys made no reply, merely entering the parlor with her head held high and moving toward the hearth to warm her hands. The priest was no longer where Meriel had left him but was sitting now at a small desk against the far wall, writing busily. He turned to look over his shoulder at her.

"Forgive me, *mademoiselle,* for not rising, but it has occurred to me that with war once more resumed between the two countries, correspondence will become most difficult again. If it is not to ask too much, I am hoping you will once more play the messenger and carry a letter to Mr. Murray. You mentioned that you go to London, so it shall be no great thing, since he is now in residence in that city. I will provide you with his direction if you will be so kind."

"It will be my pleasure, sir," she replied, glad to be able to do him even so small a service. "Have you decided what we must do?"

"Indeed, *mademoiselle.* I think the best course would be to proceed as you have, with Monsieur Deguise's so excellent papers in hand, to the port, where you will desire passage as Americans on any ship departing the harbor."

"Even a French ship?"

"No, no, that would not do, would it?" He seemed confounded for the moment. "I must think, *mademoiselle.*"

"I must point out, *mon père*, that there will undoubtedly be no English ships remaining in Le Havre, and even an American ship would present potential hazards, since an American might well recognize us as British women and say something, having no particular reason, you know, to stand our friend."

"You have the right of it, *mademoiselle.* Me, I must ponder the matter, but there is at present little danger. Fernand will show you to the small bedchamber abovestairs where you may spend the night in comfort. I am persuaded that you must be tired."

Indeed, she was exhausted, Meriel realized. The day had been long and tiring, and despite the exhilaration she had felt with each new hazard to be faced and overcome, she knew now that she needed sleep. But first, she needed sustenance. She pointed out this fact as tactfully as she could, and the little priest clapped a hand to his head.

"How I am thoughtless. I am imbecile, *mademoiselle.*"

He raised his voice. "Fernand!" As Meriel began to explain that Fernand had gone to see to the safe disposal of her chaise, there was an answering shout from the rear of the hallway, and the wiry servant appeared in the doorway a moment later. The priest said, "These ladies require refreshment, Fernand. See to it at once."

The man nodded, but then spoke rapidly and briefly in French. The priest's eyebrows came together in a beetling frown, and his mouth turned down at the corners as he listened.

"What is it?" Meriel demanded.

He looked at her, but his thoughts for several seconds were clearly elsewhere. At last he spoke. "Fernand says the postboys chattered like sparrows, *mademoiselle,* about the untoward haste with which your journey has been undertaken. Their suspicions have been aroused, *sans doute,* and Fernand has a fear that they might have spoken so before the soldiers at one of the turnpikes. Is it possible, this?"

Meriel considered the matter. "They may have chattered, sir, but would we not then have been questioned more thoroughly, even detained?"

"Not if the soldier who engaged in conversation with the boys did not have immediate opportunity to pass the information along to his superior. Were there a great many soldiers at each turnpike?"

"No, only at the first. Ater that, only two at each, and our safe conduct from the first saw us pretty quickly through the others."

He nodded. "None would wish to distress a pair of American lady tourists unduly," he said, almost to himself, "but if suspicions were aroused, someone might have been set on to follow you to see where you went. It would not do for the soldiers to come here, *mademoiselle.*"

"No, indeed, sir," she agreed, then paled as a sudden clatter of hoofbeats in the narrow street outside assaulted their ears.

11

"Good God, sir, what now?" Meriel cried, forgetting her hunger and giving thought to nothing but their immediate danger.

The priest had leapt to his feet, but even as he replied hastily that the situation was clearly altered, he continued to seal his letter. Turning at last to face her, he said tersely, "There can be no thought of your remaining here another moment, *mademoiselle,* for if they have reason to believe you are in this house, they will make a search. Fernand will take you and your maid by the back way to the river. Trust him. He will see you safely to the coast by the water route. No one will detain you, and your progress will be nearly as swift as by road, for the current will be in your favor, after all. If you depart at once—as, indeed, you must," he added, cocking an ear toward the sounds of horses and men outside in the street, "you will arrive at the village of Lillebonne at the mouth of the Seine before dawn, which is of utmost importance, because now you must not use your American papers. Fernand will find another way. There are persons—"

"Free traders," Meriel breathed, her eyes lighting with excitement.

The priest shook his head, but his lips quirked in involuntary amusement. "You are a strange one, *mademoiselle.* One expects a proper lady to be repulsed by such a thought. 'Tis more likely Fernand's friends will be fishermen, but I confess it reposes my soul to know that you will not derange yourself if an untoward eventuality should come to pass. But now, there is no time. *Allez!*" He pressed his letter into her hand and took the liberty of giving her a firm push in the small of her back, turning her toward the hallway, where Gladys Peat, fairly dancing in her agitation to be off, already waited beside the stoic Fernand.

The servant soon showed that he could bustle himself, however, for at the first creak of the front gate, he hissed a warning at Meriel and Gladys, who followed him rapidly down the hallway through a tiny but immaculate kitchen, where they found the two portmanteaux from the chaise awaiting them. Then, with Fernand snatching both of these up to carry one in his left hand, the other under the same arm, they sped out the kitchen door into a small garden. There was a scattering of stars and a slim crescent moon overhead, scarcely enough to light their way, and Meriel and Gladys followed the man more by guess than by sight. As they crossed the garden, Meriel heard a clamorous thundering on the front door of the cottage and hoped desperately that none of the visitors—for she was certain there must be an entire patrol after them—would take it into his head to look round the back.

Fernand led them past a small shed at the rear of the garden, then through a swinging spring-hung wicket gate, which led onto the towpath beside the river. Turning quickly to his left, he said over his shoulder in a low tone, "Along here, *mam'zelle,* we must hurry. We are too exposed until we reach the bend. Then there is a boat, and safety."

There was silence behind them now, and her heart was in her throat as she followed the wiry Fernand, but there was excitement within her as well. She glanced at Gladys Peat. The dim light made it difficult to see more than the woman's shape, but Meriel could tell by her rapid breathing and the stiffness of her posture as she hurried along that Gladys was deeply frightened. She reached out a hand to press the maid's shoulder reassuringly, but Gladys made no response except perhaps to move a trifle faster.

At the bend, heavy foliage overhung the narrow path,

plunging them into pitch darkness, forcing them to slow their pace. Only the reflected glitter of the stars and the threadlike moon on the river told them where path ended and water began. Thus it was that when Fernand stopped suddenly, Meriel bumped right into him. He gave a grunt, then set down with a heavy double thump the two portmanteax he had been carrying.

"The boat is here, *mam'zelle,*" he said, moving toward the shrubbery at the bank. "I regret the necessity, but I shall require assistance."

"Of course," she said briskly. "Show us."

Again by feel more than by sight, they located the boat, which proved to be a wooden rowboat that Meriel was certain could be little more than six feet long and surely not big enough to hold the three of them along with the two portmanteaux.

Despite the fact that once they had dragged it to the riverbank, righted it, and pushed it bow-first halfway into the water, the little boat proved to be closer to eight feet, Gladys clearly shared her misgivings.

"I ain't setting foot in that thing, m'lady," she said firmly. "We'll be drownded certain sure."

"Nonsense," Meriel said weakly, gulping as she watched the bow of the boat begin to bob about as the current attempted to snatch it from the shore. Indeed, the craft seemed dangerously small to carry them all along the fast-moving river.

Fernand heaved it further up onto the bank again, then turned and disappeared into the darkness, only to reappear within seconds, carrying two oars, which he fitted carefully into the oarlocks. He had said nothing in response to Gladys' refusal to get into the small boat, but now he loaded the portmanteaux, one in the bow, the other between the two seats. Straightening again, he turned to the women.

"We must go," he said simply. "To wait is to invite danger."

When Gladys balked again, Meriel said, " 'Tis this or prison, Gladys, and I won't go without you, so you needn't think it."

Gladys stared at her, then looked at the little craft. "We'll be killed."

"No, *madame,*" said Fernand calmly. "A small craft serves our purpose better than a large, more conspicuous vessel. Moreover, it moves more quickly upon the current. You will see."

He took her elbow and urged her gently toward the boat. Meriel heard Gladys give a long sigh, but the poor woman said nothing more, merely allowing Fernand to assist her into the boat and uttering a sharp gasp when it lurched with her shifting weight.

"Bend, *madame,*" Fernand suggested in that same calm tone. "Hold to the sides as you move, else will you dampen yourself."

Meriel heard a chuckle from her handmaiden then and knew that Fernand's understatement had done much to reconcile Gladys to her fate. A moment later she, too, was in the boat beside Gladys, her back to the bow, and Fernand was pushing them off. For one horrifying moment she thought he meant to send them on their way alone, but at the last possible instant he pushed off with his feet, shifted his weight to his hands, and deftly swung himself into the stern seat, facing them.

When the current seized the small craft, it bobbed and weaved for several nauseating seconds before it steadied itself and began to move forward purposefully. "Gracious," Meriel exclaimed, making an effort to keep her voice low, "we are flying."

"The current, she moves at something more than twenty kilometers in the hour when the tide flows out at Le Havre," Fernand explained, unshipping one oar in order to adjust their course when an eddy midstream expressed momentary determination to fling them toward the opposite bank. "She will slow for a time when the tide turns, but still we will go rapidly. But is best we not speak, *mam'zelle,*" he added after a brief pause. "The sound, she flies too well over water, and your voice is not that of a Frenchwoman. Best you should sleep if you can."

Meriel nodded, but how she was to sleep in that tiny boat, she knew not. She could scarcely lean against Gladys, who was as tired as she was, and with the portmanteaux beneath their feet and in front of the narrow seat upon which the two of them were perched, there was little room for experimentation. At last, when exhaustion made it possible for her to ignore such things as the corner of one portmanteau digging into her ribs, and the unnatural angle in which her body found itself, she managed by stuffing her reticule into the space between to find a nearly prone position across both seat and baggage that would allow her at least to doze from time to time.

None of these little naps lasted above a few minutes or so, for just as she would begin to doze, the creak of an oar in an oarlock or an unfamiliar sound from the shore would jerk her into wakefulness again. Beside her, Gladys Peat was faring no better. At one point, exasperated, Meriel offered to take the oars from Fernand, assuring him that she had often managed a tippy coracle on far wilder rivers than the Seine.

"No, *mam'zelle.* I do not know what is this thing, a coracle—"

"A Welsh boat made mostly of hoops and hides but surprisingly reliable nonetheless," she interposed, her smile sounding in her voice.

"Ah, then I must not doubt your ability with an oar, must I? But for you to row would be to cause comment. We have passed few other boats, and we shall likely pass fewer still as the night advances toward the dawn, but 'tis better I should keep the oars in hand. Are you sufficiently warm?"

Until he mentioned it, she had not thought of the cold. Her cloak was a warm one, but the damp chill of the river penetrated nevertheless. Only her toes and left side, the side away from Gladys Peat, were really uncomfortable. But now that he had brought the matter to her attention, she could think of little else. Mentally taking herself to task for dwelling upon what could not be helped, she assured him that she was well enough, then turned her thoughts toward London and the family, wondering if Lady Cadogan was truly finding her charges burdensome. They were a lively lot, to be sure, and her ladyship had little confidence in her ability to make them mind her. It was that lack, Meriel was certain, which gave the children to believe they could take advantage of her. No doubt one or another of them had got into a scrape by now. Really, she decided, she ought to have departed for London long since. By now the Season would be half gone, and she would not be astonished to discover that Eliza fancied herself promised to some entirely unsuitable young man or that Gwenyth and Davy had driven their aunt to distraction with their squabbles and mischief. The sooner she returned to take up her duties again, the better it would be for everyone concerned.

The breeze increased noticeably, reclaiming her thoughts to her physical discomfort. This trip was certainly nothing to compare with her earlier journey. How comfortable everything had been then, how pleasant. Then, with amusement, she recalled such details as storms at sea, a boatload of sick passengers, a shipboard assault, and a thief in the night. Odd how those matters had drifted to the back of her mind, leaving her with only pleasant memories. Breakfast on the road, fascinating conversations, her every wish seen to, her every comfort assured. Not that it would have been so, she admitted, had she followed through with her original intention to travel alone. Her regrettable experience at the inn in Rouen had proven that much. Without Sir Antony's capable assistance, she would no doubt have suffered as much on that trip as she was suffering on this one, only for a longer period of time. The chaise would certainly still have broken down. Sir Antony had proved most useful.

A small, guilty suspicion stirred that she was not being entirely fair to Sir Antony. He had made it clear, after all, that he liked looking after her. No doubt he had enjoyed their flirtation as well. He had never attempted to kiss her again after that one time, so she flattered herself that she had managed to flirt without giving him any false notion that she would be amenable to improper advances. As the thought crossed her mind now, she sighed, conscious of a strong wish that he had kissed her again. But since the mere wish set her nerves to tingling, and since Sir Antony was doubtless interested in nothing more than mild flirtation—even, she reminded herself firmly, if she had the time or inclination for anything else—it was just as well that she would probably never see him again.

Somehow this thought, too, struck her as false. She shifted her position slightly, attempting to find comfort where there was none to be found, and bent her thoughts once more to the large, lazy, but eminently capable gentleman. She wondered what had been his thoughts upon discovering that she had left Paris. Despite what she had said to Nest, she was nearly certain he would not have gone away without first being assured of her safety. Would he be distressed to learn that she had left Paris without first discussing her plans with him? She rather thought, now that she came to dwell upon the matter at length, that he would be annoyed. A smile twitched upon her lips when she decided that what would undoubtedly annoy him the most would be the fact, when he learned of it, that she had left quite half of her wardrobe behind. That, he would say, had been careless and unnecessary. She had got her priorities wrong again, he would say. She ought better to have left her reticule behind.

By imagining such foolish scenes as this, she managed to while away the hours between Rouen and the coast so well that when the little boat suddenly bumped against the shore, she was unprepared and was nearly betrayed into a startled shriek. As it was, she managed to stifle all but a small gasp, and even this noise was sufficient to bring down a reprimand upon her head.

"Silence, *mam'zelle,*" Fernand whispered, carefully removing one oar from its oarlock in order to use it as a pole, standing up to jam it into the river bottom, then pushing with all his wiry might. His energy brought Meriel to her senses. She moved to stand up also, thinking that she could turn and clamber over the portmanteau in the bow to the shore and thus help haul the boat to safety.

"No, no, *mam'zelle,*" Fernand warned quickly.

His words came too late. She had already discovered that her legs were numb and her body too stiff from the river's chill to serve her properly. Lurching sideways, she landed in Gladys' lap, bringing a loud "Oof" from that lady, who awkwardly attempted to upright her again.

Meriel giggled, then clapped her hand over her mouth,

astonished to hear such a sound from herself. Suddenly she felt like crying, but she managed to straighten herself, clasping both hands firmly in her lap and wondering how in the world she was going to get out of the little boat without making an utter fool of herself.

She felt the scrape of solid ground beneath her as the boat settled, and Fernand uttered a sigh of relief. "Now, *mam'zelle,*" he said very quietly, "if you will allow the liberty, you and Madame Peat, I must attempt to climb between you, for I fear that neither of you is in any condition to alight unaided."

They made no objection, and he was able to make his way to the bow of the boat. Once there, he leapt briskly to the shore and turned to extend a hand first to Gladys Peat and then to Meriel, who was able with such assistance to clamber awkwardly out of the little craft. Walking was another matter.

"I'm sorry," she said after her first attempt, "I cannot."

"You must, *mam'zelle,*" Fernand said urgently. "This is not a safe place. There are houses just beyond those bushes."

She shook her head, slumping down against the bank. "My legs simply will not cooperate, Fernand. They are filled with pins and needles. If you can let me have just fifteen minutes to rub some proper feeling back into them—"

"Impossible." He looked right, then left. The village of Lillebonne appeared to be asleep, but the darkness did little to reassure him. "We must still find my friends, *mam'zelle.*"

"You find them," she said, "Gladys and I will await you here. You will be safer going alone, anyway, and I believe the two of us can contrive to keep out of harm's way while you search your friends out."

He hesitated, but decided, as she had been sure he must, that she was right. A few minutes later, curled up next to Gladys beneath a leafy bush, Meriel fell fast asleep.

She was partially awakened sometime later by a rough shake, and moaned irritably when the indignity was repeated.

"Wake up, Meriel," commanded a familiar voice. "Wake up at once. What on earth are you about, to have fallen asleep like this when your very life is at stake? Unnatural brat, wake up, I say!"

She stirred, wanting to open her eyes but failing miserably. She was simply too tired. She had been ready to drop when they reached the priest's cottage, and that had been hours and hours ago. Who dared to try to waken her now? The shaking went on until her teeth threatened to fly from her head, and she opened her eyes at last to mutter indignantly, "For heaven's sake, would you kill me?"

"Cheerfully," came the unexpected response. "Sit up, damn you. At once."

She managed to obey, hearing an authority in the tone that she could not remember hearing from anyone since her father's passing. Though her eyes were open, she could not see well enough to make out the features of the figure leaning over her, a figure so large as to block out all light from the reflections in the river. Since she knew it could not logically be the one person she would most like it to be, she shook her head, trying to clear it and succeeding only in making it ache. It was protesting, no doubt, the shaking it had already endured.

"Come now, get up. We must go at once."

While she was still attempting to accept the reality of that voice, she heard Gladys say, "Come, come, m'lady, stir your stumps. It don't do to keep Sir Antony waiting now he has found us."

Meriel frowned, allowing the large man to help her to her feet, then slumping sleepily against the solid bulk of his warm body. "Sir Antony? But it cannot be. Sir Antony is still in Paris."

"The deuce he is," said the deep voice close to her ear. "Not that you might not wish he were still there when I've done with you, my girl. How dare you be so foolish as to leave without waiting for me!"

"What?" She struggled to stand upright and succeeded well enough that she was able to peer up at him through sleep-filled eyes. "You *are* here."

"Indeed, I am, but what the devil you are doing here is what I should like to know."

"We came in a boat," she said, fancying that she spoke with great precision of mind.

"Only from Rouen," he reminded her. "Before that you were on the road playing at being Americans for the entertainment of the French military. You idiotic female. For that alone you deserve to be well thrashed. Do you not know the penalties in this country for traveling with false papers?"

"We bubbled them neatly," she said, yawning and leaning gratefully against his solid body again. "You will scarcely credit it, sir, but I lost my temper twice and that answered the purpose excellently well. Are we leaving now?"

He sighed in resignation. "We are. Fortunately, your man came across us near the village harbor. I had been near frantic with worry for your safety before that. But all is well now. We have friends here with a boat, and there is a yacht waiting offshore to take us home. Can you walk?"

"Oh, yes," she murmured, still disoriented and scarcely able to take in what he was saying. "I daresay I have been able to walk for a good many years now, sir."

"Don't try me too far, my lady," he said grimly. "Within the hour we'll be where it will no longer matter if you make a bit of noise."

"Sir," said Gladys in anxious haste, "she knows not what she says. Indeed, an I mistake not, she be still more than half-asleep. Don't let go of her when she tries to walk, I beg you."

"I won't. Carruthers, get those bags, will you? It looks like I'm going to carry her ladyship."

Meriel opened her mouth to tell him that it was Fernand who accompanied them, not Carruthers, who was no doubt safely locked up in a French prison by now, but before she could form the words, an unmistakable cheerful voice sounded out of the darkness, assuring Sir Antony that everything was well in hand. What on earth Carruthers was doing there, she could not imagine, but the effort required to ask was too great. When she felt herself lifted into a pair of strong arms, she gave up with a sigh of contentment and leaned her head into Sir Antony's shoulder. That was the last thing she remembered other than vague imaginings having to do with another small boat, rough voices, and a sort of swinging sensation that made her think she had been hung out to dry in a cool breeze. The sensation passed quickly, however, and the next to come was one of softness and warm comfort. After that, there was not so much as a dream to disturb her until the soft gray light of morning touched her face through a round brass porthole in a mahogany-paneled wall.

Slowly she opened her eyes, feeling at once the rocking motion that she associated with shipboard life. She was at sea. A second, even more exciting thought followed hard upon the first. She was out of France. She was safe.

Then, as memory of the previous night returned, she remembered Sir Antony with a vague but distressing notion that he was vexed with her. Sitting up, she looked around to discover that she was in a small mahogany-paneled cabin in a narrow cot fastened to the interior bulkhead. There was another cot under the porthole, but it was presently empty. The two portmanteaux sat side by side upon the floor nearby.

Noting that she was clad only in her shift, she swung her feet to the floor, intending to search for something to wear, when a noise from the door sent her scrabbling for the gray woolen blanket. Snatching this up to her breast, she watched wide-eyed as the door to the cabin opened slowly and silently. But the face that peered cautiously around it a moment later made her grin, relaxing.

"Come in, Gladys. You needn't fear to waken me."

Gladys Peat came inside with a responding smile. "Sir Antony bade me let you sleep, m'lady. He could see as well as anyone that you was exhausted."

"A poor honey he must think me," Meriel said ruefully, "but all those late nights in Paris, and then the excitement of our journey—I suppose anyone must have been tired out by all that." She paused, regarding her handmaiden searchingly. "Is . . . is he angry, Gladys?"

"Oh, I daresay he's recovered his temper by now,

miss. If he were a bit cagged like afore, 'twas only that you gave him a scare."

Meriel nodded, but she was still wary of her first meeting with Sir Antony. As it transpired, after looking at her searchingly as though he would determine for himself whether she ought to have risen from her bed, he smiled at her and shook his head, his amusement setting his eyes atwinkle.

"You look well," he said. "Are you hungry?"

"Famished," she replied, grinning in her relief that he was no longer angry with her. His behavior, as always when she knew she had vexed him, surprised her, but she believed she was coming to know him better at last. He was simply not a man of strong emotion. Though she had seen his temper flare occasionally, it always burned itself out quickly. No doubt, for him to sustain it would be too wearing.

Still, she thought, it was as well that he did not know the power of his least frown or blandest smile to disturb the order of her mind and body. That twinkle in his eyes just now, for example, and the sensuous way his lips parted slightly as he watched her, stirred her blood and warmed her from the center of her body outward to her fingertips and toes. She felt as though he had kissed her, which was absurd, of course, since he was across the room. Her tongue darted out to dampen suddenly dry lips. Really, she decided, this warming sensation made one much too aware of one's own body and was not something a lady ought to allow her thoughts to dwell upon. She quickly turned her attention to filling her breakfast plate.

The trip across the Channel was a swift one, whiled away in the playing of backgammon and three-handed whist. The subject of their hasty flight was avoided, much to Meriel's relief. Since they were all safe now, she had no wish to hear the gentlemen's comments regarding her escape and thus did not inquire into theirs.

Only once, when they had docked in Portsmouth and Meriel, at the request of a stern-faced customs agent, produced her British passport without ceremony from her leather reticule, did Sir Antony look at her with anything other than warmth and lazy amusement in his eyes. Then, for a fleeting second, she saw what appeared to be a glint of near-fury. The look disappeared at once, however, when the agent turned to ask him for his papers, and she told herself firmly she must have imagined it.

Sir Antony booked a parlor at the George for their comfort while he arranged for a post chaise to carry them to London, and Gladys and Meriel were sitting comfortably in a sunny window embrasure enjoying tea and cakes when he and Mr. Carruthers returned. The men pulled up a pair of chairs and sat down, Mr. Carruthers immediately beginning to examine the platter of cakes, while Sir Antony poured the two of them glasses of Mountain from a decanter sitting cheek by jowl with the teapot.

He sipped appreciatively, then said, "The chaise will be ready in half an hour, ladies. 'Tis all of seventy miles and more to London from here, so I've told them we'll rack up in Guildford for the night. I hope that meets with your approval."

"Could we not reach London tonight?" Meriel asked him. "I should prefer to delay as little as possible now we are back in England."

"Even a fast chaise would take all of eight hours, ma'am, and that only if the roads are clear and in good condition."

"Well, they cannot help but be in better condition than the road from Paris to Rouen," she pointed out.

He smiled. "True, but you will not wish to arrive in Berkeley Square in the same condition that you arrived in Lillebonne, and you will be all the better for a good night's rest."

"I do not like having such decisions made for me, sir. I should prefer to make London tonight."

"Now, Miss Meriel," Gladys said firmly, " 'twould be ten o'clock at the earliest if we set forward at once and experienced no delays along the way. You'd do better to do like Sir Antony tells you, and no mistake."

Meriel's temper flared instantly, but a swift glance at Sir Antony caused her to swallow before replying in a carefully even tone, "I have been too long away as it is."

Mr. Carruthers chuckled. "You won't see anyone until tomorrow in any event, I daresay. 'Tis Wednesday, ma'am. Unless your sister has not been provided with vouchers, which I cannot think probable, she and your aunt will be at Almack's tonight, and if they return before two in the morning, they will be quite unlike any ladies of my acquaintance."

She was forced to admit the truth of what he said. Eliza and Lady Cadogan would certainly attend the weekly assembly at Almack's, for to do so was the delight of all young ladies in their first Season. To be denied the privilege was to be denied entry to the first ranks of the *beau monde*. And Gwenyth and Davy would be in bed asleep by the time she would arrive in Berkeley Square. Still, when she noted that Sir Antony was regarding her with a mixture of understanding and amusement in his eyes, she had all she could do to refrain from emptying the decanter in his lap.

"Very well," she said at last, high upon her dignity, "I daresay it will be better to arrive refreshed, rather than travel-weary."

"To be sure," Carruthers said. "I should not wish to see you so tired as you were in Lillebonne, ma'am. You quite frightened us when Sir Antony couldn't waken you."

"I have been meaning to ask you, sir," she said calmly, ignoring his comment, "how it is that you were with Sir Antony in Lillebonne. I had been given to believe that he had left Paris for a short time in order to accompany Lord Whitworth's party some distance along the road to Calais. I realize that you charmed most of Paris into accepting your presence in their homes, but surely the British ambassador did not number among your conquests."

Carruthers opened his mouth to respond, but Sir Antony's bland tones were heard first. "Devilish lucky for me that he did choose to come along," he said, "what with all those blasted soldiers at every turnpike. We left in such haste after learning that you had already departed from Paris, that without Carruthers here to show me the way to avoid the turnpikes, I'd have been dished. I had only my British papers and my original French pass, which was useless, of course. There was no time to provide myself with anything else."

Meriel said to Carruthers, "You must know the terrain well, sir."

"Well," he acknowledged modestly, "in my previous trade, you know, such intimate knowledge was rather a necessity. I was glad to be of service. Even so, we were too far behind to catch up with you before Rouen, and then we arrived after the soldiers had been to the priest's cottage—for you must know that your sister told us you had been advised to seek aid there."

Meriel turned in surprise to Sir Antony. "Than you did not speak with Monsieur Deguise?"

"No," he said. "We discovered at Maison de Prévenu where you had gone, and the good father was kind enough to direct us to the estuary at Lillebonne, where we were most fortunate in running his man to earth. You can imagine our distress when we saw that Fernand was alone." His tone was light but there was a look in his eyes that gave Meriel to understand that despite what she had thought before, he had not entirely recovered from that fright. Suddenly she was grateful for the presence of the others and for Sir Antony's strong sense of propriety.

The trip to Guildford was uneventful, and the Angel Inn proved to be neat and tidy with an excellent table. Making an early night of it, they set forth early the following morning and accomplished the remaining miles to London with admirable speed, arriving in Berkeley Square not long after eleven o-clock. Speeding around the southern end of the square, past the magnificent grounds of Landsdowne House and beneath the tall plane trees of the central garden with its statue of George III on horseback, the chaise rolled to a halt before Traherne House, located in the center of the square's west side.

The house was just as Meriel remembered it. Ordinary enough from the outside, it was four stories tall, three bays wide, and constructed of yellow brick with elaborate rustication around the deeply inset front door. As she allowed Sir Antony to assist her from the chaise, she kept her eye on that door. One of the postilions dismounted and ran up the steps to exercise the brass knocker, so it was not long before the door was opened by a porter in green-and-silver livery, who took one look at the equipage drawn up at the flagway and gestured to someone behind him. The next moment, Marwyn appeared, and seconds later Davy pushed excitedly past both servants and ran pell-mell down the steps.

"Meri, Meri," he shouted, "you'll never guess who's here!"

She had no need to guess, however, for stepping through the doorway at that very moment was a man of medium height with light brown hair and extremely broad shoulders, a man whom she could not fail to recognize, though she had not seen him in seven years. She uttered a shriek of astonished pleasure.

"Joss!"

The twelfth Earl of Tallyn had come home from the New World at last.

12

"We were afraid you would not be able to get home again, Meri!" Davy exclaimed, dancing beside her and trying to hug her at the same time as she straightened beside the chaise.

She put her arm around the boy's thin shoulders and gave him a hearty squeeze, saying quietly, "Well, we did get home, Davy." She had not taken her eyes from her older brother, and although she had not seen him in so many years, the set of Jocelyn's jaw and the tension in his powerful shoulders were as familiar to her as though he had never gone away. She knew without even considering the matter that he struggled to keep his volatile temper in check.

His gaze shifted from her to the big man beside her, then to Carruthers, who dismounted with easy grace and gave his horse's reins into the keeping of a liveried servant. When Jocelyn began to descend the broad, shallow steps, Meriel saw that he had changed from the young man she remembered. Never before had she seen him walk with such dignity. It was as though he were profoundly aware of eleven and more generations of Trahernes at his back. Indeed, he put her forcibly in mind of her father.

He did not speak until he reached the flagway. Then, meeting her steady gaze with a stern one of his own, he said. "Welcome home, Meriel. Will you have the goodness to introduce me to your friends?"

With difficulty she wrenched her gaze away and glanced first at Sir Antony and then at Carruthers, rather as though she were surprised to find them still there. Then, quickly, she said, "Of course. I'm sorry to be standing like a post, Joss, but your appearance, you know, comes as something of a shock after all this time." When he said nothing, merely waited pointedly, she hurried on, "This is Sir Antony Davies, and that gentleman is Mr. Roger Carruthers. They very kindly helped to get Gladys Peat and me out of France."

"Where you had no business to be in the first place," muttered her brother in an angry undertone. Then, recollecting himself, he turned toward Sir Antony. "Forgive my surliness, Davies. You must realize we have been sick with worry."

"Indeed, my lord," replied Sir Antony in his calm drawl, "I can think of no more normal reaction than yours to the danger her ladyship has been in. I can only be thankful that we are able to restore her to you undamaged."

When Meriel drew a breath of angry indignation, his hand tightened at the small of her back imperatively, making her swallow the words that sprang to her lips.

"You must come in for refreshment," Jocelyn said, including Carruthers in a gesture. "My late father's cellars here contain some outstanding vintages."

Shooting a rueful glance at Meriel, Mr. Carruthers opened his mouth as though to excuse himself, but before he could speak, Sir Antony said, "We'd be most grateful for a glass of something wet just now, Tallyn, thank you." There was nothing for it then but for all of them to repair inside.

The exterior appearance of the house scarcely prepared visitors for the grandeur within, so Meriel was not surprised when both her traveling companions expressed astonishment at what they saw. The house had been designed some seventy years before by William Kent in a determined and highly successful effort to arrange the interior of a London terrace house in a palatial fashion. Into its square core he had fitted, with extraordinary ingenuity, a spectacular staircase which rose in a single flight to an apse, forming a landing from which two gracefully curving arms returned upward to the first floor.

As they climbed the first flight, Carruthers looked from the ornate ironwork railings by Benjamin Holmes to the high, domed stained-glass skylight and said, "By gad, Lady Meriel, considering the small space which confines it, this is as beautiful a piece of art as can be imagined."

She smiled at him over her shoulder as her brother said proudly, "We believe the stairway is very fine, thank you." Privately Meriel thought the staircase, and indeed most of the public areas of the house, to be theatrical and over complex. She preferred the vast, rustic spaciousness of Plas Tallyn.

They emerged upon the first floor, turned right, past a screen of Ionic columns concealing another flight of stairs that wound against the apse's rear wall to an open gallery on the second floor, and entered the front drawing room through an ornate pillared and pedimented doorway. A spectacular chamber by any standard, the drawing room rose one and a half stories to a coved, tunnel-vaulted ceiling, coffered, gilded, and boasting small inset paintings designed by Kent himself in such a way as to produce a three-dimensional effect. His subjects had been the Greek gods and goddesses, whose figures were repeated in a collection of marble sculptures decking every chest and table in the room. Rich dark colors had been used throughout, and the plasterwork by Robert Dawson was as ornate as everything else.

As Mr. Carruthers expressed his pleasure at the grandeur and the three occupants of the drawing room exclaimed their delight to see Meriel, she shot an oblique look toward Sir Antony to see what his reaction would be to a chamber that had always made her feel as though she had entered an anteroom in a king's palace. His expression was as bland as always, but she was sure a twinkle lurked in the hazel eyes. Satisfied, she turned quickly to greet her aunt and sisters. After hugging them all, she suggested that perhaps Jocelyn would like to entertain the gentlemen while she went upstairs with the ladies to refresh herself. She was promptly overruled.

"We shall certainly excuse you if you have personal matters to attend to," her brother said, "but you will want to return immediately to see to our guests' comfort." He turned away then to present the two men to his aunt, leaving Meriel with nothing to say.

Eliza, having watched the exchange silently, now moved a step closer to Meriel. "Joss has been in a rare taking," she said quietly, "even before war was resumed."

"How long has he been here?" Meriel asked in an undertone, as her brother gave orders to a footman to see to the serving of refreshments at once.

"Two weeks," Eliza murmured swiftly. "Auntie Wynne would have mentioned his arrival in her last letter to you, only that he wished to surprise you and thought you must return soon."

Observing that Jocelyn was waiting for them to take their seats, Meriel moved with her sister farther into the drawing room, where a magnificent Oriental carpet and the upholstery of the comfortable chairs and glove-leather sofa echoed the rich dark colors of the paintings overhead. She stepped past the pair of tall, narrow, dark-red-velvet-draped windows overlooking the square to stand before the marble fireplace in the wall opposite the door. Though cold now, it was large enough to bring cheer and warmth to the chilliest day, but it was not the fireplace that drew Meriel's attention. It was the painting above the chimneypiece, a haunting picture of the great house at Plas Tallyn, seen through a light mist and set against the magnificent peaks of Cader Idris. Staring mesmerized into the picture, she felt a sudden strong longing for the mountain.

"Meriel, do you intend to keep everyone standing indefinitely?" her brother asked sharply.

She looked around at the others vaguely to see that although Gwenyth, Eliza, and Lady Cadogan were already seated, the gentlemen and Davy were not. "I beg your pardon. I didn't realize—"

"Come, sit by me," recommended her aunt, patting the place beside her on the wide claw-footed sofa. "I wish to hear all about your adventures."

"Tell us first how you managed to escape from Boney," said Davy. "I'll wager that was something like."

"Yes," agreed Jocelyn, casting an enigmatic glance at Sir Antony, who stood patiently beside a wing chair near the empty fireplace. "Do tell us about that."

Meriel moved to sit beside her aunt, her thoughts speeding as she tried to think how best to describe her escape, but once again, before she could speak, Sir Antony forestalled her.

" 'Twas nothing very alarming, you know," he said blandly, sitting and arranging his coattails to his satisfaction as he spoke. "The Lady Meriel was fortunate enough to have made the acquaintance, through your sister, the Comtesse de Prévenu, of one of Napoleon's ministers of state. Monsieur Deguise appeared to have a fondness for both your sisters, my lord, and was kind enough to warn Lady Meriel of her impending danger and to provide identity papers to see her safely to the coast."

"I see," said Jocelyn, looking at him searchingly. "Then just how did you figure in her escape, sir?"

Davy and Gwenyth, who had clearly thought Sir Antony's explanation rather flat, stirred excitedly, and Davy said, "Yes, there must have been something else. Meriel said you got her out."

Sir Antony shrugged gently. "Mr. Carruthers and I, not being fortunate enough to have been granted safe conduct by the French ministry, took a rather more circuitous route to the coast, but once there, we encountered Lady Meriel and her maidservant, who would no doubt have experienced a certain amount of difficulty, despite their papers, in finding a boat to bring them to England. As my yacht was awaiting me offshore, I was able to accommodate them."

While Jocelyn was digesting this glib explanation, Meriel cast Sir Antony a look of gratitude. She did not understand why he was attempting to protect her from her brother's displeasure, but she had no doubt that that was precisely the case. Why else had he not mentioned that the magic papers he described so casually had been entirely false and might well have resulted in arrest rather than escape? Considering that he had been incensed with her himself and had scolded her fiercely for what he had callously described as idiotic behavior, he ought by rights to be siding with Jocelyn, not intervening on her behalf. She glanced at Mr. Carruthers and discovered a gleam of amusement in that gentleman's eyes. She hoped Jocelyn would not see it. Her brother was no slowtop.

He was speaking now. "I must assume that my sister Nest decided to remain with her husband's family. Is she reasonably safe, do you think?"

"Entirely safe," Meriel replied, seeing no reason why Sir Antony should answer this question as well. "André is home again, and the Depuissant family has taken her entirely under its wing. She has the full protection of their power."

"Power is a sometime thing," said Jocelyn, frowning.

"Well, that hasn't been so with them. Monsieur Deguise said the Depuissants are like cats, always landing on their feet."

He nodded, then seemed about to say something else when Carruthers said mildly, "Our adventures must seem tame beside your own, my lord. The Lady Meriel has told us that you have been for some time in America. Indeed, she said she had been unable to reach you through the medium of the post, so you must have traveled well into the interior, unless of course you were captured by those wild savages we hear so much about and rendered incapable of communicating with your family."

"Yes," said Meriel, straightening as she favored her older brother with a glare, "just where have you been, Joss, and why did you not have the goodness to respond to any of my letters?"

To her surprise, his expression changed to a rueful one, but he did not respond immediately, for the butler chose that moment to usher in a footman and a maid with a selection of excellent wines from the late earl's cellar for the gentlemen, tea and lemonade for the ladies, and platters of tiny sandwiches and iced cakes for all.

"Gracious," Meriel said appreciatively, " 'tis a prodigious fine spread, Marwyn, thank you." But the moment the servants had departed, she turned to her brother again. "Now, Joss, tell us. And your tale had best be a good one, sir."

He smiled then, and the expression altered the planes of his face, showing him to be a ruggedly handsome young man, rather than the harsh disciplinarian he had looked before. The smile reached his blue-gray eyes, lighting them, softening his entire demeanor. "I knew when I saw the dates on the letters I did receive that I'd be giving my head to you for washing. You sent them to Philadelphia, Meri, and I had not been there since the first year. Mr. Carruthers is right. I went into the interior at the first opportunity, to a place called Kaskaskia, in point of fact, in a part of the country then known as the Northwest Territory. Now, of course, it has been divided into what they call the Indiana and Illinois territories, and indeed, what with negotiations being in train when I left to acquire a much larger block of land from France, the interior of that great continent will no doubt soon be entirely in American hands. 'Tis vastly exciting, I can tell you, and I suffered more than one qualm at leaving it all behind."

"When do you mean to return?" Meriel asked with a grimace.

"He doesn't," said Gwenyth brightly.

To Meriel's astonishment, Jocelyn flushed like a guilty child and would not meet her gaze. "As to that," he said, "I haven't precisely decided." Then, straightening and unconsciously smoothing the sleeve of his well-cut coat, he said in a rather more lofty tone, "I believe my duty lies here for the moment, certainly."

"It took you a precious good time to remember that," she said tartly.

He shot her a warning look from under this thick brows. "Less of that, my girl, if you please. I tell you I learned only five months ago of Papa and Mama's deaths, and crossing the Atlantic in winter is no easy thing to arrange. For all that, getting to the east coast wasn't simple. I was back in Kaskaskia, after nearly three years of exploring unmapped territory to the north with a Welsh expedition, and found your letters awaiting me. They'd been brought to Kaskaskia by a fellow who'd picked them up in Kentucky. That won't mean much to you, I daresay, but I can tell you he'd brought them the devil of a distance. When I left Philadelphia, I traveled south to Virginia and through the Cumberland Gap. Then, one way and another, I made my way up the Mississippi River until I got taken up by the French as a spy, of all devilish things."

"How perfectly thrilling for you, dear," said Lady Cadogan placidly, "but I thought you were quite friendly toward the French. Seems to me that's what all the fuss was about between you and your dear father, unless I've got my facts mixed. Surely they must have been kind to you."

He snorted. "They took me for a damned Englishman, of course, no matter that I told them I was Welsh and that even if I weren't, no person of quality would involve himself in something so underhanded as spying. But of course, thanks to that fellow Fouché having sent spies all over the place like he did before Bonaparte got rid of him, the French don't see the matter as we do. It was all quite beyond their understanding." He glanced at Meriel then, and the irritation she had seen earlier was back in his eyes. "That's why I was in such a taking when I learned you were in France, my girl. With the political situation in such a turmoil, as it was, I should have thought you'd have had better sense than to go flitting across the Channel. The French don't seem to recognize their allies when they fall over them."

"I cannot say I was ever a particular ally of theirs, you know," Meriel said thoughtlessly.

Sir Antony spoke rather more quickly than usual. "How did you manage to convince your captors of your good faith, my lord? I confess to a quite unbecoming curiosity on that point."

Jocelyn, glaring at his sister, turned to him and said curtly, "Oh, I didn't do anything. A lawyer in Kaskaskia, name of John Rice Jones—fellow Welshman from Merioneth, in point of fact—spoke to the commandant on my behalf. Being just across the river, they had come to know one another, and the commandant was perfectly willing to take Mr. Jones's word that I was the deuce of a fine fellow. It was Jones who kept your letters for me, too, Meriel."

"He sounds to be a kind gentleman," said Lady Cadogan. "Do have some more of these little cakes, Mr. Carruthers."

"Thank you, ma'am." As he leaned forward to help himself, Carruthers caught her ladyship's shrewd, somewhat thoughtful gaze and smiled mischievously at her. Meriel, intercepting that smile, grimaced, thinking the last thing she needed to have added to her dish was to see her aunt succumb to the man's fateful charm.

Sir Antony asked another pointed question just then, turning the conversation back to Jocelyn's sojourn in America and adroitly keeping it there for the next twenty minutes, at which time Marwyn opened the tall double doors to the drawing room and announced, "Captain Halldorson, my lord."

A fair, wedge-shaped young man in the bright red-and-blue jacket and pale gray trousers of the King's Dragoon Guards entered the room, carrying his brass-trimmed black helmet under his arm. His gaze swept over Meriel and the others to come to rest upon Eliza, who sat blushing in a chair beside her elder brother. With a dazzling smile the gentleman turned to make his bow to Lady Cadogan and Lord Tallyn.

"Good day," he said. "I see that I am interrupting a family party. Your man ought to have denied me."

"Oh, no!" exclaimed Eliza before either her aunt or brother might speak. "Marwyn knows he must never do such a thing as that, Freddie . . . that is, Captain Halldorson," she added hastily with an oblique glance at Meriel. "You must come in and meet my sister, the Lady Meriel, and . . . and her friends." These last words faltered when she encountered her sister's frowning gaze.

Jocelyn had arisen, however, and began to make Captain Halldorson known to everyone. Meriel realized from her brother's cheerful demeanor that he welcomed the newcomer and thought highly of him, so she nodded graciously when Captain Halldorson bowed to her, and continued to regard him thoughtfully from beneath her dark lashes.

He was certainly a handsome young man, and by the grace of his manners she was certain that he had had a decent education. When she learned that he was a member of the Dragoon's' second foot, that famous regiment known popularly as the Coldstream Guards, she was sure his antecedents must be excellent and thought for a brief time that at last her capricious sister had discovered a suitable young man. She was disabused of this notion some moments later when Sir Antony commented casually that he rather thought he knew Captain Halldorson's oldest brother.

"Oh, do you, sir?" inquired that young man politely. "He's years older than I am, so I daresay you might."

Sir Antony blinked as though he had felt a twinge of pain, but he replied calmly, "He is Ribblesdale, is he not?"

The captain nodded his fair head. "Yes, sir, and he's grown dashed proper since he inherited the title. Use to cut his capers with the best, so they say."

"A dashed fribble is what *I'd* say," murmured Mr. Carruthers under his breath.

Hearing him, Meriel favored him with a quelling glance, but he grinned back, quite unabashed, confirming her opinion of him as one who would take advantage of his betters at the least encouragement. She turned her attention pointedly back to the conversation between Sir Antony and Young Halldorson.

Sir Antony was saying, "You come from a large family, do you not, captain?"

"Don't I just," agreed that young man with a droll look. "Twelve others between Ribblesdale and yours most sincerely, and two-thirds of them males, all clamoring for post and position. 'Twas a fortunate circumstance for me that my mama chose her great-uncle Frederick for my godpapa. He purchased my colors for me and set me on the road to success."

The conversation became general after that, and when the visitors had departed, Jocelyn informed his sisters and aunt that he had business to attend to in his library. Before taking himself off, he said briskly to Meriel, "I know you must be wishing to rest after your journey, but make no plans to go out tonight, my girl, for I've several things to say to you."

When he had gone, Eliza let out a long sigh, but Gwenyth said angrily, "He takes too much upon himself, Meri, coming back like he has and assuming he can tell everyone what they can and cannot do, just as though he had never gone away and left the whole to you to manage."

"Well, I for one," said Lady Cadogan, rising from her chair and gathering her fancywork, "was prodigiously glad to see him, and so I do not scruple to tell you." She bent a stern eye upon Gwenyth. "And you should not be speaking so of your brother *and* the head of your family, for if he does not have the right to order things as he likes them in his own house, then I should like to know who has. I am persuaded, moreover, that he would not like to hear you speaking of him in such an uncivil fashion."

Gwenyth flushed deeply at the reprimand, astonishing her eldest sister, who had expected to have to take Lady Cadogan's side in the matter. In the past, Gwenyth might well have been stirred to impertinence by such a rebuke. Instead, she now offered a swift apology, which Lady Cadogan accepted graciously before suggesting that she take her younger brother up to the schoolroom.

"No doubt Mr. Scott has been wondering this age where you have disappeared to. For you must know," her ladyship added in an aside to Meriel when the two younger children had taken themselves off, "that Davy's very excellent tutor has agreed to teach Gwenyth as well, until it can be decided where she shall go to school. For now that the French have so unfortunately taken up arms against England again, we can scarcely send her to Mademoiselle Lecolier."

"No, ma'am," responded Meriel, hiding a smile, "but how is this? Am I to understand that you have succeeded already in finding a proper tutor for my brother? I was persuaded that you would rely upon Mr. Glendower's services until my return and that my first duty would be to interview a number of intimidatingly brilliant young men in an attempt to find someone suitable."

"Oh, I had little to do with it, my dear. No sooner did

dearest Jocelyn return than he saw that dear Mr. Glendower was no longer able to cope with young Davy's mischievous ways. Indeed," she added with a small, sad grimace, "I fear that both Davy and Gwenyth had got distressingly out of hand."

"They behaved dreadfully, Meri," Eliza interposed, taking pity on her aunt, who was beginning to wring her hands at the memories now assailing her. " 'Tis a wonder there's a servant left in the entire house, for what must they do first but lock one of the between maids into the wine cellar, where she had no business to be in the first place."

"She told Mrs. Peabody—your brother's housekeeper, you know—that that young limb of Satan told her Marwyn had given orders that she was to dust all the wine bottles."

"God have mercy," breathed Meriel, hardly daring to think what her brother must have said when he discovered that his father's precious wine collection had been disturbed.

"Just so," responded her aunt, nodding wisely. "Most fortunately, Davy slammed and locked the cellar door before she had so much as reached the bottom step, thereby frightening the poor girl so much that she never dusted so much as a single bottle but went into a screaming fit instead, a fact which Marwyn seemed to greet as a heaven-sent miracle when he discovered what had occurred."

"And the very day Joss arrived," Eliza continued wryly, "both those young scamps gave Mr. Glendower the slip and took themselves off to view the circus riders at Astley's Amphitheater. Marwyn was on the point of sending several of the footmen in search of them when he opened the front door to see Joss stepping out of a hired chaise. His shock was nothing, though, to what Gwen and Davy must have felt when Joss was there to greet them upon their return."

"Oh, such a scene as there was!" said Lady Cadogan, shaking her head. "But I must say that both those young'uns have behaved themselves a deal more circumspectly since his return."

"Well, I should think so," said Eliza, shooting a look brimful of amusement at Meriel. "When one considers the alternative to good behavior, I daresay anyone might take care to behave circumspectly—anyone with experience of Joss's temper, at any rate. Isn't that right, Meri?"

Meriel grinned at her. "From your superior tone, I take it that you at least have managed to deal happily with our brother."

"Oh, Joss is not difficult to manage if one but makes the effort, you know, although he does not properly understand the difference between prices here in London and those in backwoods America, I might say."

Lady Cadogan chuckled. "That he don't. Why, how he thinks Eliza can be rigged out for an evening's entertainment for any less than what she is and not be looked down upon for a dowdy is more than I can tell you, Meriel. But he has been perfectly reasonable about it, for all that. Indeed, he has been a great deal too forbearing in some areas, more's the pity."

Eliza lifted her chin. "You are only saying that because he likes Freddie and you do not. Oh, Meri," she went on, turning impulsively toward her sister, "do you not think that Freddie—Captain Halldorson, you know—is the handsomest, most charming of gentlemen? Please, please say that you have not taken him in dislike, for I must tell you that I have fallen quite madly in love with him, and even if you do not quite like it, there is nothing to be done, for Joss says he is the very man for me, and Joss is my guardian, after all, so there is no more to be said, is there?"

13

Fortunately for the course of pleasant relations between the two sisters, Marwyn chose that particular moment to announce the arrival of two lady callers who were particular friends of Lady Cadogan. Since they were also influential hostesses, she insisted that Eliza must stay at least long enough to greet them and be civil, but Meriel, pleading travel fatigue, was able to make good her escape before the butler showed the callers up to the drawing room.

She half-expected Eliza to come in search of her as soon as she was free to do so, but for one cause or another that young lady did not get upstairs until it was time to change for dinner, so Meriel was able to greet her in the drawing room, where the family gathered first, with their good relations unimpaired. The entire family was present in celebration of her safe return, including Davy and Gwenyth. Meriel discovered that so glad was she to be with her family again that she could even welcome the presence of Mr. Glendower; however, the feeling lasted only until that gentleman made his way to her side.

"My dear child," he said, his full voice carrying his words to the others with ease, "how grateful we must all be to the Almighty for having brought you safe amongst us again. You can have no notion how worried your beloved aunt was for your safety. We must hope you never have cause to do such a thing again, indeed we must. Not," he added with ponderous humor, "that everyone agrees with you that there *was* cause."

"Good evening, Mr. Glendower," she said calmly before adding in a raised voice, "Gwenyth, do smooth your skirts before you sit down, dear. If you plop into a chair in that hoydenish fashion you will rumple them sadly."

Mr. Glendower chuckled. "I daresay we all have our work cut out to turn that one into a lady, do we not?"

Meriel looked at him. "Indeed? You must excuse me now, sir. I see that my aunt wishes to speak with me."

He bowed, his good cheer quite undisturbed by her snub, and she moved quickly past him. "Oh, Auntie Wynne," she said, coming up beside that lady's chair, "I feel as though I never left the home fires at all."

Her aunt smiled up at her. "Do you, my dear? I believe that is often the case when one travels abroad. So like a dream, you know, when the journey is done and one is returned to that which is most familiar to one. I like that gown," she added, peering at Meriel critically. "You had it made up in Paris, I daresay."

"Yes, indeed. Is it not elegant?" She turned a little, this way and that, showing off the peach-colored, gaily embroidered skirt with its blond lace edging, and holding her arms away from her sides to give the full effect of the high waist and the little puffed sleeves that flattered her round arms so well. She wore elbow-length white gloves buttoned tightly at the wrists and peach satin slippers over white silk stockings. Her hair was piled high on her head, except for three neat ringlets tied at the nape of her neck with a narrow peach ribbon. Her only jewelry was a simple necklace of aquamarines.

"The color of that gown becomes you exceptionally well," said her aunt. "Do you not agree, Tallyn?"

"Certainly," said Jocelyn, stepping up beside Meriel. "A devilish fine rig, Meri." He was smiling, making it clear that for the moment, at least, he had declared a truce between them.

Meriel, with Eliza's earlier declaration still echoing in her mind, was not feeling altogether charitable toward him, but she had better sense than to take him to task then and there, so she responded lightly and moved on a moment later to join in conversation with Davy and Gwenyth.

"Oh, Meri, I adore special occasions," Gwenyth said when she approached them. "Dining with you is far nicer than dining in the schoolroom, truly it is, and I am by far too grown-up for that sort of thing now, you know."

"To be sure," Meriel said, squeezing her hand as she sat down in a chair beside her, "you are growing up very fast, are you not?"

"Hmmph!" said Davy, slouching in his chair.

"Sit up," Meriel told him, grinning. "You are growing up too, and must learn to behave like a gentleman."

"I've seen gentlemen," the boy informed her. "They wear spotted neckerchiefs knotted round their throats and lean against walls with their arms folded over their chests instead of dancing. I've no great opinion of gentlemen."

Meriel chuckled. "In Paris they wear gold earrings in their ears, and some of them clearly forget to wash. We must hope those particular fashions do not find their way here. But how do you know how gentlemen look when they might be dancing, sir?"

He shot her a sapient look from under his thick eyebrows. "There was dancing here one night after a supper party, and Gwen and I hid in one of the window embrasures and peeped at the guests."

"Goodness, that must have been a large supper party. How fortunate that no one wished to open a window for fresh air."

"Well, it was rather a big party," Gwenyth acknowledged. "Auntie Wynne did not wish to have a proper ball, you know—not when you were away, and without a gentleman host—but she could not think there would be anything amiss with a buffet supper, and there were not above fifteen couples for dancing afterward. And Auntie Wynne does not approve of London's night air, you know, so we had little fear of discovery."

"Well, you ought not to have spied upon the guests,

nonetheless, but I expect you will know better if we ever do have a proper ball here."

"We are having one," Gwenyth informed her. "The invitations have gone out already—almost as soon as Joss got home, in fact—and Auntie Wynne was afraid the whole thing would have to be canceled if you got thrown into a French prison. Only you did not," she added complacently. "I wish I were old enough to attend."

"Well, you are not," said Meriel, hiding a smile and repressing the urge to comment upon how fortunate it was that Lady Cadogan's pleasure was not to be spoiled by the inconvenience of her imprisonment. "Here is Marwyn to announce dinner. I confess, I am quite famished."

She followed the others across the gallery to the dining room. There the conversation was desultory for the most part, although Davy asked Meriel more than one question about her French adventures, and Eliza wanted to hear all about the fashions and social life in Paris. Twice Meriel caught her brother's eyes upon her in such a manner that she avoided looking his way again for several moments afterward, and it was only a chance remark of Eliza's toward the end of dinner that, by stirring her temper, restored her customary self-confidence.

"It seems a pity that the fighting had to start again," the younger girl began harmlessly enough, "for I should like to visit Paris. Still, I daresay it will all be over by the time Freddie and I are married, and we shall pay Nest and dearest André a lovely, long visit."

Meriel controlled her voice with an effort. "Have I missed something?" she inquired faintly. "Surely you have not already announced your engagement to Captain Halldorson."

"No, no, nothing of the sort," Jocelyn interposed in jolly tones. "I've told the minx she oughtn't to speak so until Halldorson requests my permission formally and the announcement has been placed in the *Gazette*. Of course, the match has my approval, so when Halldorson comes up to scratch, as I make no doubt he will—"

"I should not like to see such an announcement before the Season is done," Lady Cadogan said gently.

Jocelyn shrugged, casting a wary glance at Meriel, but she folded her lips tightly together, determined to say nothing more on the subject until they were alone. Realizing that Eliza was also looking anxiously her way, she forced a smile. The younger girl relaxed visibly.

"I think Captain Halldorson is very handsome," Gwenyth said thoughtfully, "but he is not the sort of man I wish to have for a husband, I can tell you that."

"No one asked you," Eliza pointed out, frowning at her.

"Fellow's no more than a dashed show-off," said Davy scornfully. "Saw him from the schoolroom window when he rode into the square today, and even the veriest nodcock could tell at a glance that he fancies himself a pretty fine fellow on horseback. Jabbed the bit down the poor nag's throat and made him rear up like one of the trick horses at Astley's when he brought him up at the door. Probably thought you was watching from the drawing room, Liza."

"Hold your tongue, sir!" commanded Jocelyn in a sharp tone.

"Well," said Meriel fairly, "he is entitled to express an opinion, Joss, but I do see that the less he says about Astley's the better it will be for him. How do you like your new tutor, Davy?"

The boy shot her a grateful look and launched into a description of Mr. Scott's attributes grand enough to persuade her that the man was a vast improvement over Mr. Glendower. She glanced at that gentleman, now engaged in a low-toned conversation with her aunt, and was glad to see that although he had indeed heard Davy's words he showed no sign of jealousy. Since he had considered the boy his special charge for a good many years, Meriel would not have been surprised to learn that he felt displaced by Mr. Scott.

Lady Cadogan signaled at last that the time had come to leave his lordship and Mr. Glendower to enjoy their port in masculine solitude. However, when everyone stood up, Jocelyn turned to the chaplain and said, "I hope you will excuse me, sir. I have business with my sister that must not be put off any longer. Do not let me prevent you from enjoying this excellent port, however. Remain here as long as you like." Then, following the others onto the gallery landing, he said quietly to Meriel, "If you will be so good as to come downstairs with me, we may be private in my library."

She said nothing, for by now she had as great a wish to speak to him as he had to speak to her. Laying her hand lightly upon his arm, she excused herself to the others, who were on the point of entering the drawing room, and allowed him to take her down the stairs and into the library.

This chamber was quite as grand as any of the other public rooms of the house. Its walls and tall bookshelves were painted white with gold trim, while a groined vault, which Meriel thought particularly Gothic in character, helped to fill the space between the bookcases and ceiling, where good pictures would have been wasted. Indeed, the only picture in the room was an antique Roman mosaic of a lion savaging a leopard, which had been acquired by an earlier Traherne during his Grand Tour and incorporated into the ornate overmantel.

Jocelyn crossed the white-and-gold floral Wilton carpet to the library table, which was in fact a walnut desk with a broad flat top, boasting drawers, cupboards, and kneeholes on each side. Taking his place at the far side of this massive but elegant piece of furniture, he gestured toward one of a pair of Chippendale chairs near the crackling fire.

"Sit there, Meri. The room's still chilly, so I daresay the fire has not been going long. You will be warmer if you take that chair."

Meriel eyed the chair, with its pierced splat-back in the shape of a lyre, and shook her head. "If you will draw up that Kent chair from the window, Joss, I should prefer it. I have never understood why Papa insisted upon keeping those Chippendales in here. They are elegant but dreadfully uncomfortable, as you would know if you had ever sat in one."

The look he shot her gave her to understand that she was merely being contrary, but he said nothing until he had drawn up the blue velvet Kent chair trimmed with tiny brass nails to a position near the hearth for her. Then, when she had settled herself comfortably, he moved to his own deep leather wing chair behind the massive library table, sat down with his elbows on the desktop and his fingertips pressed together to make a steeple in front of his chin. Then, folding his lips together tightly, he peered at her in silence for several moments. Just when she had begun to think she would have to speak first, he said abruptly, "I should like to hear just why you thought it necessary to travel into France at such a dangerous time."

Meriel returned his steady look, no longer feeling the least bit nervous of his temper. "I believed the trip was necessary, Joss, and I am home again. There is no more to be said unless you wish for further news about Nest and André."

A curt gesture waved away that notion. "France is at war, my girl. You'd no business there."

She lifted her chin. "It is perfectly true that France is now at war with England, though they were enjoying peace when I departed. Perhaps I ought to have realized when we reached Barmouth and began hearing more recent news than had reached us at Plas Tallyn that war was imminent. However, by that time I had already fixed my purpose and the arrangements were made. No one warned me that I might be in danger, Joss, although I did begin to think before ever I saw the school that even with Nest in Paris to look out for her, Gwenyth would do better to remain at home."

"Going to France was a crackbrained thing to do," Jocelyn said sharply, leaning forward and pointing his fingertips at her. "You'd no business to be traveling alone, and don't play off your tricks telling *me* that Gladys Peat was chaperon enough. I won't stand for it."

"What you will or won't stand leaves me supremely indifferent, Joss," she told him calmly. "I suppose you would have had me engage someone to look over the school for me, but that is not my way and never shall be. And if you think I would simply believe Nest when she assured us of her safety, all I can say is that you have changed even more than I can see, for you would certainly never have done so, yourself."

"No, and had I been here, no doubt I should have gone to see her just as you did," he said grimly, "and perhaps even have had a look at that blasted school—"

"But you were not here, Joss. That decision, like every decision these two years past, was mine to make, and I made it. You have no business to be telling me now what I should or should not have done."

"I have every business, Meri. Dammit, I am the head of this family."

"Yes, indeed, and how very kind it is in you to have returned to take up your duties at last. You cannot know how grateful I am to be able to place the family in your capable hands after all these years."

"Here now, don't go throwing that in my teeth again. Papa's only been gone two years, and I explained how I missed your blasted letters."

There was a moment's silence. Then Meriel said gently, "If you had had the consideration to write to us occasionally, I should have known where to direct my letters, Joss."

He stared at her resentfully for a long minute, idly rearranging a penknife and letter opener on the desk pad. Then, his jaw tightening, he straightened where he sat. "Look here, Meriel, we did not come in here to discuss my travels, but yours. You cannot begin to comprehend the danger you were in. Who is this dashed fellow Sir Antony Davies, I should like to know?"

She was nearly betrayed into a chuckle at the thought of Sir Antony being classed among the dangers she had faced in France, but she managed to answer calmly, "He is a friend of Lord Uxbridge. I believe he is also well-acquainted with Lord Hawkesbury, the foreign secretary. His family comes from Shropshire, and I met him at a supper party in Barmouth before we sailed."

"Good God, do you mean to say you traveled the entire time in his company? Meriel, surely you must realize your reputation is seriously compromised."

"Fiddlesticks," she retorted. "I was never once in his

company alone, except aboard the packet when everyone else was ill, and then we were in a public room with servants in and out. As for his kindness in escorting us on the road, there was nothing in the least compromising about it. In Rouen he stayed in a different wing of a very large inn, and in Mantes-de-Jolie, the village where our chaise broke down, Gladys was with me every moment." She saw no reason to mention her moonlight walk or her meeting with a would-be thief; therefore, she fell silent.

Jocelyn's grim expression had relaxed. "I cannot like it, Meri, but at least on that damned yacht and during your journey from Portsmouth to London, you were accompanied by Carruthers. His addition to your party must certainly lend it a little more respectability."

Meriel stared at him, not daring to trust herself to speak. She knew he meant only that two male escorts made a less singular appearance than one, but her sense of mischief urged her to assure him that Mr. Carruthers had been with them a deal longer than he realized. Wisdom kept her silent, however, and Jocelyn took that silence for acquiescence. He said quietly, "All will be well, I suppose, if you do not encourage Davies to haunt the house now you are home again. If you will oblige me in this matter, my dear, I will engage to say no more about your journey."

But he had already said enough to fire her ready temper. "You have not the least right to tell me how I should go on," she informed him roundly, "and if I choose to welcome Sir Antony to this house, that is all that anyone shall say about it. Not only am I of age, Jocelyn Traherne, but I have been my own mistress and mistress of this family for far too long to answer to you or to anyone else for my behavior now. No, don't say another word," she added furiously when his brows snapped together and his mouth opened. "You shall not speak against Sir Antony, whom you do not know at all. And considering your poor judgment of men, you would do better to keep silent altogether. What on earth are you about to have encouraged that idiotish soldier of Eliza's to haunt the house?"

"What?"

"You heard me," she retorted. "Eliza thinks herself as good as engaged to that penniless Halldorson fellow, and all you can see is his fancy uniform and gold braid. He is as unsuited to marry our sister as that Bugg Dewsall of hers back in Dolgellau."

"Dewsall? Don't tell me she had a fancy for him? His father's nothing but a miner. I hope you won't say Halldorson's antecedents are anything comparable to that."

"Oh, no, for he is the son of an earl, is he not?" Meriel said, her tone scathing. "The fourteenth child, if I did not mistake him, with a mere eight brothers betwixt himself and the earldom. For the love of heaven, Joss, even Dewsall will have more money than Halldorson. How do you suppose the captain will support Eliza, if I may make so bold as to ask such a question?"

"You are impertinent, Meriel," Jocelyn said, adding loftily, "You must know that I do not care for such paltry stuff as rank or position, but only for the character of the man. I believe Halldorson to be a man of ambition who will go far."

"Yes, all the way to France, I make no doubt. The Coldstream Guards are generally among the first regiments to be sent into battle. What will Eliza do then, do you suppose?"

"Why, she will live here with us, of course." But he was frowning slightly, and she knew he had not before considered the probability that Halldorson might have to take part in the escalating war. "He is stationed at St. James's now. Will he not remain on palace guard duty?"

"You must ask him," Meriel said, her voice calmer now. "I do not know. I do know that he is not at all the sort of husband I should pick for Eliza. You scarcely know her, Joss, so you cannot be blamed for not realizing that she is nearly as shatterbrained as Nest. She always has her nose in some foolish novel and believes life marches along page by page."

"Well, I cannot think what you were about to have let her read such stuff," he said, disgusted.

Meriel shrugged. "Plas Tallyn offers little by way of entertainment during the long winters, you know, particularly since Eliza does not enjoy long brisk walks in the cold."

"Up the mountain, I suppose you mean," he said, a tiny reminiscent smile flickering across his face. "Do you still enjoy your private rambles, Meri?"

She nodded.

"What will you do in London, my dear? You cannot mean to continue them here."

She sighed. "No, of course not. Things I can do at home, even things I could do on the Continent, will not do for London. I do know that, Joss, and I will not make a scandal here by behaving as I do at home. Though why I should not be able to walk alone in one of London's lovely parks, I do not know."

"Yes, you do, Meri. London's rabble does not haunt the slopes of Cader Idris, nor yet the banks of the Wnion or the Dovey. A lady walking alone in a London park must expect to be molested. Even," he added, smiling more broadly now, "a lady so stricken in years as you are."

She returned his smile, feeling more in charity with him now. He was Joss, and she loved him. Despite his odd notions about the sort of man who would suit Eliza, she knew she could handle him if she could but manage to keep young Halldorson from coming to the point for a day or two. And she was certain she could manage that easily enough.

When she left him, she returned to the drawing room, where she ordered Davy and Gwenyth off to bed and then sat chatting with her aunt and Eliza until Joss joined them when the tea tray was brought in. Later, in her own bedchamber, wearing a charming confection of sea-green satin and forest-green velvet, she paced the carpet for some time, trying to put her recent journey into perspective. But try as she would, here in London in this elegant house, surrounded by her lively family, she could not make her recent experiences seem real.

Their reality became clearer the following morning, however, when Marwyn stepped into the sunlit morning room to announce the arrival of Sir Antony Davies and Mr. Roger Carruthers.

"I have put them in the downstairs saloon, my lady," the butler informed Lady Cadogan, who was engaged in writing graceful replies to a flattering number of invitations. "Shall I tell the gentlemen you are not at home?"

Meriel set aside the copy of the *Monthly Mirror* she had been idly perusing, prepared to speak up if her aunt should answer in the affirmative, but it was Eliza, casting aside her embroidery, who responded to the butler.

"We will come downstairs at once, Marwyn," she said quickly, adding with a self-satisfied toss of her head, "I daresay there will be any number of callers before the morning is done, so don't sit like a stick, Meri, bustle about. I daresay these two have come to see you, after all."

Meriel exchanged a speaking look with her aunt, but in the butler's presence she forbore to reprove Eliza.

Lady Cadogan said, "Show the gentlemen to the drawing room, Marwyn. We shall be down directly. No, Eliza," she added quickly, when that young lady jumped up to follow in the butler's wake, "you must tidy yourself first."

"Yes," Meriel agreed. "Your sash has come untied, and your hair wants brushing before you present yourself to gentlemen callers. And henceforth," she went on sternly when the door had shut behind Marwyn, "you will not again put yourself forward as you did just now. Such behavior is most unbecoming, as I'm persuaded even your foolish books must tell you. Auntie Wynne is the one to reply when Marwyn wishes to know if we are home. When she desires you to express your wishes, you may do so. Otherwise, you will abide by her decision."

Eliza pouted. "Am I never to do as I please? First, Joss orders me to practice my needlework and not read my books, and now I am not to have gentlemen callers only because you and Auntie Wynne do not wish to encourage Captain Halldorson to call."

"Eliza, really," said Lady Cadogan, "you ought not—"

"No, Aunt, let me," interposed Meriel with a spark in her eyes. "Eliza Traherne, you should be ashamed. I told you only to tidy yourself and mind your manners. I did not say you could not go with us to the drawing room. As for your precious captain, certainly I am at one with

Auntie Wynne, for you can do a great deal better for yourself than that. And although neither of us would forbid you to see him if he calls, your present behavior leaves me to wonder whether I ought to inflict your presence upon any visitor. Where, may I ask, have you come by such pretty manners in so short a space of time?"

Eliza's eyes welled with tears. "On, Meri, I beg your pardon. And yours, Auntie Wynne. Everything just seems to get bigger and more overwhelming, the longer we stay in London. There are so many parties, and so many people, and I want to do everything and see everyone. Only people are forever saying I must do this or I mustn't do that, and I begin to wonder whether I am on my head or on my heels. I cannot think why I spoke as I did. The words just tumbled out as though someone else were speaking them."

"There now," Meriel said, moving to put an arm around her sister's waist. "During my first Season, I felt like a doll Mama had brought along with her to London. 'Twas the oddest thing, but I fell into distempered freaks occasionally too, Eliza."

A watery chuckle greeted this admission, and Eliza accepted Lady Cadogan's lacy handkerchief with a muttered expression of gratitude. "Distempered freaks, indeed," she said. "Will you wait while I tidy myself?"

"Certainly we will," her sister assured her.

"But do not take all day," advised Lady Cadogan. "Gentlemen do not enjoy being left to kick their heels."

The two gentlemen who rose to their feet when the ladies presented themselves at last in the drawing room did not show any sign of impatience, however. Both were smiling, and both greeted all three ladies with every indication of pleasure.

Meriel was astonished at the feelings that swept through her upon seeing Sir Antony. Her whole body seemed to sigh with relief, as though it relaxed for the first time since her parting with him the day before. Indeed, the only feeling to which she could compare it was the feeling which overcame her whenever she left her cares and worries behind to climb her special mountain. Though there was no crisp, clean breeze here to ruffle her hair, no sound in the distance of water tumbling over stones, and no soaring ravens overhead, still when her gaze met Sir Antony's she experienced the same surging sense of tranquillity that she experienced on the rugged slopes of Cader Idris.

14

If Meriel was surprised to see Sir Antony once again in company with Mr. Carruthers, the matter was quickly explained.

"Seems we both took the fine same notion into our heads this morning," said Carruthers as they seated themselves near the fireplace. "Met Sir Antony on the flagway as I was giving my nag into the keeping of one of your lads. Come to think of it, all some enterprising young fellow'd have to do is appear dressed in plausible-looking livery, and most anyone would hand over the finest of horseflesh to him, never for a moment thinking he was giving the poor beast into the hands of a thief."

Meriel had all she could do to keep her mouth from falling open at this insouciant observation, and she was careful to avoid Sir Antony's gaze.

Eliza chuckled appreciatively. "I do believe you are what my little brother, Davy, calls a complete hand, sir," she said, fluttering her eyelids and peeping at him through her thick dark lashes in a way that made her older sister yearn to shake her.

Carruthers grinned at Eliza. "People have said worse of me, my lady."

"I don't doubt that," muttered Meriel, adding in a normal tone when the drawing-room doors opened, "Ah, here is Marwyn with refreshment. Will you take a glass of Madeira, Sir Antony?"

"Thank you, ma'am," that gentleman replied evenly. "I should like that very much."

His quiet tone made it possible at last for her to look directly into his eyes, but she wished at once that she had not done so, for what she saw there was a disconcerting glow of tender warmth. At first she told herself he merely laughed at her for being flustered by Mr. Carruther's bland reference to horse thieves, but she knew his expression meant more than that. A blush crept into her cheeks. When she began to lower her eyelids, merely as a shield against that confounding, steady gaze, she suddenly realized she must look very like her idiotish sister. Her eyes snapped open on the thought.

Sir Antony smiled at her, lifting one eyebrow in gentle query. But since he turned almost at once to accept his glass of wine from the butler, Meriel was free to return her attention to Carruthers. That gentleman had taken not the slightest exception to her comment and was talking animatedly with her aunt and sister about the mad dash he and Sir Antony had made from Paris.

"I assure you, ladies, neither of us had the least desire to spend the war—which may last for years, after all—interned in Verdun. Why, there's no saying who might be stuck there. I don't doubt we'd have found ourselves rubbing shoulders with the scaff and raff right along with the *beau monde*." He chuckled at this sally and took his own glass from Marwyn before continuing his tale.

Meriel watched him carefully as he chatted, telling herself as she had many times before that however he had managed to learn the manners and dress of a gentleman, he had done the thing very well. Perhaps, she mused, Nest had been right and he was a cast-off younger son, or one who had simply chosen housebreaking over the church or the military as a career. His casual impudence certainly lent credence to the latter possibility. Still, she had come to like Carruthers very much and was in several ways beholden to the man, so she had no wish to snub him, despite his faults. Nevertheless, as she watched him flirt with her sister Eliza, she could not help but think that Sir Antony ought to have dissuaded Mr. Carruthers from visiting her brother's house.

The gentlemen stayed only the requisite half-hour, but before they departed, Sir Antony begged the pleasure of Lady Meriel's company that afternoon to drive in Hyde Park. Accepting his invitation, she gave him her hand in farewell, allowing him to retain it for some seconds longer than was customary, merely to indulge herself in the sense of warm security his touch provided. When the gentlemen had gone, she realized that her sister was watching her rather narrowly.

"What is it, Eliza?"

"Nothing at all," replied that young lady with an arch smile. Then, as though she had no wish to be questioned further, she added with studied nonchalance, "Meri, do you still have that paper the French soldiers gave you—the safe-conduct thing?"

Nodding, Meriel realized that Mr. Carruthers must have given away more of the details of her escape than she had seen fit to tell her family, and she quickly expressed a strong hope that Eliza would not mention these to Jocelyn.

"Oh, of course not," Eliza said quickly. "I am not such a ninnyhammer. Only I should like to see what a safe conduct looks like. I have read of them from time to time and always wondered."

"Well, it is in my leather reticule," Meriel said. "I can fetch it, if you like."

"Oh, do, Meri, and before we have more callers, or we shall forget all about it."

So Meriel went upstairs to her bedchamber and turned out upon the counterpane the leather reticule she had carried into France with her. The safe conduct lay beside her British passport, and as she picked it up, she saw beneath the pile of documents not only her little pistol but also the letter Père Leclerc had entrusted to her the night of her escape. Staring at the missive now, she wondered how on earth she had come to forget about it. That night seemed strangely long ago, to be sure, but the little priest had trusted her to deliver his message, and it might well be the last one Mr. George Murray would have from him until the war ended. And as Mr. Carruthers had pointed out, that date might be years and years away. Her duty was clear.

Even as these thoughts tumbled through her mind, she picked up the safe conduct, the letter, and her reticule, stuffing its other contents back inside. Collecting a dark green pelisse from her wardrobe and slipping it on over her primrose muslin frock, she hurried downstairs again to the drawing room.

"Here is that paper you wanted to see, Eliza," she said giving it to her. "I have remembered an important errand that I must attend to, so you and Auntie Wynne must excuse me for the present. I shall take the landaulet."

"Merciful heavens," said her aunt, blinking at her. "Where are you off to in such a hurry, my dear? I am persuaded you said nothing of errands earlier."

"No, ma'am, because I quite forgot. I shan't be long."

As she turned toward the door, Marwyn entered to announce the Ladies Jersey and Cowper for Lady Cadogan. Meriel, greeting these two haughty dames on the landing, made glib excuses, wished them both a good day, and hurried down the stairs, her gloved hand light upon the wrought-iron railing.

In the hall, she found a footman, but even as she opened her mouth to order the landaulet brought round immediately from the mews, she remembered that she would have the company of her brother's coachman if she did so. If the coachman should mention anything about her destination to Jocelyn, that gentleman would certainly ask some pointed questions, and he would not be fobbed off with such vague excuses as she had offered upstairs. He would wish to know, for example, why she had not simply sent a footman to deliver the priest's letter, and she did not know that she could explain the matter clearly to him. She wished to deliver the message herself, and that was all there was about it.

She had no idea where her brother was, but she rather hoped he had gone to his club and would not walk in upon her before she had made good her escape.

Quickly she explained to the footman that she required a hackney carriage because she had no wish to dawdle about waiting for one of her brother's carriages to be got ready. It was not until she was being assisted into a shabby coach at the front door that she realized the footman expected to relay her orders to the coachman. Thinking swiftly, she commanded that she be taken to Bond Street.

"A little shopping," she added casually for the footman's benefit. He looked surprised, as well he might, she thought, cursing her lack of imagination. But he said nothing, and the carriage moved forward toward the south end of the square. She waited until they had passed along Hay Hill into Dover Street before she pulled the checkstring and let down the curbside window.

"Yes, m'lady?" the coachman called back over his shoulder as he drew his horses to a walk.

"I have changed my mind," she said, giving him the address in the King's Mews at Charing Cross where Père Leclerc had told her she might find Mr. Murray.

The coachman looked down at her. "I know the place, m'lady, and it ain't b' no means no back slum, but didn't you ought to 'ave brung that there starched-up footman o' yourn along o' ye?"

"I shall do quite well enough on my own, but thank you for your concern. 'Tis merely a matter of a brief errand, and if you will be so good as to wait for me, I shall endeavor not to keep you waiting above a minute or two."

He nodded his grizzled head. "Aye, miss, I'll wait. Like as not, ye'd not wish to be standin' in the street a-whistlin' up another 'ack."

She agreed to this understatement with a smile, shut the window, and settled back again. Twenty minutes later the hackney coach was drawn up before a tall, narrow brick building with white trim. Climbing to the pavement unassisted, Meriel looked up at her coachman. "You will wish to walk your horses. There is a chill in the breeze."

"Aye, m'lady, and perhaps I'd best give a penny to some lad to 'old 'em and come along o' you m'self."

She laughed. "Indeed, you are very kind, but you need do no such thing. I daresay I am in no more danger here than I would be entering a bank."

"Which wouldn't be no more proper for a lady to do unescorted, I'm thinkin'," said the coachman dourly.

Grinning saucily at him, she turned away toward a pair of tall doors. As she approached these, one of them opened and a young uniformed soldier stepped out. Regarding her in some surprise, he seemed to realize that she meant to enter and stood aside, holding the door for her. Thanking him, she stepped inside.

The sole occupant of the rather plain office she found herself in was not wearing a uniform, but he wore with a certain military air the dark coat and buff breeches that constituted a gentleman's morning dress. His neckcloth was simply tied, and his shirt points were of a conservative height. He sat behind a large, dilapidated desk and regarded her with raised brows for a moment before he seemed to realize that she was a lady and came to his feet.

"May I be of service to you, ma'am?" he inquired with a startled air.

"I am looking for Mr. George Murray," she said simply.

"He is no longer here, I'm afraid," the man said. "Perhaps I can be of some service to you."

"No, I have merely brought a letter to him from a friend. If you will tell me his new direction, I will send it to him."

"That won't be necessary," the man said. His attitude was more alert now, and he moved several steps around the desk toward her, holding out his hand. "I'll be happy to take care of it for you, ma'am, if you will just give that letter to me."

The change in his manner disturbed her, and she stepped back. "I have been asked to give it to Mr. Murray," she said, replacing the letter in her reticule and hoping he would not attempt to wrest it from her as, indeed, he looked perfectly capable of doing. "If you will tell me where he can be found— "

"Mr. Murray has rejoined his regiment," the man said, "and is no doubt at this very moment on his way to the Continent, where his services are needed. So you see, you must entrust that letter to me. It will have to be sent with the diplomatic post."

"I don't see that at all," Meriel said, taking another step backward. "This is merely a letter from an old friend, and I cannot see that by giving it to you I should be doing the right thing. What is Mr. Murray's regiment, if you please? Surely I can simply send it to his regimental headquarters."

With a sigh of reluctant resignation the man turned back to his desk, pulled a green record book toward himself, and flipped two or three pages before finding the information she required. His entire posture made it clear to Meriel that he was not pleased with her. Still, she experienced a certain amount of satisfaction at having bested him. Armed with Mr. Murray's regimental address, she left the office and returned to the street, where she found her hackney coachman patiently awaiting her.

Telling the man she wished to return home, she allowed him to hand her inside, where she settled back, thinking furiously. The attitude of the man in the plain little office had stirred her suspicions, and although she certainly hoped she was wrong, she could think of only one way to discover the truth. Containing her soul in patience until she reached the safety of her bedchamber, she shut and bolted her door to ensure privacy. Then without so much as taking off her pelisse, she pulled the letter from her reticule and stood staring at it for some moments. Every ounce of breeding told her that no acceptable reason existed for opening someone else's letter, but every instinct screamed to open it. Scanning her memory rapidly from that first evening in Barmouth, she remembered all the messages she had carried. First the letter from Murray to the priest, then the letter from the priest to Monsieur Deguise. Next there had been the letter of explanation from Deguise to the priest, and now this letter in her hand—a letter that a perfect stranger had seemed rather more than ordinarily interested in taking from her. Altogether, now that she came to reflect upon the matter, she appeared to have been more courier than tourist.

No more than an instant of such reflection was necessary before Meriel broke the seal and unfolded the letter, to find that it was written in English and that there were scarcely more than ten lines. The brevity surprised her, for she had been certain that the priest had scribbled rapidly and at some length, that the letter had been crossed and recrossed. Moreover, considering the fact that he had made such a point of hurrying to get a message to Mr. Murray, the contents were certainly innocuous. Indeed, it was no more than an inane description of the priest's health and the French weather. Meriel read it again, looking for possible hidden meaning. There seemed to be nothing at all out of the ordinary.

Holding it up to the light from one of her windows, she saw that there were indentations and scratch marks between the lines of writing. No doubt it was simply the way the paper had been made that caused it to appear so, but now that her suspicions were aroused, she wondered if there might be more to the message than first appeared.

On that thought, she removed her pelisse, tidied her hair, and went to find her aunt. Lady Cadogan, having seen the last of her morning callers, had ordered a small luncheon served to her in the drawing room, and there it was that Meriel found her, enjoying her meal in solitary splendor.

"You are all alone, ma'am?"

"As you see. 'Tis prodigious peaceful, my dear."

Meriel chuckled. "I am persuaded that you found your charges very troublesome, Aunt. It was thoughtless of me to have left you with them for such a long time."

"Nonsense, my dear," Lady Cadogan replied as she applied a thick layer of butter to a bit of roll. "Once Tallyn arrived and took the children in hand, there was nothing for me to do at all, except enjoy myself taking dearest Eliza about."

"Well, you were a week or more alone with them before that."

"Ah, but they behaved rather well until they got their London feet, as it were. The two younger ones were in such awe, you know, and didn't know how to get about. And dear Mr. Glendower was able to manage quite nicely for a time, though Mr. Scott has more energy when it comes to that scamp Davy, I must say," she added, smiling. "Did you wish to speak to me about something in particular?"

Meriel pulled up a chair beside her and helped herself to a cup of tea from the tray. "As a matter of fact, I do," she said, thinking rapidly and coming to the conclusion that there was no way in which to ask her question that would not stir her aunt to ask a number of awkward questions of her own. "I cannot give you a reason," she said, "but I wish to know if you have ever heard of a way by which one might write something that others could not see. Have you come across such a thing in all your reading? A kind of ink that would fade after one had written what one wished to write?"

Lady Cadogan chuckled. "I daresay there are any number of ways, you know. I have read of invisible ink, though I do not know that it is any such thing at all. I believe lemon juice can be used. If one heats it later, over a candle, you know, then a sort of brown writing appears. Schoolboys use such a method, writing notes to one another in school. I daresay most masters know the trick of it now, however," she added placidly.

"I do not think the method I am looking for would be so simple as that," Meriel said thoughtfully.

"I should suggest asking Tallyn," said her ladyship. "He no doubt learned a number of odd things in America."

But this Meriel could not bring herself to do. She could not imagine any way in which she might question her brother on the subject without having him cross-question her in such a way that she would end up showing him the letter. And she wanted to know what it contained before she gave it into anyone else's keeping.

Thus it was that she kept her own counsel until later that afternoon when Sir Antony came to take her out driving in his curricle. By then she had thought of a way to ask her questions that she hoped would not lead to that gentleman's suspicions being aroused. She waited, enjoying the expert way he managed his team of roan geldings, until he had negotiated the traffic of several narrow residential streets and turned into Park Lane. Then she began to chat about commonplace things till they passed through the gates to Hyde Park. As the curricle bowled gently along Rotten Row, she mentioned that her sister was once again reading a lurid romance, despite her older brother's orders that she was to forgo such pleasures.

"Tallyn disapproves of gothic romance?" Sir Antony said, turning to smile at her.

"He says 'tis devilish stuff, unfit for feminine minds," quoted Meriel, laughing. But she shifted her gaze forward, unable to meet his as she continued, "This one, Eliza says, is full of such stuff as spies and secret writing and posion rings—all that sort of muck. I daresay all of it comes straight out of the author's imagination and has no basis in fact whatsoever." She shook her head. "All those dreadful poisons the ancients supposedly spilled out of their rings into their unsuspecting guests' mugs of ale. And secret writing! I ask you, sir, how could anyone write something and have it disappear as soon as the ink dried? And even if such a thing could be done, why, how would the person the letter was sent to read it? It all seems most idiotish to me."

Sir Antony chuckled. "I daresay it does in such books as your sister must read. I cannot blame Tallyn for trying to put his foot down on the matter. I am ignorant on the subject of ancient posion, I fear, but I know for a fact that invisible writing has been used, even by governments. Indeed, the Americans were notorious for using it in coded letters sent back and forth to England as part of the intelligence-gathering they indulged in during their revolution."

"Truly? But I do not see how such a business could be managed. Surely anyone could decipher the letters once the secret is known. I know," she added sapiently, "that school boys use lemon juice and then heat the message over a candle, but since every master must know the trick as well, I cannot see that it does anyone a bit of good."

"Oh, there are a number of methods," he replied casually, lifting a hand in greeting to a passing acquaintance as he spoke. "The greatest trick would seem to me to be keeping those you don't want reading the letter from realizing there is anything the least peculiar about it. The Americans in question were supposedly writing gossip to relatives in England. The secret stuff was scribbled between the lines. Or so I am told."

Meriel found that she was holding her breath, and let it out slowly. Hoping her voice sounded perfectly normal, she said. "Just what did they use to scribble between the lines, and how could the recipient read the results if what they wrote became invisible?"

"My," said Sir Antony, looking down at her again, "You really are interested in this little topic, are you not?"

She shrugged. "It just seems like another child's game to me, sir, and not possible to think of seriously."

"Well, it was dashed serious to the Americans," he said. "That was how they got a good deal of their information about what was going on in England."

"They were spying?"

He nodded. "Oh, they weren't listening at keyholes or pretending to be what they weren't. Mostly, the information came from sympathizers to their cause, who saw no harm in telling them certain things that might help."

"No harm? Then why was it necessary to use invisible ink?"

He turned and smiled at her again. "A home question, is it not? I daresay their consciences smote them from time to time, and they certainly realized that others might take a dim view of what they were doing. So they wrote their messages with milk or lemon juice or whatever seemed the best way to them."

"Milk works like lemon juice?"

He nodded. "So I'm told. Either one, heated, comes up with writing. But there are other methods, as well, some much more sophisticated, because, as you say, anyone knows enough to try heating a suspect message. One method I heard of," he added, speaking more slowly now, "used a real ink to do the writing. At least, it would look real to anyone overlooking the writer. Must be a bit odd to see someone writing in lemon juice, you know. But this ink is made up of chemicals that fade away when they dry, leaving nothing but blank paper in their wake."

"And heating achieves nothing?"

"Not a thing. In this case, another chemical is required to react with the first mixture and bring the writing up again."

"A chemical?" Dismay filled her. How could she possibly come by an unknown chemical?

But Sir Antony was nodding again. "Usually it is something entirely simple, like an alcohol compound or milk. I once heard of a message coming to light because a man spilled his whiskey on it. And I know the British have used a chemical that reacts with milk. But I can't pretend to know much about that. Does that book of your sister's not tell how the message may be read?"

"Oh, she hasn't got that far in the story," Meriel responded, thinking hard. When she looked at him again, to discover that he was regarding her somewhat searchingly, she smiled. "This is a lovely day for the park, sir. Thank you for bringing me."

His expression softened. "You do me honor, my dear. How do you find your family, by the by? Were their affairs in such turmoil as you expected to find them?"

She chuckled, relaxing. "Why, no, sir, my brother had matters well in hand. You must know that he has been home for two weeks already, and the first thing he did was to engage another tutor for my brother. At present Gwenyth, too, takes lessons from him, but Joss says she must go to school at Michaelmas term. And she must go to school in England, of course. He was not best pleased with me for going to France."

"I daresay he lacks your sense of adventure," Sir Antony said dryly.

"Well, what a thing to say, when you must know he went off to America and had all sort of adventures himself."

"I stand corrected. I should rather have said he disapproves of adventuring for the fair sex. But what of your sister Eliza? As I recall, you were concerned that she might have made an unsuitable alliance in your absence. Was Ribblesdale's young brother—?"

"Oh, yes," Meriel said, not waiting for him to finish. "Captain Halldorson, as you must have seen for yourself, sir, is entirely unsuitable, and what must my idiotish brother do but decide he is the very thing for Eliza. Joss thinks himself a very democratic fellow, you know. Such thinking does not interfere with his notion of what is due his title, mind you, but it gives him some odd notions of what will do for his sisters. I daresay," she added, much struck by the thought that crossed her mind just then, "that he and Napoleon Bonaparte have more in common than one might think to look at them."

Sir Antony chuckled. "But you do not think Halldorson will prove himself worthy of your brother's faith in him?"

"I do not wish to see Eliza making and scraping whilst he seeks his fortune in the army," Meriel said tartly. Then she added with a grin, "Not that I believe it will be necessary if we can but keep him from coming to the point yet a while."

"You believe your sister's affections will alter?"

"They always do," Meriel said. "Indeed, she was flirting with Mr. Carruthers only this morning, sir, as you must have seen for yourself. And that, I can tell you, will not do at all. I wish you will speak to him for me. He must not encourage her folly."

But this Sir Antony would not engage to do. Reverting to his customary languid manner of speech, he recommended that Meriel let matters take their natural course. "No doubt you may trust to your sister's fickle nature," he said, smiling gently at her, "but there is no cause for distress, my dear, nor any reason that I can imagine to trouble yourself over your sister's many flirtations."

She looked up at him in protest. "But—"

"No reason at all," he repeated firmly, his steady gaze catching hers and holding it. His horses, ambling along at a lazy pace quite at odds with their powerful appearance, took no notice whatsoever of their master's sudden inattention, even though it was to continue for some time.

Meriel's breath stuck in her throat, and all thought of Eliza's affairs vanished as smoke from her mind. She could think of nothing but the hazel eyes looking so deeply into hers. So lost was she in that gaze that she did not even sense movement before his hand touched her chin and his fingertips moved in a gentle caress along her jawline. No more than the slight pressure of his little finger in the softness beneath her chin was necessary to make her tilt her face to a more convenient angle for his kiss. When his lips touched hers, she leaned toward him, a tiny moan sounding deep in her throat. The tip of his little finger moved, tracing a line down the center of her throat to the neat collar of her moss-colored carriage dress, then dipping beneath the collar, lightly tickling her skin as his hand moved around to a point beneath her left ear. This sensuous movement brought a gasp to her lips that separated them, allowing his tongue to gain entrance to the soft interior of her mouth.

Involuntarily she pulled back, only to respond immediately and with a passion that surprised her when his hand moved quickly to the nape of her neck to hold her where she was. But his sudden motion had had another effect. The hand holding the reins jerked suddenly, and Sir Antony's horses surged forward as a result, forcing him to return his attention to them at once.

Brought thus suddenly to her senses, Meriel glanced around quickly, her cheeks flushing in fear of discovering that her wicked behavior had drawn every curious eye in the park. To her immense relief, there appeared to be no one in their immediate vicinity, but for some moments she avoided looking at her companion. When she turned her glance upon him at last, she found that he was smiling lazily at her as though what they had done had been a perfectly natural thing and not at all the outrageous, if perfectly delightful, contravention of public morals that she knew it to be. She was uncertain whether to be relieved or indignant when he chose a perfectly harmless topic of conversation to while away their return to Berkeley Square.

15

Not until the following day did Meriel find time to put her newly acquired knowledge to good use, although she did wave the priest's letter several times over her candle that night, to no good effect. Since she had come to the conclusion after speaking with both Lady Cadogan and Sir Antony that the key to the letter would not be so easily come by, she was not so disappointed as she might otherwise have been.

The great difficulty, she discovered, was in obtaining a glass of milk and the privacy in which to work at one and the same time. Her first thought had been to request the chambermaid to bring milk with her morning chocolate, but it occurred to her that although the maid would certainly oblige her, she could not prevent Gladys Peat from entering her room while she was in the midst of attempting to decode the priest's letter. And to leave the milk standing until she could be certain of her privacy would not do. The chambermaid would certainly carry it away with her when she took the other dishes. The best she could do was to plead an incipient headache when Lady Cadogan requested her company on a round of morning calls.

Since Eliza did accompany her aunt, and the children were safely in the schoolroom with Mr. Scott, Meriel took the opportunity to order a cup of tea served to her in her bedchamber.

"Right away, m'lady," said the obliging footman. "I'll send one of the maids up directly."

"I'll take a small pitcher of milk with it," Meriel said casually, "and perhaps some sweet biscuits."

"Yes, m'lady," he replied with only the slightest hitch in his brows to indicate his surprise at such a request.

Realizing that he knew she never took milk in her tea, Meriel said with a smile, "I didn't eat very much breakfast, you know, but I begin to think perhaps some food will help my headache. But I don't want anything heavy."

"No, indeed, m'lady. I'll see to it right away, and perhaps you would like me to send Mrs. Peat to you, as well."

'That is not necessary. I shall simply read for a bit, drink my tea, and then rest for an hour or so," she told him firmly.

Twenty minutes later, the letter spread out carefully upon a folded towel, Meriel carefully spread milk upon it with the corner of a clean chamois. At first she treated only a tiny portion of the letter, but it was not long before pale brown letters began to appear between the neat rows of black ink. Excitedly she treated the entire letter, then sat impatiently waiting for the whole to dry.

At one point she had to whisk the letter, towel and all, under her pillow when she heard footsteps approaching her door along the corridor. When Gladys Peat cautiously opened the door, she found her mistress curled up against a pile of pillows on the bed, a quilt over her knees, reading one of Eliza's books.

"What's this I hear of a headache, Miss Meri?" the woman demanded.

"Oh, 'tis but the merest trifle," Meriel told her. "It has been coming on since I awoke this morning, and I decided to coddle myself instead of accompanying Auntie Wynne and Eliza on their morning calls. I daresay you will tell me I am being wickedly lazy."

"I'll tell you no such thing," stated Mrs. Peat, peering at her suspiciously. "What I will say is that it ain't like you to give in easily to illness. Indeed, m'lady, I cannot recall the last time you was indisposed like this. 'Tis my opinion you be more ill than you be lettin' on, and no mistake."

Meriel's smile hid her dismay. What Gladys said was true. She was never ill. But she said in a rallying tone, "You needn't fret, Gladys. There is nothing amiss with me that a morning of quiet reflection will not cure. I daresay I have not entirely recovered from our mad dash out of Paris. You will recall that I was exhausted when we reached the coast. No doubt I have simply not given myself enough rest."

"Then you ought to be laid down upon your bed and not reading that muck," said Gladys frankly.

"Oh, but 'tis most diverting muck," Meriel told her. " 'Tis about a gentleman's travels in France and all the adventures he had there. There's a mysterious monk and a beautiful lady, and would you believe, Gladys, he got all the way to Paris without a passport, merely by claiming to be part of a French count's party upon landing."

"Yes, and all lies, no doubt," said Gladys with asperity. "Not to mention the circumstances of his traveling no doubt being a sight different from our own."

"Well, he did travel some thirty years ago, but France and England were at war then too. At least," she added, trying to remember her history, "he says they were. But he says also that he quite forgot that little fact when he decided to visit Paris."

"Humph," retorted Gladys, moving to plump her pillows and smooth the coverlet. "Never mind that, miss. Just you lie back there and have a rest. I don't mind tellin' you I don't like the sound of this headache o' yours."

Obediently Meriel lay back against her pillows, hoping that Gladys had not ruined the letter in all her ministrations. The tirewoman moved from the bed to the window, drawing the curtains. Then, seeing the tray on the table, she picked it up, saying, "I'll just take this along o' me, so that chambermaid won't be disturbing you, m'lady."

"Thank you, Gladys," Meriel said meekly.

The moment the woman was gone, however, she sprang up from her bed, flung the curtains wide again, and rescued the priest's letter from under her pillow. It was a little wrinkled, but a satisfactory webbing of pale brown ink now appeared all over its surface. She hurried to the little table in the window embrasure and carefully smoothed the sheet of paper out upon it. Wishing she had a magnifying glass, even Sir Antony's quizzing glass, she peered carefully at the writing.

At first it was difficult to tell if it was French or English, for the scrawl was Continental and not very neatly contrived. However, once she had found the beginning, she was able to make out enough of what was written to make her sit back in her chair with a gasp. Père Leclerc wrote that Napoleon had immediate plans to invade England from Boulogne.

She remembered hearing more than one person speak of the number of ships gathering at that port, and she thought now that perhaps such talk was one reason Napoleon had been so insistent upon interning English tourists, that they might not repeat what they had heard or seen. But surely any number of persons knew of the armada at Boulogne. There had been rumors of invasion since before the peace treaty. What was more disturbing was what Pere Leclerc had to say about a network of French spies operating in England under the guidance of Napoleon's ex-minister of police, Joseph Fouché. Meriel knew that England's leaders had congratulated themselves more than once upon being rid of Fouché, but here he was again, and if the priest could be believed, Fouché had detailed knowledge of a royalist plot against Napoleon and meant to use that plot to his own end. Leclerc wrote as though Mr. Murray were already familiar with such a plot, giving Meriel to believe that one was known by the British authorities to exist. But what authorities? And how was she to get this information to them?

Her first thought was to ask Sir Antony for his advice again, but she did not wish to vex him, and she was certain he would be as appalled as she was herself at the activities she had been unwittingly involved in. The fact that she had been manipulated by others unbeknownst to herself would not weigh any more heavily with him than it would with anyone else who might discover what she had done.

She had spied for England. Well, she told herself fairly, perhaps that was to refine too much upon the matter. But she had certainly been allied with spies, for she had no doubt now that the other letters she had carried had been no less innocent than the one she held before her. But all she had to help her find George Murray, to give him a piece of her mind as well as his devilish letter, was a regimental address. If the man at the office in the King's Mews could be believed, Mr. Murray was on his way to the Continent.

Perhaps she could return to that office. Certainly the man she had spoken with there had evinced interest in the letter. Still, she had no way of knowing that he wasn't one of the very spies Leclerc mentioned. She could not chance giving the letter into unknown hands.

That left Sir Antony. But even as the thought came to mind, she set it aside. Despite their agreeable flirtation, he would be disgusted, repulsed. Had she not been told more than once that any red-blooded Englishman would be revolted by the unfairness of spying? To deal with spies was to cheat at the game of war. She had heard the argument more than once. Surely Sir Antony would not easily accept the notion of a lady of quality soiling her hands or reputation in such a way. Much though he appeared to care for her, he must be repelled. And she had an increasingly strong desire to retain his good opinion of her. Moreover, if her activities should become known to others, she and her family might well be ostracized by the *beau monde*. Eliza, for one, would never forgive her.

Thinking of Eliza made her smile, for here was just the sort of romantic adventure that young lady would revel in if she were to find it between the covers of a book. But Meriel did not delude herself into thinking that her sister would wish to be snubbed by all the persons whose good favor she had so carefully cultivated these past weeks. Books were one thing. Life was quite another. With a small sigh, she folded the letter again and tucked it into a smaller reticule, that she might keep it by her.

She would have to consider the matter carefully before taking action.

In the week that followed, she scarcely had a moment to give thought to her problem, for her aunt had accepted a number of social invitations on her behalf, and she found the days filled with activity. Besides the necessity of planning for their own ball, there were afternoon charade parties, evening ridottos, balls, and an expedition to Vauxhall Gardens to hear a concert. On several occasions Sir Antony and Mr. Carruthers were invited to join. Meriel had been unable to think of any reason short of the truth that might prevent her brother or her aunt from enthusiastically accepting the latter's company on these occasions, and if she was grateful to him for the fact that neither Jocelyn nor Eliza continued to sing the praises of Captain Halldorson quite so loudly, she found herself wishing on more than one occasion that Mr. Carruthers would not respond so easily to her susceptible sister's flirtatious overtures. After a particularly trying evening of watching Eliza stand up for no less than three dances with him, she attempted to take the younger girl to task and failed miserably.

"I don't wish to discuss him, Meriel," said Eliza quietly, turning away from her in the coach. "Auntie Wynne, did you not think that Sally Fane's gown was quite the wickedest you have ever laid eyes upon?"

"I did," said Lady Cadogan, and the moment was lost as she launched into a lecture on proper ball attire for young women in their first Seasons.

Since Eliza was generally one to fly into the boughs when reproached, her quiet reply startled her sister, but when Meriel mentioned the matter to Lady Cadogan in that lady's dressing room after Eliza had been sent off to bed, her ladyship tended to shrug all concerns aside.

"He is a charming gentleman, that Mr. Carruthers," she said, "and comes, if I don't mistake the matter, from an excellent Somerset family. Eliza could do a deal worse. Certainly he is an improvement over that dunderheaded dragoon your brother encouraged to haunt the place. We see a deal less of him, thanks to Mr. Carruthers."

Meriel opened her mouth to inform her aunt that a

dunderheaded dragoon must at all times be preferable to a gentleman who had been known to make his living through housebreaking, but she found she was quite unable to say such a thing to her. Instead, she determined to go to the source of the problem, especially since Sir Antony continued to refuse to interfere in Mr. Carruthers' affairs.

Accordingly, the following morning when Marwyn stepped into the morning room and informed Meriel, who was sitting there quite alone, that Mr. Carruthers was below, she said calmly, "Pray tell Mr. Carruthers that I will be down immediately, Marwyn."

"Very well, m'lady, and if you can tell me where Lady Cadogan may be found, I shall send one of the footmen at once to inform her of the gentleman's presence in the house."

"That will not be necessary, Marwyn. Nor are you to inform his lordship, if you please."

"His lordship, m'lady, has gone to White's."

"Good, I mean to speak privately with Mr. Carruthers on a matter of importance, Marwyn, so I desire you to tell no one else that he is here—particularly not the Lady Eliza."

Understanding dawned in the butler's eyes. "Very good, ma'am."

She found Carruthers lounging against the chimneypiece in the drawing room. He straightened, stepping forward to greet her with his usual cheerful impudence.

"Mr. Carruthers," she said, cutting him off without apology, "I have no very good idea how many minutes we may have before we are interrupted, so pray let me say what I have to say without interruption."

His eyes twinkled, but he made her a little bow and said, "You wish to know if my intentions toward your sister are honorable, ma'am? They are, but would it not be more proper for your brother to be conducting this interview?"

"Perhaps, but I have not told my brother all I know of you, sir," she said frankly. "Surely you cannot imagine that I will continue to allow you to pursue my sister as you have been doing."

"I have mended my ways, my lady, I promise you. You see before you an honest man."

"That's as may be, sir, but your past cannot be condoned. I should prefer for my own reasons not to have to divulge your secret, but rather than allow my sister to believe herself in love with you, I must do so."

He frowned. "I see. I had hoped your silence thus far meant you'd not speak of past indiscretions."

"Mr. Carruthers, you are not a fool. My sister is the daughter of an earl. Surely you cannot think I would permit her to marry a thief. Every feeling must be revolted."

"I am not a thief, Lady Meriel."

"Very pretty, sir. The downcast eye is particularly appealing. I should recommend that you try that manner with my brother, once I have told him how I made your acquaintance. He will be prodigiously amused, I make no doubt."

" 'Twould be better at this present if you say nothing about that meeting, ma'am," Mr. Carruthers said quietly, all trace of amusement now gone from his countenance. "Perhaps you had better sit down, that we may converse quietly."

His quiet manner aroused her curiosity, and she moved to obey him, saying only, "Do you mean to threaten me, sir? I promise it will do you no good."

"I am not such a fool as that, Lady Meriel. I have long since taken your measure, and I am convinced that nothing but the truth will do for you." He sat beside her on the glove-leather sofa, leaning back a little into one corner.

She turned to face him, folding her hands in her lap. "Well, then, sir, let us have the truth if you please."

"I doubt you will find it much more appealing than what you already believe of me, but I assure you that what I have done in the past, I did for a good cause." He paused, then took the plunge. "I was involved in what might tactfully be called 'intelligence gathering' for the British War Ministry."

Meriel stared at him, somehow not as surprised as she might have been. Was it possible that Carruthers might provide the answer to her problem? Carefully hiding her excitement, she said calmly, "Am I to understand that you are a spy, sir?"

"You take the news mighty well, ma'am. There are those who would not be so calm, I assure you. I worked in France for a new department of the British War Ministry, which was organized by Quartermaster General Brownrigg, who got the notion from Napoleon himself. General Brownrigg organized what he called the Depot of Military Knowledge, which was to have separate branches to look into troop movements, keep track of past and present operations, maintain a library, and collect maps. During the peace, it occurred to the head of the operations department that it would be easy for gentlemen of the so-called upper classes to travel about in France and acquire information. I was one of those whom he approached, and I agreed to help."

"And was Sir Antony one of those whom you expected to have information?" There was scorn in her tone. "Surely you did not think to acquire knowledge of French troop movements from an Englishman, Mr. Carruthers."

He smiled at her. "No, certainly not, but I knew, for one of our agents had discovered the fact, that Sir Antony had been assaulted on board the packet ship after having come from Wales, where he had been present at a gathering my own chief attended. I thought perhaps—"

"Can you tell me the name of your superior, Mr. Carruthers?" Meriel interrupted with a new surge of excitement. She was certain she knew already what he would say.

He regarded her speculatively for a rather long moment before saying, "No harm in that, I suppose, now that the whole department has been completely disbanded. They've moved a procurement officer into poor George's office now, I hear."

"George Murray?"

He nodded. "Do you know him? Poor fellow's been posted back to the Third Foot, and last I heard, was on his way to the Continent. And General Brownrigg's in Surrey with York, trying to determine the best course to follow now. He's had too much else dumped on his plate to worry about his intelligence depot. Too bad. The notion was a good one, but for now it's been dished."

Realizing that he would be of little use to her, she returned to another line of thought. "I interrupted you a moment ago, sir. Did you mean to say that Sir Antony was also involved with this mysterious intelligence depot?"

"I was going to tell you no such thing, and what I have said about my own activities, I trust will go no further. You must realize that while I might think the gathering of intelligence against an enemy is a good thing, there are many more good folk who disagree with me. And we weren't even at war when I was in France, ma'am. That makes it all the worse. I'd most likely be socially ruined if my activities were to become public knowledge. Somehow we have come over the years to look upon spying as a despicable act—cheating, in fact."

"Yes, sir, I have heard all that before, but there must be times when it is necessary to have at least a notion of what the enemy intends to do, even during a so-called period of peace."

"You have a head on your shoulders, and no mistake, my lady," he said approvingly, "but you cannot change what everyone else thinks overnight, and I for one will thank you not to attempt it. My family, though it will shock you to hear it, is quite respectable—"

"Somerset," Meriel murmured. "My Aunt Cadogan knows them, I believe."

He grinned. "I know. And please believe me when I tell you that my father, for one, would be very much shocked to learn that I have been engaged in trying to keep one step ahead of Boney and his lot. He thinks the French are no-account sneaking creatures, but he would not let that keep him from castigating my actions, believe me. Furthermore, both my parents and my sisters would suffer socially. Do you understand what I am telling you?"

"Better than you know, sir," she told him slowly. Then, gathering her wits, she straightened and smiled at him. "I will tell my aunt and my sister that you are here, and you need not fear I shall betray your secret, for I will not."

When she rose, he stood beside her, taking her hand and bestowing a light kiss upon it. "You will not regret your decision, Lady Meriel. I am utterly out of the business now, of course, but perhaps one day it will become more respectable. Who can say?"

Her smile this time was brief, and she quickly took her leave of him. After telling Marwyn that he might now inform Lady Cadogan and Eliza that a visitor awaited them below, she hurried up to her bedchamber to think.

Casting her mind back over the strange interview she had just taken part in, she realized that Carruthers had never actually said that Sir Antony was not part of the new intelligence department. Certainly Sir Antony was a frequent traveler in France. He had said as much himself. Therefore, would he not have been precisely the sort of gentleman to appeal to George Murray for his purpose? And for that matter, had she not seen Mr. Murray and Sir Antony in company with one another? The only thing which made her think perhaps Sir Antony had not been one of Murray's minions was the fact that Murray had given her his letter to the priest. Surely, if Sir Antony had been his agent, he'd have entrusted the letter to him.

She had come full circle. It would be pointless to give the letter to Mr. Carruthers, for he had said he was no longer part of the intelligence department. Indeed, he had said the department no longer existed. Did that mean that no one would be interested in the information Père Leclerc had provided? Surely that could not be the case. But she resisted the temptation to put the problem before Carruthers or to ask his advice. In the first place, she could not imagine taking advice from one whom, despite his confession, she still thought of as an impudent ne'er-do-well. His attitude was capricious, and although she readily saw that such an attitude must have served him well in his late profession, she simply could not imagine throwing her problems into his lap.

Thoughtfully she considered her brother. Jocelyn was resourceful, there could be no doubt of that. He had survived in a far wilder, more dangerous country than France for seven years. But he was still her brother, and she could not think he would look upon the matter constructively. He would be more likely to rip up at her for her actions in not having taken the letter to him when her suspicions were first aroused. Nor could she imagine his doing anything more than flinging it upon the nearest fire. His sympathies, for the most part, were more likely to be with the French than with the English.

Her thoughts kept returning to Sir Antony. She remembered how capably he had handled every mishap during their journey, how tolerantly he had looked upon the most outrageous of her behavior. Even the fact that she carried a pistol had not overly distressed him. She simply had not been thinking clearly when she had assumed that he would respond as other men would to what she had done. He was not like other men. With a smile she recalled dining with him on shipboard and vagabondizing with him in Paris. Then, with warmth flooding her cheeks, she remembered their more recent and most improper interlude in Hyde Park. He would scarcely dare to chide her for the impropriety of her actions. Indeed, only when she had attempted to act alone in a way that might endanger her safety had he ever been vexed with her. She bit her lower lip at this thought, realizing that she wanted more than anything else to avoid vexing him again. She could not deceive herself into believing that the information she held was not valuable. Even the fact that she had delayed acting for this long might prove disastrous. She could not know. But the more she came to think, the more certain she was that Sir Antony was the man to deal with her problem.

Fetching her standish from the shelf it occupied in her wardrobe, she placed it upon the little table in the window embrasure and wrote a graceful note requesting that Sir Antony call upon her in Berkeley Square that very afternoon, as she had something of a private and most urgent nature to impart to him. That, she thought, underscoring "private and most urgent" with two bold black lines, would keep him from bringing anyone else with him. Having dispatched a liveried footman to deliver this message, her next matter of business was to ensure that her family would be otherwise engaged when he arrived.

Since Lady Cadogan had already expressed the intention of taking Eliza to her dressmaker for a final fitting of the gown she meant to wear to the upcoming Traherne House ball, those two ladies presented no problem. And they would not expect her to accompany them, because Meriel had already convinced Lady Cadogan that the exquisite lace-trimmed lavender ball dress she had had made up in Paris would do excellently well for the occasion.

Getting rid of Davy and Gwenyth was nearly as easy, for she simply told Mr. Scott that she thought a visit to see the beasts at the Exeter Exchange in his company would be very educational, and that admirable young man agreed with her wholeheartedly. Thus it was that she saw them off soon after her aunt and Eliza had driven away in Lady Cadogan's elegant barouche. Turning to Marwyn in the hall, she said calmly, "Is my brother expected soon?"

"Not before dinner, m'lady. He means to dine at home this evening, however. Shall I tell him you wish to speak with him upon his return?"

"Oh, no," she returned airily. " 'Tis merely that we have seen little of him these days, and I wondered."

The butler permitted himself a smile. "If I may say so, m'lady, the young master has fallen rather quickly into his new position. I doubt he misses his American adventures in the least."

She chuckled. "No doubt you are in the right of it. He is fairly wallowing in his earldom, is he not? I daresay Papa never enjoyed being Lord Tallyn half so much as Joss does."

The butler bowed, and she took herself upstairs to the drawing room, hoping Sir Antony would not keep her waiting long. She could not depend upon Lady Cadogan and Eliza to loiter once their errands had been attended to, nor could she be certain Jocelyn would not come home early for once. Thus it was that she fairly leapt to her feet when Marwyn opened the drawing-room doors at last. But the figure behind him was not large, nor did he instill any wish in her to fling herself upon his chest and pour out her problems.

Peter Trent slipped past the butler even as that outraged worthy was announcing him, and executed a graceful bow. "Your message to my master brought me to you, ma'am," he explained quickly. "Sir Antony is, most unfortunately, out of town, so I took the liberty of scanning your note, which was not sealed, you know. Your footman had said it was most urgent and must be delivered at once to Sir Antony. I hoped perhaps I might be of service in his absence."

"Well, it is certainly distressing that Sir Antony is not at home, but I do not know what you may think you could do for me, Trent. The matter is one that I can discuss only with him, you see."

Trent glanced at the butler. "If you please, m'lady, I should prefer to speak to you privately."

Marwyn, becoming more stately than ever, stepped nearer to the valet. "You may prefer such a thing, my man, but you may believe me when I tell you that her ladyship will not be entertaining the likes of you without a proper chaperon."

Trent said nothing. He merely looked at Meriel with an odd glint of conspiracy in his eyes that intrigued her at once. She smiled at the butler and said, "It is all right, Marwyn. Mr. Trent and I became acquainted, you know, upon my journey into France. I am certain he may be trusted to keep the line. You may go."

"I'll just bring refreshment, m'lady."

She saw Trent give a slight negative movement of his head, and instantly took the hint. "No need for that, Marwyn. I'll thank you to see that we are left undisturbed until I ring."

"Very well, my lady," the butler said, every line of his majestic body stiff with disapproval, "it shall be as you request."

"I thank you, your ladyship," Peter Trent said smoothly, moving a step nearer when the butler had gone. "Now, perhaps we may speak freely. I am aware that certain information has come into your hands, and I assure you that you may confide in me. I am the very embodiment of my master."

His smooth self-assurance unaccountably annoyed her, and she rather wished she had not sent Marwyn away. "I cannot think what gave you the notion that I might confide in you," she said, turning toward her chair again. "Indeed, your attitude is unseemly, Mr. Trent. I assure you that I merely wish to ask Sir Antony's advice upon a matter that is entirely person—"

Her last word ended in a startled squeal as the valet's muscular arm came round her throat and a knife flashed before her eyes.

"I believe there's more to the matter than that, my precious lady. Until this very day I thought I must have mistaken my man. But now you'd best hope that butler of yours don't take it into his head to disturb us before I get to the right of things, or this day's light will be the last you ever see."

16

Meriel drew breath to scream, but the knife point pricking at her throat turned the scream into a sobbing gasp instead.

"Not a sound, m'lady," Trent growled in her ear, "for I shan't hesitate to use this, and I assure you, that old puffguts butler of yours would be of little use to you once you was dead. Now, quickly, have you got a message for Sir Antony? Did the priest give you something, is that it?"

"He told me nothing," she gasped. "He merely helped my maid and me to escape the soldiers. You must realize we were running for our lives!"

Trent allowed himself a grim chuckle, but the pressure of the knife against her throat did not relax. "I don't doubt you was escaping, but don't try to bamboozle me into thinking that priest ain't hand in glove with the English and didn't give you a message to relay to Sir Antony Davies. I can't think of any other reason you'd have run to him from Paris, and I know for a fact you did that, for I was with Sir Antony when he went there for news of you. I didn't leave their sight for a minute, howsoever, so I know the old man passed nothing along to Davies or to that other fellow that was with him—Carruthers."

"Well, Père Leclerc gave me nothing for Sir Antony either," Meriel said truthfully. "In any event, if he had, don't you think I'd have given it to him at once?"

"Perhaps, if you had been conscious when 'e found you. Or even if you'd been alone with him aboard the yacht. But you wasn't. And maybe you wasn't supposed to pass it along at all, now I come to think about it. Only reason for you being involved at all as I see it is that no one'd suspicion a female might carry an important message. Perhaps Sir Antony was naught but dust thrown in my eye to keep me from considering you, all along."

His body relaxed a little as his thought processes stirred, and Meriel could no longer feel the knife at her throat. With her head held back as it was, she could see very little other than the ornate ceiling above, but her arms were relatively free, and she began to reach out with the right one carefully, feeling for some object that might aid her. Knowing she must be quite near at least one of the occasional tables that littered the room, she was not altogether surprised a moment later when her seeking hand came into contact with one of the Grecian sculptures. Thinking the marble might prove too heavy for her purpose, and realizing that she would have only the one opportunity, she braced herself and heaved the statue with all her might, bringing it up and over as much by guess as by awareness of where Trent's head must be. Her aim was admirable, however. The base of the statue caught Mr. Trent just over the eyebrow as he wrenched his head around in a belated attempt to see what she was about.

The knife fell from his limp hand as he sank into oblivion, and Meriel stepped quickly away, feeling much as she would have had she stepped upon a viper. As she turned to see what she had done, her hands flew to her mouth, for there was blood upon Trent's forehead and she very much feared she had killed him. She tried to call out, but the words refused to form themselves upon her tongue. Her throat seemed to have shut tight, making it difficult to breathe.

From some distance away she heard voices, masculine voices. She shook her head a little, thinking she was imagining them, but they only grew louder. There was a clattering, too, as of footsteps upon marble. Drawing a long breath, she straightened her shoulders and faced the door onto the gallery. Her heart was pounding, but she willed herself to be calm, certain now that the noise heralded the arrival of friends, not more enemies.

When the tall doors were thrown open to reveal Sir Antony, with Mr. Carruthers, Lord Tallyn, and a visibly anxious Marwyn just behind him, Meriel looked straight at the only one who mattered and said quietly, "I'm afraid I've killed your valet, but indeed, I did not know what else to do."

At first she had been so distraught herself that she had imagined Sir Antony was breathing hard, that he was frightened at what he might see. But now she realized she had quite mistaken the matter. As his gaze met hers, he appeared to be as calm as ever, and although there was a certain enigmatic glint in the hazel depths, there was strength there as well. She drew from that strength as she had done before, and when he moved toward her, stepping around the prostrate Trent, she held out her hands to him, expecting him to take them in his own. To her surprise he crushed her into his arms instead, and the action seemed perfectly natural to her. She snuggled there willingly, certain her troubles were over.

"My poor girl," he said gently. "Trent acted much more quickly than we had any reason to expect. I hope you will forgive us."

Shock raced through her, stiffening her body in his embrace. She raised her head from his chest and looked searchingly into his face. "You knew he had come here? You expected him to do so?"

Sir Antony nodded, but before he could speak, Jocelyn said angrily from the doorway, "What goes forward here, if I may ask? Who is that fellow on the floor and why is no one attending to him? I daresay it makes no never-mind to the rest of you, but I for one would as lief he not bleed all over my carpet. What were you about, to be alone in this room with a man like that, Meriel? Your conduct wants correcting, my girl, and so I tell you. As for you, Davies, what do you mean by such behavior, sir? I daresay the girl was a trifle upset when this fellow collapsed at her feet, but as she'd no reason to be here with him in the first place, I'd take it kindly if you was to release her at once. You've taken a number of liberties that I don't hold with, now I come to think about it, liberties you oughtn't to take without you pleaded your case to me first, sir. London manners must have changed these seven years, dashed if they ain't."

Sir Antony released Meriel, exchanged a glance with Carruthers, who stood near the butler just inside the doorway, and then addressed himself to Jocelyn. "I cannot explain the whole business to you, my lord, without discussing it first with some others more directly concerned, but I can assure you that your sister did not entertain this fellow by choice. It would certainly have been better had he not been left alone with her. Your butler ought to have remained in the room." A choking sound from the indignant butler drew his eye toward that worthy. When Marwyn folded his lips and glanced at the ceiling, however, Sir Antony's gaze shifted to Meriel, and there was enough steel in the look to send a shiver racing up and down her spine. He continued in a harder tone, "We—rather foolishly, as matters transpired—assumed that Lady Meriel would simply give into his keeping that which he came for. That she would refuse him, or that he would do anything to harm her if she did, never occurred to us." He glanced down at Trent, his jaw tightening. "That knife on the floor belongs to him, does it not?"

This last was addressed to Meriel, and she nodded, nibbling at her lower lip and wishing he would behave more as she was accustomed to see him behave. Gone was his languid manner, along with the lazy look in his eyes. He was angry, and she very much feared, despite his comforting hug earlier, that she was the one who had angered him. She glanced at Carruthers and saw him looking at her, his expression a mixture of amusement and compassion. She glared back at him, and he gave a little shrug, moving to take a closer look at the man lying on the floor.

Lord Tallyn spoke again, petulantly. "I do not understand you, Davies," he said. "What business had my sister with a man who carries a knife upon his person? And who is that fellow? I demand an answer to that much at least."

"My valet," returned Sir Antony curtly. He glanced at Carruthers. "I shall leave you to deal with this—as quietly as possible, if you please. No doubt the butler will know how to remove him with the least disturbance to the household."

"Indeed, sir," said Marwyn at his stateliest. "You may with perfect confidence leave everything to me."

"Thank you," said Sir Antony with a slight smile. "Just don't lose him. I've a few questions to put to that lad if her ladyship hasn't put him beyond answering them."

"He's still alive, Tony," said Carruthers, kneeling now beside Trent.

"Well, thank goodness for that," said Jocelyn, eyeing his sister. "At least you won't have to stand trial for murder, Meriel. I shall have a few things to say to you later, my girl, but for now I daresay you'd best take yourself off to your bedchamber until we get this business cleared up."

Meriel turned on him indignantly, prepared to tell him precisely what she thought of such an order, but just then Sir Antony said calmly, "If you please, Tallyn, I should like a few moments of privacy with Lady Meriel before I depart. There are certain matters I wish to discuss with her."

"Oh," said Jocelyn, looking at him in surprise but with a light of dawning understanding in his eyes. "It's like that, is it? Well, I must say I've expected no less, Davies. You pick a damn peculiar time for it, but I suppose if she does not object, we needn't be too finicking about that. You may take her down to my library if you wish, sir. She knows the way. And as for you," he added, turning to his sister and ignoring her gathering fury, "you must count yourself fortunate, I suppose, that Davies here is prepared to see that all your damned odd behavior don't destroy your reputation altogether."

"How dare you!" Meriel sputtered, taking a step toward him, then whirling to face Sir Antony, who was regarding Jocelyn in mild astonishment. "How dare the lot of you! 'Tis bad enough that I have been used as a mere puppet by persons to whom I have no connection whatsoever, but to have been used in that same manner by two men who pretended to be my friends is the outside of enough. You, Mr. Carruthers," she added, shooting a glare at that gentleman, whose eyes were twinkling irrepressibly with unholy glee, "you laugh to think how clever you have been to have played games with all of us. But you, sir"—and here she planted herself firmly in front of Sir Antony and pushed a hard, sharp-nailed finger straight into his broad chest—"for you to pretend to my brother now that you mean to offer for my hand and that there is no more than that left to discuss, when not two minutes ago you made it perfectly clear to me if to no one else that you as good as arranged for that abominable toad to come here like he did, is going beyond what anyone might tolerate. You used me just as Mr. Murray and the others did. Indeed," she added, her fists flying now to her hips, "I should not be at all surprised to discover that the entire plan was of your devising from first to last. Well, I shall not go to the library or anywhere else with you. Moreover, I shall not ever speak to you again, and I pray you may take the greatest possible care of Trent. The two of you deserve each other!"

Turning upon her heel, she pushed past her astonished brother and strode straight toward the doorway, forcing Marwyn to step quickly to one side to let her pass. As she crossed the gallery she heard Jocelyn say, "What the devil—?" but the rest of his words were lost to her as she ran up the curving stairway behind the Ionic screen to the second floor. Once inside her own bedchamber, she slammed the door behind her and strode quickly across to the window, her breasts heaving with anger, disappointment, and dismay.

Tears filled her eyes, but she brushed them furiously away. She would not cry. Nothing Sir Antony had done was worth crying about. Of course, if she cared about him, then perhaps she might be more upset. But she didn't care. Not in the slightest. She told herself so over and over again as she peered through watery mist, sobbing deep racking sobs and trying to pretend she was merely observing the view from her window. A moment later she realized her hands were clenched into two fists and pressed into her skirt, and she forcibly relaxed them. Then it was necessary to brush the tears from her eyes again. Still angry but breathing more calmly, she turned to search her dressing table for a proper handkerchief. All she could find was a tiny dab of lace that was of no use to her at all.

She ignored the first knock at her door. It was no more than a light tap and deserved to go unheard, although she believed it must be Lady Cadogan or Eliza returned from the dressmaker and wishful to know what all the commotion was about. The second knock was firmer, clearly not the knock of a feminine hand. Meriel bit her lip.

"Go away, Joss," she said gruffly.

"It isn't Joss."

Meriel stared at the door, then glanced quickly around to assure herself that she was truly in her own bedchamber. The knock came again, harder yet, and she stepped swiftly back toward the window, coming up hard against the little table in the embrasure. It rocked, and she grabbed at it to keep it from falling over.

There was panic in her voice. "You cannot come in here. Whatever are you thinking about? You ought not even to be on this floor. Go away!"

"I am coming in, Meriel."

"You can't!" she shrieked as the handle began to turn. Torn between the urge to fling herself at that door and an equally strong urge to flee, though she knew not where, she stood where she was, clutching at the table behind her and watching.

The door opened, and Sir Antony stepped inside, firmly shutting it behind him. "As you see," he said, "I can do precisely as I say I will do."

"My brother will kill you," she muttered.

"I sincerely hope he will not try. His experiences in the wilds of America notwithstanding, I can give him twenty or thirty pounds and a few years of practice in the art of self-defense." He was not smiling, but there was a look of understanding in his eyes. "He will not interfere, my dear. The task was not an easy one, but I have convinced him that to do so would serve no good purpose. I left him, in fact, trying to keep your aunt in hand. She and your sister have returned from their expedition to Bond Street, and Lady Cadogan, I am persuaded, would prove to be a much more formidable opponent than Tallyn."

"You choose to jest, sir, but what you have done is no laughing matter."

"I will not pretend to misunderstand you, Meri," he said gently. "I do not think you refer to my invasion of your bedchamber. May I sit?"

"As you please." She gestured toward the two chairs on either side of the little table behind her and moved to sit in one of them, still watching him warily. "I do not know what you mean to accomplish, Sir Antony, but I shall never forgive you for what you have done today."

He did smile then. "I hope you will at least listen to me."

"Very well," she replied ungraciously, "though I cannot think what you might say to the purpose."

"I think you might if you give it some thought," he said easily. "Carruthers told me he explained to you about the department we both worked for." When she nodded, he continued, "It is unfortunate that over the last century or so, our upper classes have developed an absurdly sanctimonious attitude toward the gathering of information about our enemies. 'Tis sheer foolhardiness to pretend that we are above that sort of thing, when our survival as a nation depends upon seeing the matter in a clearer light. Do not think, however, that I was anything other than opposed to the notion of employing an unsuspecting female to deliver that first message to Leclerc."

"Why did you not carry it yourself, if you were working for Mr. Murray?"

"I had already done a great deal, and it was feared

that I had aroused a suspicion in some quarters by my frequent, often brief trips into France. Though I managed to see you quickly through the French customs, you will recall that I was not so fortunate myself. Indeed, I was thoroughly searched, as was my luggage. I might well have carried Murray's message in my head, as I have done before, but we could not be certain I would not be detained. Then, too, we wished to see if our suspicions were correct. As you know, they were. I was assaulted on board the *Albion*."

"By your own valet." She grimaced. "Did you suspect him at once?"

He shrugged. "I was certain of it when I realized I had not been robbed, but I had suspected him even before that. My previous man left without notice, and Trent appeared rather too providentially to take his place, you see. I might have turned him away, but we thought it would be more educational to have him where we might watch him. With Fouché out of favor as he was, we wanted to know just what the French would be up to."

"Fouché is not so out of favor as you thought," Meriel said quietly. "He may no longer be minister of police, but he is just as active as before. He has organized an entire network of spies here in England, and some sort of royalist plot appears to be in jeopardy. Here, I will show you." She got up and went to get the letter out of her reticule. Handing it to him, she said, "I doubt not that Peter Trent is one of Fouché's agents."

Sir Antony nodded. "His real name is Pierre Truquer. We were able to learn quite a lot about him in France."

"But why did he attack you on deck? He might just as well have done so at any time in your cabin."

"He did not sleep in my cabin," Sir Antony said. "Nor did I, if you will recall, when we were aboard the *Camden*. Your sister Gwenyth did. And I took good care, as well, never to let him take me unawares. Once he had searched my trunks, as he had ample opportunity to do, I suppose he thought he must search my person, and it never occurred to him, of course, that a woman would have the message he searched for. I daresay he never suspected you until your message was delivered to my house."

"He said I must have got a message from Père Leclerc. Does that mean the priest is in danger?"

"No, for Trent cannot be certain, and no one else knows anything. Apparently the soldiers acted upon suspicion and nothing more. They were gone before we arrived, but the good father was not, I believe, anticipating an arrest. Trent merely guessed from your message to me today that you were somehow involved in the business. I daresay he might have thought before that if you had been sent to the priest to help you get out of France, it must be because the priest was an English agent. He was with Carruthers and me, but he must have realized there was no time for a message to have been passed then, for once I learned you were somewhere on the river between Rouen and Le Havre, I wasted no time in an attempt to speak further with the good father. We left on the instant. For that matter, Leclerc didn't so much as try to tell me there was a message, though I might have guessed it for myself had I chosen to consider the matter."

"How?" she asked, now drawn into his story despite herself.

He grimaced. "You do not think you were meant to act as courier all over France, do you? Leclerc brought you his letter in the innyard and presented it to you right under my nose. Short of telling you the whole and demanding that you give me his letter, there wasn't much I could do about it. Fortunately Trent did not see you receive the letter. I had set matters in hand to gather evidence against him, but until I did, I did not wish to do other than give him his head."

"You were not so surprised as you pretended to be to find Mr. Carruthers in Mantes-de-Jolie, then?"

He shook his head. "He was searching Trent's things. Pocketed a few of my belongings in order to make it look as though he were a thief if Trent walked in upon him. Instead, you captured him with Trent right there to see you. I was afraid, despite everything, that Trent might suspect you were carrying information, and I can tell you

I was in a quandary, wondering if you'd be safer if I left you to travel alone and carried Trent away with me. I decided at last that it was better to know the enemy and to keep you under my eye. And that was also why Carruthers joined the party. Two of us to keep an eye on Trent seemed safer than one. There was also your reputation to consider. To travel into Paris under my protection alone might have looked odd even to your delightful sister. And when we reached Paris and you had seen Deguise, I assumed your involvement was ended. I was wrong, clearly, but until you questioned me about invisible inks and Carruthers told me about your interview with him, I did not realize that either Deguise or Leclerc had decided to use you again to send messages back to England." He smiled ruefully. "Carruthers had the devil of a time to keep you from giving this damned letter into his keeping, you know."

"You wanted it for bait."

"We did. Once we decided such a letter must exist, we determined to make Trent attempt to get hold of it. Finding it in his keeping was all we hoped for. It never occurred to me, my little idiot, that you would refuse to give it to him if he asked you for it. That, may I tell you, was quite as stupid as carrying your British passport right in your reticule while you were jauntering across France."

She stared at him. "Was that why you were vexed with me when we reached England? I remember wondering. I never thought about it, but I see now that we might have had a bad moment or two if any of those soldiers had insisted upon searching us."

"You might well say so. But to get back to today, I also misjudged Trent, and for that I must apologize. The thought that he would be so stupid as to attempt to murder you in your brother's house with a dozen servants nearby simply never entered my head. I do realize, by the by," he added, regarding her rather sternly, "that you take great pride in your independence of spirit, but why did you not scream for help at once?"

A rueful smile touched her lips. "I could not," she said. "When first he grabbed me, I seemed to have no voice, and by the time I might have screamed, his knife was at my throat. I believed he meant it when he said he would kill me."

"Than what possessed you to struggle with him at all?"

"I didn't. I found that the statue was within my reach and I simply hit him with it."

He got to his feet, reaching for her. Though she had a strong notion he meant to shake her, she made no attempt to elude his grasp, but let him pull her from her chair. When she stood before him, however, she found that her courage had deserted her. She could not make herself look higher than the center button of his waistcoat.

"It is done now, Meri," he said quietly. "Have I put myself entirely beyond forgiveness?"

She caught her lip between her teeth, wondering how it was that she could still misjudge his temper, and how it was that the mere sound of his voice could stir a warm glow within her body. After a small silence when he made no effort to press her for an answer, she looked up at him to find that he was regarding her with a peculiar tension in his demeanor.

"Perhaps not altogether beyond it, sir," she said, smiling at him and raising a hand to smooth away the tension from his face. "I believe you wished only to protect me."

He caught her hand in his and pressed it to his lips. A moment later she was in his arms again, and there was nothing languid about his embrace. Nor was his kiss as gentle as the last time he had kissed her. Unfamiliar but entirely delightful sensations threatened to overwhelm her. She made one feeble attempt to push him away, and then, finding it impossible, grasped his coat with both hands and clung to him, responding with a fierce passion to match his own.

"Protection was not all I had in mind," he murmured against her cheek. "I fell in love with you on the coastal packet when I discovered you had thrown coal all over the floor of the ladies' saloon."

"I didn't!" she protested.

"But you did," he reminded her, "when Gwenyth was ill."

"Oh, dear, so I did," she said somewhat distractedly.

"What you must have thought of me! I keep expecting you to be angry or at least irritated by things I did—traveling alone, carrying a pistol, and the like—only you never were."

"I was, on more than one occasion," he countered, "but the feelings never lasted. I loved you for what you are, my sweet. 'Twould be folly to seek to change you."

She leaned her head against his shoulder. "That's twice you have mentioned love, sir. I meant only to enjoy a mild flirtation, but I'm afraid I have fallen in love with you too. What on earth shall we do?"

He held her away from him, looking down at her in amusement. "Considering that your brother was convinced to allow me to come up here only by virtue of his strong conviction that I mean to offer for your hand, I think we had better get married, don't you?"

"But I cannot. The children—"

"Meri," he said gently, drawing her close again, "Tallyn is perfectly capable of looking after them, and it is his duty now, not yours. You will, I trust, soon have children of your own to look after. The only thing I cannot promise you is a mountain to match your Cader Idris. Is that an obstacle too great for us to overcome, my love?"

She knew he was right about the children. Jocelyn handled them well, and he would look after Plas Tallyn too. Her duties were done. As her body stirred in response to Sir Antony's gentle, idle caresses, she realized that she was ready to take on new duties. She looked up into his face, imagining him striding beside her up the slopes of Cader Idris. The vision came easily to her mind, and she realized that she wanted to show him all her favorite views along the way. She smiled. "I suppose we may visit Wales from time to time, sir, may we not?"

The door to her bedchamber was flung wide just then to reveal her brother upon the threshold, his face creased in an angry frown. "What goes on here, Davies? I said you might come up and speak to her, not make love to her. Good God, man, turn her loose, I say! 'Tis not the thing, sir, and I don't scruple to tell you so."

Lady Cadogan, entering behind him, peered rather

shrewdly at Meriel and Sir Antony, then turned to Jocelyn. "I think you need have no concern, my lord."

"Do you not?" Jocelyn inquired with heavy sarcasm. "I suppose I will be the judge of that."

"But your aunt is perfectly correct in her assumption, Tallyn," Sir Antony said, looking down at Meriel. "Unless I am much mistaken, your sister has just agreed to be my wife."

"Indeed? Is this true, Meriel?" Jocelyn demanded.

She looked up at Sir Antony. "Completely, sir," she said.

About the Author

A fourth-generation Californian, Amanda Scott was born and raised in Salinas and graduated with a degree in history from Mills College in Oakland. She did graduate work at the University of North Carolina at Chapel Hill, specializing in British history, before obtaining her MA from San Jose State University. She lives with her husband and young son in Sacramento. Her hobbies include camping, backpacking, and gourmet cooking.